FATE OF ECHOES AND EMBERS

C. L. MECCA

Boldwood

First published in Great Britain in 2025 by Boldwood Books Ltd.

Copyright © C. L. Mecca, 2025

Cover Design by JD Smith Design Ltd

Cover Images: Shutterstock

A CIP catalogue record for this book is available from the British Library.

Paperback ISBN 978-1-83656-307-5

Large Print ISBN 978-1-83656-306-8

Hardback ISBN 978-1-83656-305-1

Trade Paperback ISBN 978-1-80625-853-6

Ebook ISBN 978-1-83656-308-2

Kindle ISBN 978-1-83656-309-9

Audio CD ISBN 978-1-83656-300-6

MP3 CD ISBN 978-1-83656-301-3

Digital audio download ISBN 978-1-83656-304-4

This book is printed on certified sustainable paper. Boldwood Books is dedicated to putting sustainability at the heart of our business. For more information please visit https://www.boldwoodbooks.com/about-us/sustainability/

Boldwood Books Ltd, 23 Bowerdean Street, London, SW6 3TN

www.boldwoodbooks.com

For everyone who believes love is worth the risk, even when the tides threaten to pull you under.

1

MAREK

Valewood Bay, Estmere, Elydor

"She lives less than a full day's ride from here." I stopped, waiting for the serving girl to clear our meal. She'd not taken her eyes from me last eve when we arrived or this morn, but I wasn't interested in a dalliance.

Not today, at least.

"How long will it take to secure your lady's acquiescence?" Kael asked, leaning back into the wooden seat and stretching out his legs. His partner, Mev, watched him with a look that I knew well. One of desire.

I'd been introduced to the Gyorian prince and Aetherian princess only a fortnight ago but could appreciate their tight bond, even if partnering wasn't in the cards for me.

"Attempt to secure it," I clarified. "There is every likelihood she won't come with us."

Mev took a sip of ale. No one at The Maiden's Rest seemed to notice anything unusual about her. By outside appearances, she was an Aetherian woman... Princess Mevlida's long pearl-white hair overshadowing that she was also half-human. If patrons knew the long-lost daughter to King Galfrid sat in the same tavern as them, we would be surrounded. As it was, the few that remained this early in the morning were more interested in their own ales than us.

"That's not the first time you've said as much. What's the deal?" Mev, the only human to have come through the Gate from the human realm in nearly thirty years, often used words not familiar here.

"The deal?" I asked.

The corners of Kael's mouth lifted. "The scoop. The dealio," he said in his best Mev impression.

"Pretty sure he won't know those either. Besides, I've never used 'the dealio' before."

Kael's brow raised. "No? Then would you care to tell me where I learned it?"

"Oh, I don't know. Maybe from one of the other humans in Elydor? We're in an entire kingdom of them." She waved her hands around. "If you haven't noticed."

"I don't associate with any other humans. As you know."

"Not true. You associate with Issa."

My hand froze. I put down the mug of ale and asked Mev to repeat herself.

"Did you say... Issa?"

"It's short for Isolde. She's literally one of the only humans, besides me, Kael likes. Actually, when I first met her—"

"Lady Isolde Hawthorne?" I asked.

Kael answered. "You know her?"

Oh, I knew her well enough. "I'm certain I mentioned going to Hawthorne Manor when we arrived in Valewood Bay. You made no mention of being familiar with it."

Kael sat up in his chair. "I'm certain you didn't."

"I'm pretty sure," Mev cut in. "Your exact words were, 'After we drop off Rowan, I need three days in Valewood. There's a woman there who might be useful for this mission.'"

"And when we asked," Kael added, his gruff, Gyorian manner more on display now than it had been before Issa's name had been mentioned. "You refused to say any more."

That was entirely possible. I didn't talk about Issa.

Ever.

To anyone.

"How do you know her?" I asked, half-afraid of the answer.

"I would ask you the same."

It was a story I had no intention of sharing.

"Uh, guys. Can we put the measuring tape away?"

Both Kael and I looked at Mev, neither of us having an idea of what that meant.

"Never mind. It would take too long to explain. Kael is friends with her. But I have a feeling she was more than a friend to you?"

Fucking humans. "A feeling? Because you're reading me?"

No human could enter the Aetherian Gate without some type of intuitive ability. Typically, once they came through, those abilities were heightened due to the magical qualities of our realm. Mev, the daughter of a king, had apparently become quite powerful in her short time here and could sense both emotion and intent in others.

"I'm not reading you, Marek," she said calmly. "But women's intuition is real."

Kael and I exchanged a glance. He shrugged.

"Issa is the woman I intend to ask for help," I said.

"You're going to Hawthorne Manor?" Mev asked.

"I am."

Kael cleared his throat. "Correction. *We're* going to Hawthorne Manor. Issa is a good friend, as Mev said."

From what I knew of Kael, that was surprising, to say the least. Gyorians and humans were very rarely friends, especially when the Gyorian in question was the son of the king who hated humans with a vengeance.

"It a long story," Mev said. "Which it seems like we'll be able to tell you on the road. I can't believe Kael's Issa is the woman you're asking for help." Her eyes widened. "Oh my God, of course. She senses magical qualities. Kael..."

He was looking at her with amusement.

Mev pretended to scowl at him. "You figured it out already."

"More than that," he said dryly. "I thought of asking her as well, especially when Marek said we were porting here."

"Why didn't you?" she asked.

I was still reeling from the fact that Kael was a friend of Issa's.

"Because she won't do it."

I tended to agree but remained silent.

"Even if we tell her the situation?" Mev argued. "If she can sense the Wind Crystal." She lowered her voice. "Which I assume is something she's capable of doing since it's apparently the strongest of all magical artifacts. It would be nice if Marek can verify it really is in the Maelstrom Depths before risking his neck to retrieve it."

"Precisely my thinking," I said, leaving it at that. Assuming "risking my neck" meant risking my life, it was actually much worse than that. Surviving the Maelstrom Depths would be nearly impossible. "It would be helpful to know the Crystal was there for certain." I turned my attention to Kael. "You don't believe she'll do it? Even if finding the Wind Crystal is the only way to reopen the Gate?"

Popping his last piece of bread into his mouth, Kael sighed

heavily. "She'll not want to leave Hawthorne Manor. The border has become more unstable since Mev's return. Her people are everything to Issa. Keeping them safe is more important to her than anything, including the Gate."

I didn't argue his point. Kael was right about Issa's love for her people, but I could think of one thing even more important to her than that. Either way, I was going to Hawthorne Manor to at least try to convince her to accompany us.

"You're not going to tell us how you know her?" Mev asked.

"No," I answered. "I'm not."

Kael waved the serving girl to us. "I'll simply ask Issa."

"Maybe he doesn't want us to know, Kael," Mev countered.

While her partner gave the serving girl coin for our meal, I offered Mev a smile. The Aetherian princess was as kind as she was fearless. Unfortunately, the same couldn't be said for Kael. He may be fearless, but "kind" wasn't the first word that came to mind to describe the Gyorian warrior. He might have sworn allegiance to Mev's father, pitting him directly against his own, but the man glowered more often than not.

I stood as Kael and Mev did the same.

"We will need to find you mounts," I said, spotting the very person who might secure them for us. Kael followed my gaze and groaned.

"What?" Mev asked.

"Rhett Damaris is a known human smuggler, even in Gyoria. I suppose I shouldn't be surprised Marek knows him."

"I'll choose not to take offense to that," I said, making my way to Rhett. He owed me a favor. A big one. And it was time for him to pay up.

"Too bad," Kael called. "Since I meant it as that."

Thankfully, my back was turned so Kael couldn't see me smiling. He was growing on me, but even so, I would be depositing

King Balthor's son in Aetheria before making my way to the Maelstrom Depths. The question now was, would I be heading there alone? Or would Lady Isolde be accompanying me? And more importantly, could I survive another encounter with her? Because the first one had nearly brought me to my knees.

2

ISSA

Hawthorne Manor, Border of Estmere and Gyoria

"Fall back."

The order came from my commander, one I trusted with my life. But that didn't mean I always listened to him. As Lady of Hawthorne Manor, the welfare of its people was my responsibility. I would not surrender these animals to our enemy when they were relied on by the farmer who owned them.

"Lady Isolde."

Pretending not to hear him, I continued to pursue the reivers, spurring my mount forward. The Gyorian raiders were headed for the trees, dangerously close to the border. I knew that was the reason my commander attempted to pull us back. But if they did make it to the border, I was prepared to deal with the consequences. It was the largest herd of sheep they'd stolen yet and one I refused to allow.

Mindful these reivers were Gyorian and could manipulate the land and eliminate us easily, if they so chose, I relied on my knowledge of the terrain to anticipate their movements. Their most likely path was a choke point, a narrow path by the stream where they could herd the sheep through.

"We need a diversion," I yelled to Warren, who rode beside me. He wasn't thrilled with me, but I could deal with my commander later.

As he called for two guards to loop around and draw the reivers' attention, the remainder of our party rode into the trees. "We need to block the path at the stream," I yelled.

Unfortunately, as the reivers became aware of our advantage, tree roots suddenly snaked across our path. Navigating through them and an innocuous rockfall that proved the reivers meant to intimidate rather than harm us, we stayed the course.

Thankfully, the diversion worked. As the reivers hesitated, we seized the opportunity to block the narrow path at the stream. The Gyorians, realizing they had lost the advantage and the herd, retreated. Regrettably, I couldn't do the same. Warren wasn't pleased. I rode ahead as he gave a command for the others to herd the sheep back where they belonged.

"They could have killed you. Easily," he said, catching up to me.

"True enough," I admitted. "But they wouldn't risk King Balthor's ire in doing so."

I could sense by Warren's expression he didn't agree. "Balthor would not mourn the loss of a few humans."

I pointed to the roots we circumnavigated. "Those men have little regard for law, or Elydor. Balthor hates us, but he has a deep respect for Terranor."

Their god, like all others in Elydor, demanded one thing above all. Balance. Creating, without taking away, was strictly forbidden.

"Perhaps they will return to right the land they've disturbed."

I laughed, earning a smile from my stern commander.

"Or perhaps not," he admitted. "Even so, I'd not see you come to harm and would have been pleased—"

"If I remained at the keep," I finished for him.

He smartly remained silent, for that was the truth of it. Despite the fact that my father trained me himself like the son he never had, Warren disliked whenever I used that training. It was an argument we'd had so many times, I tired of attempting to dissuade him. Instead, I let him believe what he would about my role as Lady of Hawthorne and continued to think and act according to the values my parents taught me. And if that got me killed one day?

So be it.

The ride back was as terse as I expected. While my men returned the stolen sheep to their owner, we passed through the gatehouse and spoke again only when both Warren and I dismounted in the courtyard outside Hawthorne Manor's great keep as the steward hurried toward us, blurting, "You have guests."

That was not unusual. Hawthorne Manor often entertained guests. Warren immediately joined me. Though we did not always agree, my commander, once my father's commander, was as loyal as they came.

"Who?" I asked, handing the stableboy the reins of my mount.

"Prince Kael and Princess Mevlida." His eyes darted between Warren and me which made little sense. I adored Kael and was glad to see him. I'd only met Mevlida once, but the spark between the two of them was undeniable. Even so, I was surprised when rumor reached us that they were partnered. Their fathers were bitter enemies. Kael pledging himself to King Galfrid had been a shocking development indeed.

I removed my riding gloves and took a step toward the keep.

"I'll be glad to see them both." When my steward cleared his throat, I stopped. He was acting unusually odd.

"There is another guest."

Master Edric, the son of a tenant farmer who my father befriended as a young boy, had been the steward of Hawthorne Manor for as long as my memory served. As loyal as Sir Warren and sharp-witted as any man or woman I knew, he and his family had served me well, especially after the sickness that spread through Estmere claiming both of my parents' lives.

The look on his face now was typically reserved for the direst of news.

"Who?" I asked.

"The Thalassarian Navarch."

If Edric punctured my leather armor with a broadsword, it would have been less painful. I knew it for a fact since I'd experienced it once in an unfortunate training accident.

"Marek is here?" I asked. "With the others?"

I couldn't even manage their names. Or remember my own. If not surrounded by my men, I'd have easily succumbed to the desire to sink into the ground. Instead, I channeled the woman who'd once told me, "You're stronger than the storms that seek to break you." My mother's voice echoed in my mind, steadying the whirlwind of emotions swirling around inside me.

"He is, my lady. They await you in your solar."

Resisting the urge to rearrange the errant strands of hair that had escaped my braid, or, worse, hurry to my chamber to change from riding clothes into something more presentable, I thanked him. Telling Edric I had no need of his assistance, I made my way into the keep.

Hawthorne Manor could have been called a castle as it was built for defense, but for some reason that neither my parents nor my grandfather, when he was alive, could explain, it had always been named as a manor house.

Such was the way of things in Estmere.

Our ancestors who first came through the Gate brought their ways with them. Over the course of a few hundred years, some were replaced by more modern human traditions and ideals, but more of Estmere remained the same than it had changed. Elydor was a strange place for humans, its requisite need for balance allowing very little technology to pass through the Gate reminding everyone that this world was made for immortals, and humans were their guests.

Some of us, myself included, never quite believed that. If native Elydorians simply accepted we were a part of their world, we would have less cause to worry for our safety from their elemental abilities.

Each step I took toward the solar chamber was heavier than the last. Why could I face a band of Gyorian reivers but the thought of seeing Marek again made me want to lose my last meal? My leather boots crushed the newly replaced and scented rushes beneath my feet. Standing in the corridor, my gaze focused on the light of the wall sconce as it flickered against the weathered stone wall behind it.

The last time I saw him, the meeting hadn't gone as planned.

My entire journey to Thalassaria, I imagined seeing him again, not knowing if it would even happen. Though I planned a detour to the tavern he frequented whenever in port, there was every possibility he would be out to sea. But instead, Marek was right where he'd once told me he spent much of his time when home: seated at The Moonlit Current, ale in hand. Also unsurprising, he was with a woman. A beautiful one at that. What happened next was not something I could have predicted.

I looked down at my hand, remembering the slap as clearly as if it was this morn and not years ago. The rage that had built up, seeing him again, was as unexpected as my action. I'd never struck another man, or woman, in my life, outside of training. But the look he'd given me... it had been worse than the flippant smile Marek so often wore.

It was one of regret.

Anger welled inside me. He had no right to feel regret when he'd been the one to leave, without a word. It had taken the entire journey home for me to calm myself, to wonder how I could have actually been in the same room with him but not spoken a word to the only man I'd ever loved.

What a fool I had been.

Not for loving him. Marek was an easy man to fall for. But to hear his stories, laugh at his conquests and bad behavior, and then believe I was different? If Kael and Mevlida were not in that chamber, I'd not be reaching my hand out toward the door. But they were, and the reason all three were together had me curious enough to turn the knob, take a deep breath, and step inside.

3

MAREK

I thought I was prepared to see her for the first time since The Moonlit Current.

I wasn't.

Disheveled, her dark-brown hair pulled off her face with strands escaping everywhere, she was dressed for battle and looked as if she'd just come from one. Those piercing hazel eyes were trained directly on me, Issa's expression exactly as I'd imagined it would be. Her lips, fuller than on any woman I'd ever known, parted, as if she would say something to me.

Instead, she turned to Kael and Mev.

It didn't matter that it had been my fault I'd lost the right to have her look at me the way she did them. This had been a bad idea from the start. But I had known that all along.

"What," she said, as Kael rose and hugged her, "are you doing here?"

Mev did the same. For my part, I remained seated. Issa was more likely to stab me than hug me, more's the pity.

"Have you eaten?" she asked them, the wine goblets Master

Edric gave us already filled. He was a fine steward and even managed to be cordial to me. Without knowing what Issa had told him, I'd expected a cooler welcome.

"We have been fed," Mev said, sitting beside the fire in one of four plush chairs that had been arranged before it, the intricately carved, wooden table at the center holding our wine goblets. Even without windows, it was a welcoming space, not unlike the rest of Hawthorne Manor. Issa prided herself on the care she and her staff took to make it a home despite its size. A fortress nearly as large as any in Estmere, it was one of the first built when King Galfrid carved out a portion of his own Aetherian land for the humans.

"I'm uncertain," Issa said, sitting back, "if I should ask first if the rumors of the two of you are true or"—she looked at me— "how you come to travel with him."

"Hello, Isolde," I said, not daring to give her the same sort of smile I once had. Instead, I willed myself to forget how beautiful a woman Issa was. Forget how her lips felt against my own. Pretend she was simply a human noblewoman whose help we needed. "It is good to see you."

"I cannot say the same."

"Well." Mev put her wine back onto the table. "I for one can't wait to hear what the hell happened between the two of you. Marek told us squat on the way here." She added, "Sorry, he told us nothing."

"Squat. That's a new one," Kael murmured. "She's a constant source of surprise," he added for Issa's benefit. "And while I can't account for which rumors you've heard, I can tell you Mev and I are partnered. And I did indeed pledge myself to her father."

Issa didn't hide her surprise. "Those are the rumors. Would you care to tell me how that happened? The last time I saw the two of you, Princess Mevlida's name was Mia, she claimed you kidnapped her and I'm certain," she said to Mev, "your hair was not white."

Mev's side-eye to Kael confirmed part of that as true. "Oh, he kidnapped me alright. Totally rude. Long story short, after we left, I started being able to do strange things and"—she tugged on her hair—"this."

"Mev knew when she came through the Gate," Kael said, "that she was King Galfrid's daughter. And smartly hid the fact from me, for as long as she was able. Hence, Mia."

"Basically, he fell head over heels for me. An Aetherian noblewoman named Lyra found us and began to train me. The two of them brought me to my father."

"I've heard of her, from Kael." Issa avoided looking at me, but I couldn't seem to do the same. Was that blood on her tunic? Had she been injured?

"Prince Kael of Gyoria," Issa said, her smile to Kael one of warmth, "falling in love with King Galfrid's daughter. Fate has a way of intervening in mysterious ways. Although I doubt your father appreciates the irony of your current situation."

"He does not. He sent my brother to intercept me. Took me most of an afternoon to convince him and his men to stand down so that I could follow Lyra and Mev north."

"I did hear that you battled your brother."

I'd spoken to Kael about that very battle. Prince Terran was known as a ruthless defender of Gyoria, and some said nearly as strong as his father. From talking to Kael, it seemed he was less bothered by the severed relationship with his father than being at odds with his brother.

"I did."

"He will never accept you again."

I assumed Issa spoke of King Balthor. Did she refer to Kael's brother, Terran, as well?

"No, he will not. Somehow, it took meeting Mev to appreciate how extreme my father's views had become. Before you say it." He stopped Issa. "I know you tried to tell me. But he is my father."

I knew something of complicated father–son relationships myself and could sympathize with him even as I agreed with Issa. The Gyorian king had never recovered from the loss of his queen to a human disease and all knew his hatred for humans had grown throughout the years. Did I agree with the king's decision to kidnap Mev's mother and close the Gate? Not many did, outside of Gyoria, of course. But I could understand well the need for revenge against those who hurt someone you loved.

It was what drove me, and what would probably have been my downfall. Now, it seemed, the Maelstrom Depths would have that honor.

"Interesting you mention the Aetherian Gate," I said, wanting Issa to give her attention to me.

I'm sorry.

I should have told her that night. After she slapped me, which I deserved, I should have followed her from the tavern and said those words. To this day, I couldn't explain why they'd stuck in my mouth. Why I remained silent.

"That's the reason we're here. What we are about to tell you cannot leave this chamber."

Issa's brows raised. "My integrity is not in question, Marek."

Hearing my name from her, even in that tone, was something I didn't realize, until now, I craved.

"No," I agreed. "It is not. I want you to know," I said, "the woman you saw me with is my friend Nerys."

Issa's hazel eyes flashed. "Nerys, the woman who just challenged Queen Lirael? The new queen of Thalassaria?"

"News travels fast, even among humans."

Issa's chin tilted upwards. "We have our ways," she said. I'd not meant it as a slight but should have realized Issa would take it that way. She truly did hate me.

"Yes, that Nerys. As you may have also heard, she partnered with a human by the name of Rowan of Estmere. My shared mission with him and Nerys, along with Mev and Kael, is the reason we're here. We need your help."

Issa's laugh wasn't at all like her. It was harsh, and bitter.

"You are the very last person in Elydor I care to help, Marek."

"Then do it for us," Kael said, leaning forward, elbows on his knees as if prepared to pitch our plea. "Though we still don't know how Mev was able to pass through the Gate, she's been unable to return."

Issa's eyes widened.

"You tried?" she asked Mev, who nodded.

"Kael and I were... not in a good place. I did try, and I am still desperate to get back to assure my mom and my friends that I'm okay. But as long as the portal... the Gate... stays closed, I can't do that. How much do you know about how my father opened the Gate? Or how Kael's father closed it?"

Issa looked back and forth between them.

"As much as most others, which is not a lot. They say both men relied on the elders and their deep knowledge of Elydor's magic. I know your father had attempted to create a pathway to the human realm for hundreds of years before he was successful. And that it took King Balthor nearly thirty years to close it. I assume the fact that the two of them are the most powerful in their respective clans isn't a coincidence?"

No one who knew me would believe it, but that was what

most attracted me to Isolde. I heard her voice, appreciated her intellect, before I even saw her face. A brilliant strategist, Issa was as smart as she was beautiful.

"It is not," Mev verified. "But neither of them, as strong as they are, could have done it without their clan's most powerful artifact. And not just their own but all three."

I watched as Issa took in that bit of information. Her eyes narrowed.

"I suppose... that makes sense. To open such a gateway... having the artifacts from all clans would symbolize an acceptance of Elydor for such a thing to come into existence."

I never thought of it precisely that way myself, but it did make sense. I could tell Mev and Kael were equally as impressed. Also, if Issa was going to look so extraordinarily beautiful when deep in thought, it was probably a better idea that I perish in the Maelstrom Depths than have her accompany me on this voyage.

"There is more to it, of course," Mev continued. "But essentially, to reopen the Gate and reunite my parents, along with all other humans who were separated when..." She cleared her throat. "Someone's father closed it..."

Kael's expression nearly made me laugh, but I didn't dare. Issa was fully invested in Mev's story and would not appreciate my levity.

"All three artifacts are needed. My father believes my ability to come through, even though the portal is closed, means it is entirely possible to reopen."

Issa looked at me.

It was as if I'd just successfully smuggled enchanted crystals past a contingency of Gyorians. At least, until her neutral expression turned into a frown.

"That's why you are involved. Your friend, the queen, has

offered use of the Tidal Pearl. And now you seek the Stone of Mor'Vallis?"

Impressive. "Close. Nerys has indeed pledged use of the Tidal Pearl when the time comes. And getting the Stone of Mor'Vallis from King Balthor will become necessary as well. But that's his job." I nodded to Kael and reached for my wine. Taking a sip, I relished Issa's attention on me. "In the meantime, we need to find the Wind Crystal. Apparently, when King Balthor stole it to close the Gate, he returned a fake to Galfrid and still has the original."

Her eyes darted to Kael. His grimace confirmed my words. "I returned it to King Galfrid myself," he said. "After a long, drawn-out negotiation, having no knowledge that it was not the real Crystal. Mev's father knew immediately but never acknowledged it."

"King Galfrid has been without the real Wind Crystal since..." Issa's eyes widened.

"Yep," Mev said. "Apparently, he's performed enough extraordinary feats since, on his own accord, that no Aetherians suspected it was missing. He's been unable to locate it, until now. It's another long story, how the Wind Crystal was discovered, but it has been. And Marek volunteered to go get it."

"Where is it?"

"Deep within the Maelstrom Depths."

Issa's jaw dropped as she turned her attention back to me.

"And you're planning to... go get it?"

"I am."

"Marek. You will be killed."

I couldn't resist asking, "Would that displease you, Issa?"

She opened her mouth, but closed it. And glared at me.

Clearly wanting to say, *"Nay,"* something held her back. She hated me. Despised what I had done to her. Obviously wished I was anywhere but in this solar chamber with me. But she didn't want me dead.

That was at least something.

The thought of not surviving this mission wasn't one I relished, but it was one of those things that just had to be done. Dying with Issa still angry at me? Not the way I wanted to go. And it seemed like I might just have an opportunity to turn those tides before our mission.

4

ISSA

I despised Marek of Thalassaria, Navarch of the Tidebreaker Fleet. Charming opportunist. A smuggler who was as reckless as he was daring. As ruthless as he was charismatic. It should not surprise me that he'd volunteered to retrieve the Wind Crystal from a place none were known to have ventured to and survived.

But neither did I want him to die, a certainty than none but me in this chamber seemed to appreciate.

"No one has made it out of the Maelstrom Depths alive," I said.

"That we know of," Marek quipped.

"You will allow him to do this?" I asked Kael and Mev.

"None are more qualified to attempt it." Kael sat back in his seat, wine in hand. Mev appeared as worried as I felt, but she said nothing. For her, the stakes were higher than most, and it seemed she was willing to risk Marek's life to reopen the Gate. And maybe I could not blame her for that, but neither could I so easily accept it.

"It is a death sentence."

That smile. The same one that had so captivated me the day

we met. He was unmistakably Thalassarian, the sun-bleached hair and tanned complexion only part of his clan's giveaway. From his clothing— a loose, linen shirt and leather boots, more than one dagger ever-present at his hip, that he hardly needed courtesy of Marek's water-wielding abilities— to his carefree attitude, he embodied the free spirit most Elydorians associated with his kind.

It was much more than just a smile. The combination of Marek's strong jawline which emphasized an internal determination he kept closely guarded and his easy manner made it difficult not to be drawn in.

Never again.

"Not wanting to see you dead does not mean I wish you well." I addressed Mev and Kael. "I am sorry you've come all this way, and I sympathize with your plight. I too wish desperately that those who travelled to Elydor, thinking it would be a temporary journey, could get back to their families. I want you to be able to reunite with your family and friends," I said to Mev. "And for your parents to do the same. But, as you may have surmised, there is a history between us that makes it impossible for me to bear his presence."

"Ooh, that hurts, Issa."

"It's honesty," I shot back. Without going into the details of our situation, I tried to explain to Mev and Kael. "Some wounds never heal. Instead, they change you, and not always for the better. Some might argue that even deep pain teaches us something, but the mark Marek left the first time we met is one not easily erased. It was a lesson I could have done without."

No one spoke, at first. If my words were dramatic, there was no help for it. Each and every one was true. Willingly going on a journey with Marek would be akin to opening the gates to an enemy force who intended to overtake you.

"Our intelligence places the Wind Crystal in those caves." Mev's eyes were pleading. "But there is no way to be certain. Marek could be risking his life unnecessarily. If you were to accompany us, we could be certain."

My shoulders dropped. The battle I prepared to fight fled my body instantly. Without revealing my thoughts, I listened, already knowing the outcome.

"When Terran attempted to stop me from taking Mev north, Adren was among the men. He defected and joined me," Kael said. "But after learning what had to be done, he agreed to return home and attempt to locate the Wind Crystal."

Kael's right-hand man was as loyal as any in Elydor, so Kael's story did not surprise me.

"He was welcomed back?"

"Mostly. Some suspicion remained. All know of his loyalty to me, but pledging myself to King Galfrid, partnering with his daughter, was the excuse he needed to publicly sever ties."

"This is an extraordinary turn of events," I admitted.

"You were right, Issa, to have criticized me over the years. I allowed my father's hatred of humans to influence my thinking. I never agreed my mother's death was the fault of your entire race, but I did unjustly believe humans were inferior to native Elydorians in many ways. For that, I owe you an apology."

Princess Mevlida had influenced Kael's thinking more than I could have thought possible.

"You owe none to me, Kael, as well you know."

He inclined his head. "I offer it nonetheless."

By the way Mev grinned, I could tell she was proud of him, as she should be. Changing one's thinking after so many years of influence by your own parent was not an easy task.

"Thank you," I said simply, unable to stop myself from glancing at Marek.

He was no longer smiling.

If anyone in this chamber owed me an apology, it was him. But I doubted one would be forthcoming. Nor would I accept it anyway. There were limits to my ability to forgive.

"If I refuse to help?" I asked, knowing his answer already.

Without warning, the memory of our first kiss popped into my mind. It had been summer, the garden at Hawthorne, once a source of my mother's pride, in full bloom. He'd taken me in his arms, and I went willingly, even knowing by then how many women he'd courted—or seduced, to be more accurate. That kiss had been everything I'd expected, and more.

How long had it been that I dreamed of Marek's kisses?

You know the answer to that already, Issa. It has been precisely the same number of years since the day you met him.

"I pledged to my queen," Marek said, "and to Mevlida, that I would attempt to retrieve the Wind Crystal. When I arrive in Gyoria and meet with Adren, if he still believes it is hidden in the Maelstrom Depths, that is where I will go."

Our eyes held each other's as Kael and Mev fell away. It was just the two of us, and the crackle of the fire.

There was no hope for it. "I would speak with you alone." Gritting my teeth, I stood and made my way to the door. Opening it, I found Edric there, as expected.

"Will you see Prince Kael and Princess Mevlida to their chambers. If they need anything at all—"

"I will see to it, my lady."

Kael and Mev were already standing.

"Also, my lady, Lord Draven would like a word."

Mev stopped before walking past me.

"He is here, in this keep?"

I looked between her and Kael. "Aye. He resides at

Hawthorne Manor," I said, curious. "Did you meet him on your last visit?"

"I did. Briefly."

Kael reached up, placing his hand on Mevlida's arm, as if stopping her from saying more.

"Thank you, Issa, for your hospitality. We do not wish to impose on you for more than one eve."

"You would leave on the morrow?"

"Aye," he confirmed.

I had little time to decide.

"We will speak again in the morn."

Kael's eyes darted to Marek. I nodded, but said to Edric, "I will need more wine, please."

At that, Marek laughed.

It was a deep sound, one of pure merriment and joy. The sound of a man with few cares, as if he was prepared to be lost in the Maelstrom Depths because of a life well lived. A sound I'd heard in my dreams, willing it away as the sun rose.

Closing the door, I spun toward him.

"You will notice, I am not laughing, Marek."

Neither was he now, but the bold Navarch's smile still lingered.

"I notice that, and much more, Issa."

He dared his tone to be suggestive, and didn't my traitorous body respond? Willing it to heel, I gave him my most stern and unforgiving expression.

"As do I, Marek. If only I'd done so the first time we met."

Sitting, I said nothing at first. When Edric returned a moment later, Marek seemed relieved. Unfortunately for him, my steward remained long enough to fill our pewter goblets, replace the now empty wine flagon, and give me a final look of pity before leaving.

"I'm sorry, Issa."

And there it was. Finally, after so many years. I had naught to say to his empty words. They meant nothing to me. Less than nothing. I took a long sip, wishing for a hot bath but then cursing the memory of Marek telling me what he would do to me the first time we found ourselves in a tub together. One of many promises he never kept.

"I would prefer we discuss the matter at hand."

"I'm sorry for—"

"Stop," I said, unable to bear it. "I have little desire to hear your apologies now, Marek. The reason you left, without a word. The reason you never contacted me, or returned to Hawthorne Manor, later. The reason you said nothing to me at The Moonlit Current. None of it matters. Not anymore."

"Of course it does."

"No," I argued. "It does not. You are here because of Mevlida and Kael. And for your queen. Not me. So I would prefer not to pretend otherwise or this will never work."

He didn't reply.

The intensity of his stare, the absence of an ever-present smile, often bordering on a smirk, almost had me shifting in my seat. Instead, I took a sip of my wine, held firm, and tried to forget his many more years of experience. Dealing with immortals was immensely draining at times.

This was one of those times.

I am Lady Isolde Hawthorne, daughter of two nobles who traced their roots to the origins of humans in Elydor. And before that, to kings in the human realm. I cannot control Marek's thoughts or actions, but I can control my own and will not back down. He will never have my heart again.

"I'll say nothing more on it than this," Marek said finally. "I was a coward to leave as I did. If I could have trusted myself to say goodbye and not stay, I'd have done so. Should have done so. I should have said that in The Moonlit Current but was taken aback by your presence. By the time I'd gathered my wits about me, you were gone. And by your reaction, I thought staying away was for the best."

I could hear the thud of my heart in both ears. How long had I craved for such an explanation? How many questions did I construct in my mind, wishing I could ask? There was a time, not long after he left, I'd have given everything to hear those words. But that time was long past.

If I could have trusted myself to say goodbye and not stay.

A weaker version of myself would ask what Marek meant by those words.

"Were you injured?"

I followed his gaze to the hem of my tunic. If it were anyone but Marek, I'd have apologized for receiving him in such a state.

"Trexan blood," I said instead.

"Sir Warren still spending his days attempting to persuade you to remain inside the castle walls?"

I would not be lulled into conversation. I refused to be charmed a second time.

"Aye," I said simply. "How do you envision me helping your mission?"

Marek sighed, apparently resigning himself to my refusal to engage in anything but discussion of the Wind Crystal's retrieval. He placed the wine goblet on the wooden table my father had hand-carved himself, an embodiment of one of the many reasons I could not leave Estmere, even if adventures like the ones Marek promised called to me.

"I plan to drop Mev and Kael in Aetheria before sailing to the Gyorian coast."

"Why?"

"Mev will continue to learn Aetherian ways and train with

her father. Kael has been working with King Galfrid and his elders to unearth vital knowledge about his own father and the Stone of Mor'Vallis. Once the Wind Crystal is returned, such knowledge will become vital as he takes it back from Balthor."

"And the rest of your crew?"

"A crew requires provisions, accommodations, and time. All luxuries I cannot afford."

No. Absolutely, no.

"You travel from Aetheria to the Depths alone?"

"Alone. Or with you. I will rendezvous with Adren first and then take you as close to the Depths as possible without putting you in danger. Once you confirm the Crystal's presence in the caves, I will enter them alone."

And likely die before he reached it, but I kept that to myself.

"The Maelstrom Depths are unpredictable," he continued. "Even on the outskirts. The air itself carries a charge, the water churning as if it was alive. If the Wind Crystal is inside, its magic will amplify the chaos. You should be able to sense it several leagues out, perhaps more."

"You are overly confident in my abilities."

His brows rose, Marek's skepticism apparent. "You sensed the amulet I carried before I stepped into your hall. If I remember correctly, after I learned of your abilities, you told me you'd sensed it well beyond Hawthorne's gatehouse."

He'd almost pulled a smile from me at the memory.

"The amulet that nearly had you detained for smuggling?"

"Not smuggling. A strategic relocation. That relic would have been locked away in a vault, forgotten, if not for me. Besides, it served its purpose."

I had no wish to revisit the day we met. "I would imagine," I said, concentrating instead on the task at hand, "I could sense the Wind Crystal from quite a distance away, notwithstanding the turbulence of the Maelstrom which will surely complicate matters."

Marek rubbed his thumb across his lower lip, something he did when deep in thought. I remembered the movement well. Suddenly, the wine in my goblet became the most interesting thing in the chamber. I stared at it, cursing myself for allowing, again, the thought of kissing him to enter into my mind.

"I will not be sailing anywhere near the Maelstrom with you on board."

I was forced to look up, but thankfully, Marek's hands were now occupied as he reached for his wine.

"How can I sense it, then?"

"Perhaps you cannot. But I will not take that chance."

He didn't wish to put me in danger. "Then it seems my skills will be only marginally useful. I cannot guarantee sensing even the Wind Crystal from such a distance."

"I do not ask for guarantees. Just a chance at ensuring my mission will be executed with just cause."

There were many reasons not to agree to accompany him, besides my limited capacity to help and the most obvious one... traveling in tight quarters with the man who awoke a passion within me I didn't know existed and then left, without word or warning, breaking my heart and leaving me on a longer path to healing than I could have imagined. To even consider such a thing was madness.

And then there was Hawthorne Manor.

"I have little wish to leave my people at such a tumultuous time, though I could appoint Lord Draven in my stead."

When Marek had first come to Hawthorne Manor, Draven was in Aetheria so the two had never met. He had been my father's right-hand man and had held Hawthorne in my name when I'd traveled before. Even so, our Gyorian borders were as turbulent as ever.

"It will be a sacrifice, for certain. We do not ask you this lightly, Issa."

"Whose idea was it?" I asked, suddenly curious. "To come here?"

His gaze did not waver. "Mine. I realized only this morn Kael knew you as well. He admitted considering asking for your aid but thought it was too dangerous."

"And you do not?"

"No, because I have no intention of putting you in danger. You will remain with Adren on the Gyorian shore during the mission."

A human in Gyoria could be a danger in itself, but not nearly as much as the one Marek intended. But it wasn't that danger that held me back. Draven was here and would be as good a substitute for my presence as any. Truly, there was only one reason I hesitated.

But that was not reason enough to deny Mevlida and Kael. My sacrifice would be small compared to Marek's and there was really only one answer I could give.

"I will come with you," I said, "if you promise not to make any mention of our time together."

He paused. Gritting his teeth, Marek clearly unhappy with my request, he opened his mouth and then closed it.

I waited. That concession was not negotiable.

"You have my promise."

5

MAREK

I turned in my saddle, just having passed the gatehouse but sensing someone was following me. Waiting for him to join me, I greeted the commander.

"Sir Warren."

"Navarch," he said, stiffly.

"Captain will do. Or Marek, if you prefer."

We rode in silence, our horses' hooves kicking up gravel.

"You've had little rain, of late?"

"Very little. Lady Isolde has considered sending for Aetherian aid."

Issa disliked asking anyone for aid. "I could summon water from the tide pools near the cliffs."

Sir Warren stiffened, skeptical. "Seawater?"

"It can be purified. Or..." I hesitated, feeling mischievous. "If your need is urgent, I can call upon the mists themselves to fill your reservoirs."

The man blinked. "You are serious?"

"As serious as a Thalassarian drought."

He wanted to smile but it seemed Sir Warren Calder had

caught Issa's affliction for hating me. "A rather impractical, dare I say, theatrical, display of your abilities."

"Perhaps," I admitted, "it might be simpler, especially given my short stay here, to send an emissary from Aetheria. I head there straightaway and will see to it since I know Issa won't ask."

"Thank you." He sped up alongside me.

Sir Warren appeared so much older than when we first met. There were times I envied humans for their mortality, but others when I felt poorly for the frailty that came with such rapid aging, though I would never hint of that to the commander.

"Do you have a destination?" he asked.

"No," I admitted. "It just seemed prudent to step away from the manor until mid-day."

"When my lady will join you and your companions?"

"She briefed you?" I asked, moving to the side of the road as a wagon came toward us with what appeared to be a shipment of fruits and vegetables.

"Aye. Said only that she was needed for an important mission relating to King Galfrid's attempt at reopening the Gate. Lord Draven was not pleased she refused to reveal the exact nature of her mission."

"And you are not displeased by the lack of information?"

Sir Warren greeted the wagon rider as our road opened up once again. "No. But then, I have no ambitions beyond my current station."

"But Draven does?"

He made a sound of disgust. "He will not be content until he's named King of Estmere."

"There is no king of Estmere," I pointed out.

"Precisely."

We rode in silence until a stream, where I slowed, unable to resist. Coming to a stop, I raised both hands and manipulated the water into the air, allowing it to fall on the plants and flowers along its banks.

"Braggart."

Because he said it with the faintest hint of a smile, I didn't take offense. Not that I would do so anyway, since he was right.

"Perhaps, but those flowers will be thankful for it. I'm surprised we've heard little about your lack of rain in the region."

Neither of us rode away. I, for one, was content to remain along the river, never fond of being long without seeing water.

"You broke her heart. Devastated her."

His words were so unexpected from the stalwart commander, I had no response. Instead, I watched the current, allowing it to sync with the beating of my heart. When I looked up, Sir Warren was watching me.

"I devastated myself in leaving."

"Maybe so, but you had a choice in the matter. My lady did not."

I hadn't expected to have this conversation, but since we were doing it, I'd lean into it. "I was a coward and have regretted it since. Aye, we need Lady Isolde's abilities for this mission, but I also wanted the opportunity to see her. To apologize. But she's made me promise not to mention our past."

"Then do not."

"Thank you," I said sarcastically, "for the advice."

"If your intentions are to find forgiveness with Lady Isolde, then I would suggest taking her lead. And consider not breaking her heart again."

Though his words were casual, his tone was not.

"I've no intention of doing so."

His response was a deeper scowl than he'd already been giving me.

Though I did have one more question, since the commander was being more loquacious than expected. "Is she happy?"

His eyes met mine. "It is not my place to discuss such a thing," he said finally.

And there was my answer.

It had been only a sennight, my previous stay at Hawthorne Manor. But it had been enough, Issa and I spending every waking moment together during that time, to have guessed the answer without having Sir Warren confirm it.

She craved adventure. Issa's parents' untimely death forced her into a life not of her choosing and she sacrificed herself to keep Hawthorne's people safe. I didn't need her commander's answer to know the truth of it.

"Shall we return?" he asked, likely uncomfortable with my line of questioning.

If your intentions are to find forgiveness with Lady Isolde...

Of course I wanted her forgiveness, and if I wasn't headed to my likely death, I'd want much, much more. But that would have to suffice.

"Tell me," I asked as we turned back toward Hawthorne Manor, "why you mistrust Draven. And why Issa does not."

I thought the commander might not answer.

"Draven was born a farmer's son. He rose through the ranks and was knighted by my lady's father, who was not much older than him at the time. He was given the title of Warden of the Borderlands, tasked with defending Hawthorne's southern territories against Gyorian raids."

Our slow trot allowed Sir Warren and I easy conversation. "Has he been effective in this role?"

Sir Warren's expression gave me my answer. "Just this morn, we were hunting when a heard of sheep was reported stolen by Gyorian reivers. So nay, he has not. To my mind, at least."

"A dangerous proposition, to tangle with them."

"These are dangerous times," he said. "As for Lord Draven, he was fiercely loyal to Lord Hawthorne when they were boys. But power changes men. Over time, whispers grew. The taxes he collected from the border towns never seemed to match what was recorded in the ledgers. And more than one who spoke too openly against him... disappeared."

I raised an eyebrow. "You think he betrayed her father?"

"No. But he walked the line too closely for my liking. Lord Draven is an opportunist but has always been clever enough to hide behind loyalty and duty. Issa trusts him because her father did and because he saved her once when a band of Gyorian raiders breached the southern pass. He rode through the night to warn her father."

"And yet you mistrust him?"

"I was there that night. He was the hero, aye. But he didn't issue the warning until the last possible moment. When I confronted him, he had an excuse for the lapse, but I think he wanted the breach to happen so he could be the one to save her."

The silence stretched between us.

"And now?" I pressed.

Sir Warren looked up toward Hawthorne Manor, which now appeared in the distance, its walls imposing to other humans but less so to any Gyorian who truly wished to breach it.

"He waits. Bides his time, playing the loyal knight, and whispering in Issa's ear. But men like Lord Draven don't serve forever."

6

ISSA

I left instructions with Warren and Edric. Packed my saddlebags. Spoke to the staff. There was no other reason to delay except that Marek's suggestion of riding back to Valewood Bay with him made sense. Stabling my mare there was an option, but not a desired one. Worse, Marek seemed to be enjoying my discomfort.

Of course he is. The Thalassarian smuggler is as ungracious as they come.

Kael and Mev were mounted already, as was Marek, but as I prepared to reluctantly do the same, my companion's smile slipped. I looked back to the entrance of the keep where he was staring to discern the reason.

Lord Draven stood there, watching us. We had spoken at length about everything from border security to crop rotation but perhaps he wished to speak to me further? As I walked toward him, a flash of a younger Draven kneeling beside me in this very courtyard, where I had fallen and scraped my knee, gave me pause. I realized what disconcerted me about the memory. It was his smile, the same one he wore now. There was nothing remarkable about it. Draven was as even-tempered as any man I knew, rarely given to fits of anger, or bursts of joy.

"Did you wish to speak to me?" I asked as he met me in front of the keep's stone stairs.

"Nay," he replied. "I wanted only to see you off safely with your friends."

If he made the word "friends" sound as though they were unruly children, it was only because he had always carried himself as the adult in the room. I, in turn, felt like that same girl who had scraped her knee in this courtyard years ago. It was a foolish sentiment, one I kept locked away, unspoken.

"Very well," I said, preparing to rejoin the others. "I leave Hawthorne Manor in your care."

"As your father would have wished," he said, halting me with his words. "You can rest assured, my lady... it is in capable hands."

"Thank you," I replied, though something about his measured tone lingered in my thoughts as I turned to go.

Glancing briefly at Kael and Mev, the latter seemingly unpleased by something, I reluctantly mounted behind Marek, even taking his hand to do so. Though the gesture was initiated and ended quickly, the strength of his grip and warmth of his hand lingered for far too long. I said nothing, refusing to hold onto him until we lurched forward, all but making my grip on at least his tunic necessary.

"You will get yourself killed for your stubbornness, Issa."

"Please stop using my name."

Unreasonableness oozed from me, but I couldn't seem to put a stop to it. Marek appearing at Hawthorne Manor, coupled with the necessity of my unexpected leave-taking, was not boding well for this rapidly declining state of affairs.

"What shall I call you?" he asked, as pleasant as usual. But today, Marek's infernal cheer grated.

We rode ahead of Mev and Kael, but I could hear them following. Though they were unlikely to hear our conversation, I lowered my voice anyway as we made our way through the gatehouse.

"Perhaps we do not speak at all."

He laughed. "We will be gone a fortnight, easily. Likely more. Shall we not speak in all that time?"

I said nothing for a spell since there was nothing to say. No explanation would ever be adequate, and I refused to allow myself to let him back in. But having thought of little else but his words since Marek spoke them, it was perhaps better to have the matter cleared up now before we were forced onto a small ship with Mev and Kael also on board.

If I could have trusted myself to say goodbye and not stay, I'd have done so.

"I asked you not to speak of it," I began, unsure if this was the right decision, "but would amend that request."

At that moment, his mount narrowly avoided a duskrabbit. Marek spun in his saddle toward me, my heart lurching at the sight. He was as handsome as the day we met, though his carefree grin was turned downward in a rare frown.

"Hold on, will you please? Falling and breaking your neck will serve no one. And I know how precious your people are to you, Issa."

He was right, despite that it pained me to admit it. Waiting until Marek turned back around, I reached my hands tentatively toward his waist. In response, he grabbed one wrist at a time, his other hands holding onto the reins, and pulled them forward, tightening my grip.

Breathing in a scent that should not be familiar to me, after all these years, I refused to let him know how much the close proximity affected me.

"As to amending my request?" I asked in my most noble-sounding voice, the one my mother used effectively.

"I am amicable," he responded, in a tone so unlike him it nearly made me smile.

"In an effort to find some measure of peace between us"—his back stiffened at that —"I would like to know why you left without a word to me beforehand."

And there it was.

If Marek's stay at Hawthorne all those years ago—his courting of me, the words he spoke, the care he took with my innocence—were genuine, I simply could not reconcile them with waking up to finding that he'd simply vanished. No note. No message to my staff. Nothing. Like an Aetherian whisper, heard only by those trained to do so, there was no trace of him.

"As I said, it was cowardly of me to do so."

He didn't turn toward me. Or elaborate. It was as lacking of an explanation as when Marek first offered it.

"But never sent a missive later. Or spoke to me in that tavern."

Marek did turn in the saddle then. He glanced behind us, and apparently seeing nothing amiss but our companions following, he held my gaze briefly before turning back around.

Was that, possibly, regret?

"I assumed there were no words I could have uttered that would have you forgive me."

A fair assumption, since it was true.

"Then why leave that way?"

I hated the question. Hated the way my voice quivered. Hated being reduced to the very thing I told myself I would not: a simpering fool who cared for the opinion of someone who would do such a thing.

Perhaps if I was Elydorian and lived a few more centuries, I could harden my heart enough not to have asked. I was strong in so many ways, save this one.

He turned his head enough that I could see his profile, though only briefly as a fallen branch demanded he navigate around it. At that moment, a trexan-pulled wagon appeared on the horizon. The man guiding it was an elderly farmer, his shoulders hunched beneath a patched cloak as he urged the lumbering trexan forward. Marek shifted his attention to the wagon, his posture relaxing, as though relieved to have something to draw his focus from our conversation.

I greeted the farmer as we passed.

"I'm not proud of how I handled things, Issa. The reasons for my leaving... weren't simple. They still aren't."

Why had I thought breaking my own rule, talking about the very thing I told him I didn't wish to discuss, would make things better? The sting of his unsaid words settled like a stone in my chest. We remained silent then as I deflected Marek's later attempts at conversation. By the time we arrived in Valewood Bay, I was certain he might send me back to Hawthorne Manor. Marek hated silence and that was all I had to offer him. Instead, as Kael and Mev rode beside us, commenting on the speed of our return, he told them not to dismount.

"We head straight to the docks."

Dusk had fallen, and I assumed, as it appeared Kael and Mev had, we would not sail until the morning. But if Marek wanted to get the voyage over with quickly, I would not argue the point. The sooner I could get back to Hawthorne Manor, despite the mundane days and nights that awaited me there, the better. For if there was one thing worse than not living an adventurous life, it was coming to the realization Marek left without warning for one reason, and one reason alone.

I meant nothing to him. Not then, or any day since. And I would do well to remember it.

7

MAREK

"I give you, *Tidechaser*."

Issa stepped aboard, as silent as she'd been on the journey here. I imagined coming back into Issa's life would not be smooth sailing, but neither had I anticipated how difficult it would truly be to earn her forgiveness.

"It feels as if I've been aboard her already," Issa said, making her way through the main deck. "I know more of your ship than I do anything else about you, including your family."

With Mev and Kael still on the hunt for supplies, and little other movement on the docks at this time of night, I could hear every creak of the ship as she swayed beneath our feet. There was no place in Elydor that felt more like home than here.

"My family are the crew that I left behind on this voyage."

"Would it not be easier to sail with them?"

I shrugged. "Not necessarily. Most accompany me for training. All of this"—I pointed to the rigging and sails—"is to blend in with human ships. I need little to navigate *Tidechaser* beyond the abilities with which I was born."

Issa remained unimpressed.

"Come," I said, slinging Issa's bag from one shoulder to the other. "Allow me to show her to you." Without waiting for her to decline, I pointed to the various compartments. "Those house weapons, trade goods, provisions... and then the helm, of course. Where all the magic happens."

I counted Issa's rolled eyes as a win as we moved below deck.

"The crew's quarters," I said, opening a door to reveal a room with small, functional hammocks which could accommodate up to fifteen men. "And more storage," I said as we passed another door. "This is the captain's spare," I said, opening Mev and Kael's quarters.

Issa peeked inside.

"Where will I be staying?"

"That," I said, closing the door, "is for Mev and Kael. You will be in the captain's quarters." When I opened my cabin, I was surprised not to find Issa beside me. She'd halted in the corridor.

"Issa?"

"I am not sleeping in there with you."

I pretended to stab myself in the heart with an invisible dagger. "Say it isn't so?"

When she didn't so much as crack a smile, I tried again. "I will not be in there with you."

Issa inched toward me. "You won't?"

"No," I said, stepping inside. "I'll sleep in a crew bunk. Or on deck."

Putting her bag down, I waited for Issa to join me as I pulled a moonstone from my pocket. Placing the Gyorian-mined gem in a holder on the small desk in the corner of the cabin, I tried not to think about the fact that Issa had only grown more beautiful since I saw her last.

Though now dressed as a warrior, I'd also seen Lady Isolde holding court in her own hall. Neither version was more beautiful than the other. Just different. Strands of dark hair escaped from her braid and, despite it being pulled back, I could easily imagine it falling in waves around her shoulders.

Like that one night...

"Marek?"

Getting a hold of myself, I pointed out, "The bed is small, but comfortable. Use the space however you see fit, but you may not want to look too closely under the floorboards."

Issa rolled her eyes. "You've not changed a bit."

She was too close. Her expression, not as antagonistic. For a brief moment, I could pretend I had not broken her heart, as her commander suggested.

Was it true, Issa?

It was the last question I would ever ask, not knowing what to do with the answer. Not now that I was on a death mission.

"You have," I said quietly.

Issa cocked her head to the side. "To most, I am the same Isolde that I've always been. If there is a difference, it is because of our circumstance." She put up a hand. "Which we will not discuss again."

We needed to begin anew.

Taking a step backward, I bowed to her.

"Lady Isolde, I am Marek of Thalassaria, Navarch of the Tidebreaker Fleet and captain of this fine ship which will allow us to retrieve the Wind Crystal to its rightful owner and bring you back home safely to Hawthorne Manor."

The same Hawthorne Manor that weighed down Issa's true wanderlust nature. But I did not mention that. Standing, I awaited her response. Our eyes met, mine pleading for Issa to allow me to make amends.

I'd lived more than a hundred and fifty years... escaped death... foolishly loved... had adventures that still made my heart sing when I thought of them... but nothing had ever tempted me more than my desire to reach forward and tuck an errant strand of Issa's hair behind her ear. Use our closeness as an excuse to cup her face in my hands and kiss those full lips, so unusually full that anyone would be a fool not to notice them straightaway. Where she once looked at me with kindness, and longing, Issa's eyes were full of sadness and regret.

What a fool I have been.

When Issa reached out her hand, in the human way, I took it immediately. Touching her, as innocuous as our handshake was, made standing almost uncomfortable.

"I would say, 'I'm pleased to meet you,' but I've heard much about Thalassarian corsairs to be properly wary," she said, pulling her hand back.

I swallowed, hard. Those were the exact words she had said the first time we met. I'd carved them to memory, along with every other word Issa had spoken to me in our short time together.

Shaking off the heaviness that had burdened me from the moment I left, and every time I'd thought of Issa since, I brought the Marek everyone knew, and loved, to the forefront. Grinning, I offered the same response as back then.

"Navarch, if it pleases you. Or captain, if you prefer. Or I might suggest... Marek."

Was that the hint of a smile?

"We are dropping titles already, sir?"

She remembered as well. Word for word.

"If my lady so desires."

"I could say, 'I desire to know why you've come to Hawthorne Manor,' but cannot as we are clearly"—she waved her arm around my cabin—"not at Hawthorne Manor."

My very small cabin, as it turned out, even though it was the

largest on the ship. Having Issa ride behind me all day was difficult enough, but being this close and facing her?

It would be the first and last time I found myself in here alone
with her.

"No," I agreed. "We are not."

Footsteps overhead signaled Mev and Kael's return.

"I will leave you to get adjusted in your quarters, my lady. If
you care to join us on deck, my plan is to set sail after a quick
evening meal. To that end, I typically take meals in here but we
can dine in the tidehall beside the galley. Or, when weather
allows, on the main deck. Though I will warn you, without the
cook, meals will not be elaborate."

"I didn't expect them to be but will admit"—Issa's big brown
eyes scanned my quarters—"this is larger than I expected for a
'fast, sleek ship.'"

She'd remembered the words I used to describe *Tidechaser*
after so many years. I thought perhaps her commander had been
exaggerating. Even after the slap she'd delivered at The Moonlit
Current, I'd convinced myself our few days together meant very
little to Lady Isolde, and that leaving as I did likely had not
affected her.

Clearly, I had been wrong. And there was a part of me—a
diseased, flawed part of me that put my desires above anything,
or anyone—that was glad for it. Which was precisely the reason I
left Hawthorne Manor.

"I will endeavor to make this as smooth a journey as
possible."

"There you are."

Kael. Normally, I'd welcome the Gyorian warrior's presence,
but now that Issa was speaking to me again, I'd been stalling.

"I was settling Issa into her quarters," I said, usually not one to explain myself. But everything about being around her made me feel as awkward as, well, a human.

Or most humans. Isolde was more sure of herself than most twice her age. Having such a responsibility thrust on you at a young age tended to do that.

Kael crossed his thick arms. "The one you said no one sleeps in but you?"

I faced the esteemed prince, who was clearly determined not to aid me in winning over Isolde.

"Also the one," I said, wondering why everyone liked the Gyorian so much, "I offered to Mev, who refused to take it." Turning back to Issa, I added, "She refused to be separated from him, though I can't imagine why."

This time, I was able to elicit a smile. I would be taken by the Maelstrom Depths, gladly, for that smile. It suddenly occurred to me how dangerous this journey would be with a more amicable Issa. Perhaps it would be easier to garner her anger instead.

"Speaking of beds," an irritated voice behind me continued. "I could be sleeping in one on land if it weren't for your insistence we sail out 'at once.'"

Reluctantly pulling myself away from Issa, I left the cabin with Kael and made my way above deck, asking myself, not for the first time, if soliciting Issa's aid was the wisest of decisions. For even if the Depths did not take me, something darker and more dangerous threatened to do just that.

8

ISSA

"Have you sailed before?"

Not wanting to be left behind as we pushed off, I followed Marek and Kael above deck. Joining Mev along the side railings, apparently called gunwales, which Mev confessed to learning recently herself, I watched as Marek, above us on the quarterdeck, flicked his wrist.

"I have, but never with a Thalassarian." We began to move slowly away from the dock. "How did he do that?"

"By creating a current," Kael said, coming up to us. "That nudges the ship away from the dock."

Slowly drifting away from port and the lights of Valewood Bay, the clear night sky full of stars, the same surging of excitement I'd always gotten when leaving shore bubbled within me. I turned once again to watch Marek. To say he looked at home up there would have been an understatement. All Thalassarians felt most comfortable surrounded by water, but he was not just a water-wielder. Marek was a Navarch with the Tidebreaker Fleet, and the captain of *Tidechaser*, his pride and joy. Watching him take to the rigging was a sight to behold.

"What is he doing?" Mev asked before I could.

"Releasing the topgallant sail," Kael said as it unfurled. "Marek is as territorial as any ship captain I've met. Won't let me help."

Mev made a face. "Won't let you? I was under the impression Gyorians and sailing weren't exactly like peanut butter and jelly."

"Peanut... what?"

Mev rolled her eyes as we pitched forward. "I don't know how that didn't make its way here. It's not like peanut butter is a recent invention."

"Ooh!" I ducked my head, as if willing Marek to do the same, thinking for a moment he'd come close to being beheaded by the swinging boom as the wind caught the sail. But, of course, this was Marek. Quick as a tide change, he pivoted, ducking smoothly without missing a beat.

"You don't have to worry about him," Kael said gruffly. "He may run his mouth more than any Thalassarian I've ever met, but Marek certainly knows how to navigate in the open seas."

Marek's hands were extended toward the horizon, and though I couldn't see his expression from here, it was clear he was focused intently.

"So he's controlling the current?" I asked as the ship groaned while we moved, her creak of wood joining the ocean's whispers.

"In a different way than before, but yes," Kael answered, which is when I saw Mev's sly smile. We crept along, sailing further and further away from shore.

Mev lifted her hand toward the sail.

It was subtle, at first. But as we picked up speed, her manipulation of the air to create enough wind to bolster *Tidechaser*'s sails became more obvious.

"Much appreciated," Marek yelled down from his position above us.

Mev smiled up to him, the same way I might have when we first met. Marek was easy to like.

"You've been training?" I asked, unable to look away from Marek. The moonlight caught him just right, making his expression easier to see. With one hand now resting on the ship's wheel, fingers curled around the wood, a slow smile tugged at his lips as he looked our way.

I gave my attention to Mev, too late. She'd caught me staring.

"All day, every day," she said. "Between my father and Lyra, I've little time for much else."

"Not entirely true," Kael muttered, his tone teasing.

Mev swatted him playfully.

"Lyra?" I asked.

"You know," Mev said as we glided through the water, the lights of Valewood Bay long gone. "The Aetherian noblewoman who Kael once tried to kill."

"I did *not*." He emphasized the last word. "Try to kill her." Kael turned toward us, sighing. "We served on the Aetherian Gate Council together. When I escorted Mev—"

"Kidnapped."

I pursed my lips together to keep from laughing.

"After we left Hawthorne Manor, Lyra discovered us," he said.

"Can't wait to hear this revisionist story." Mev crossed her arms, also close to laughing.

"Would you like to tell it, my love?"

Mev's smile broadened.

"She began to train her and has been doing so since," Kael finished.

I inadvertently looked up to the quarterdeck. Marek wasn't even pretending to steer the ship now. Instead, he leaned on a nearby railing, flicking his wrist toward the bow of the ship, presumably controlling the water in some way.

Except, he wasn't looking at the water.

Marek was looking at me. Always me.

I spun back to Mev and Kael.

"Lyra has advised my father for many years." Mev cleared her throat, turning serious. "And has been an ally to us in many ways."

"She was raised"—Kael pulled Mev into his side—"by one of the most prestigious families in Aetheria, her lineage tracing back to the ancient air mages who first harnessed the power of the Wind Crystal that we are attempting to retrieve."

A reminder of our mission.

"Can he do it?" I asked, only partially wanting the answer.

Kael was no longer smiling. "I grew up hearing tales of the ships that were lost in the Maelstrom Depths. How my father managed to hide the Crystal there, I have no notion. None have successfully navigated those waters before, as you know."

"So why does he attempt it?"

"The friendship between you and I, Issa, runs deep," he said, something I knew already. Kael had defied his father attempting to save my parents, despite his mistrust of humans. I could not repay him sufficiently during my lifetime.

"It does," I acknowledged.

"Marek's friendship with the new Thalassarian queen runs just as deep. I believe he attempts it for her, but also because he believes Elydor is stronger unified. We have been splintering slowly for many years, but never more so than since my father..." He paused. "Since my father closed the Gate."

Mev leaned her head against her partner in silent support. The love they shared was evident, and I was glad for it. Even knowing how difficult it must be for Kael to now be an outcast among his own clan. His father's hate was poisoning him, as it was all Gyorians.

"Marek never struck me as someone who cares about the greater good," I said, avoiding looking his way. "His own enjoyment? Surely. Lining his pockets with smuggled goods? That I believe. But risking his life for the unification of Elydor?"

"What happened between you?" Kael asked as the wind swept through my hair. I attempted to pull it from my face, but a crosswind had picked up. "He refused to talk about it."

Both he and Mev watched me expectantly. Though I had little desire to talk about Marek, they deserved to know.

"It was not long after my parents had died," I said. "Marek had recovered a pendant that once belonged to my mother, the seal of Hawthorne Manor leading him to me."

Kael's brows raised. "Recovered?"

"His word," I said, remembering Marek's reluctance to tell me how the pendant had come into his possession until, a few days later, he admitted to some of his less-than-noble activities. "Later, he admitted to being curious about the 'lady of Hawthorne Manor.' Apparently, talk of the Estmere/Gyorian border and its strongholds, specifically Hawthorne, is a regular topic at port. At first, he was to just stay the eve, as my guest. But long days strategizing on how to best protect the border turned into longer evenings discussing politics and trade. He remained at Hawthorne for over a sennight, our bond..." Stopping to remember something I'd tried for so long to forget, memories of those days flooded back. "Marek had become a brief respite from my duties. Listening to his tales of adventures on the high seas and across Elydor..."

Kael understood. He knew me well enough. "Before her parents died, Isolde dreamed of becoming a diplomat for Estmere."

Mev's eyes widened. "Get out!"

Confused, I was about to question her when Mev added, "I just mean... wow. That's cool. I didn't know that."

I smiled weakly. "I woke up one morning and he was gone. No note. No word to anyone. I saw him just once since then. While in Thalassaria a few years back, I sought him out at a port tavern I knew Marek frequented. But instead of speaking to him, as I planned, something inside me snapped when I spotted him with a woman. I slapped him," I said, flexing my fingers, remembering the sting as my hand had made contact with his cheek, "and walked out. We never spoke again until you brought him into my keep. For so long I wanted an opportunity to talk to him, just once more. Ask why he left. But then when I was faced with that opportunity, I froze, leaving myself with the same unanswered questions. I realized later... maybe I didn't want the answer knowing, as I do now, there isn't one that could possibly take away the pain Marek caused."

By now, Mev looked as angry as I had felt all these years. She was glaring up at him.

"What a complete asshole."

That made me laugh. It was a word I had heard before, but rarely. "Asshole," I repeated. "I think I will use it."

"Oh, I have more," Mev continued. "Douchebag, or douche canoe if you want. You can call him—"

Kael cleared his throat.

Mev stopped, but scowled at him. "What? He deserves it. What possible good reason could he have for getting so close to her like that and then just up and leave?"

"Good question," I said. "Something I still don't have the answer to, but I can suspect it well enough." Fact was, Marek cared more about himself than anyone else in Elydor. He wanted to leave, and so he did.

I watched Kael, wondering what he was thinking as he looked

up toward Marek. Upset all over again with him, I refused to follow his gaze.

"I think I know what happened," he said finally, so quietly, Kael's words were almost lost in the wind.

"You do?" I asked, more than a little surprised.

Kael looked back at me.

"I do," he said. "Happened to me. It's scary as hell, though I'll admit, Marek didn't handle it well."

"Handle what well?" Mev asked.

He leaned down, kissed her on the nose, and said, "Falling in love."

I stared out at sea, avoiding looking at Kael. Or Marek. Refusing to let his words take root, I denied them silently, knowing he was wrong.

Marek could not have fallen in love with me. I knew it as well as I knew that I *had* fallen in love with him for one simple reason.

"Marek doesn't believe in love," I said quietly.

"How do you know?" Mev asked.

"Because he told me."

9

MAREK

As the first rays of light hit the horizon, the Veiled Sea's shades of amber and pale pink reflected off the calm water like a polished mirror. It was the kind of sea a human would curse, but I was no human and our ship sailed smoothly along the current I'd created.

Without realizing it, I'd slipped my hand into my pocket, pulling on a leather string. Tugging, the string uncoiled, its treasure was revealed. A noise below caught my attention as long shadows loomed across the deck where Isolde had been standing the night before with Mev and Kael. Laughing in a way I'd only see her do years ago.

Would she ever laugh again that way with me?

Mist began to rise from the water as the night's chill started to lift. The air was crisp, carrying the promise of warmth. I watched as Kael climbed upward, toward me.

"Did you sleep up here?"

I tightened my fingers, fisting the artifact within.

"Without a crew? Aye."

Kael leaned against the rail, looking out to sea. "I know you're reluctant to bring a crew into the Depths, but wouldn't having one be easier on the journey there?"

Shrugging, I swept away the melancholy that threatened to pull me under as sure as the Depths themselves. Planting a smile on my face, I sighed. "Perhaps. But there is not one on my crew who would agree to remain on land as *Tidechaser* enters the Depths. I would not put their lives at risk for..."

"For the good of Elydor? It seems enough of an incentive for you."

I didn't respond. My reasons for accepting this mission were many.

"She told us. How you met."

I sighed again. "You are ruining an otherwise pleasurable sunrise. I have a rule. No speaking on the quarterdeck until the sun is fully risen."

"That isn't a rule, Marek. We've spoken nearly every morning on the voyage to Thalassaria and since returning north."

"It is a new rule," I countered, flicking my wrist and veering the ship slightly east. Standing straighter, I peered over the starboard side of the ship. Kael joined me.

"I don't see anything."

"You'd make a terrible Thalassari sailor."

"Perhaps because I'm not one? Nor do I wish to be."

"Gyorians," I muttered, pointing. "Do you see that blue glow? Beneath the waves? Look closely."

Kael squinted. Knowing he couldn't see it, with another flick of my wrist, I calmed the waters, temporarily, in that area. The telltale blue was easier to spot. Even so, Kael appeared confused.

"Have you ever sailed before?" I teased.

"Only when I could not avoid it," the land-lover admitted.

"Surely you've heard of veilborn?"

Kael's eyes widened. I turned back toward the sea as we sailed past, ensuring the blue glow beneath the surface didn't follow us. Confident we'd left it in its wake, I concentrated on the horizon once again.

"They are real?"

"Quite real. Although I will admit, to see one in these waters is highly unusual. As you should know, they are more typically spotted off the Gyorian coast."

"Never seen one myself."

"With good reason. Their bioluminescence makes them appear almost translucent. That eerie blue beneath the water is usually your only warning a nasty sea serpent is about to strike. I've seen one split a longboat clean in two with its jaws."

"I suppose they are agents of the Abyss as well?"

Sunlight filled the deck now, though neither Mev nor Issa stirred. "The Abyss," I scoffed. "You believe in such things?"

Kael's brows raised. "Do you not believe in Thalassa?"

"Or Zephra? Or your god, Terranor?" I asked, skeptical. "Were they not all one before Elydor split into three clans? Convenient of them to wait for such an occurrence before making themselves known."

"So you don't believe in the Elydorian gods and goddesses. What *do* you believe in, Marek?"

I gave him a sidelong look. "Myself."

Kael tsked. "A dangerous proposition. Bearing the full weight of your choices may lead to reckless decisions."

"Many of which I've made already."

"Was abandoning Isolde one of them?"

Aware he and Issa were good friends, I needed to tread carefully. "Of course," I said, gripping the wheel even though it wasn't necessary. I'd been taught to sail by a human, a deliberate decision by my father. Later, as my magic grew, I questioned the decision until I understood its purpose.

Kael refrained from prodding me for more. For that reason, I offered the full truth. "I was foolish. We grew close, given the short time I remained at Hawthorne Manor. I'd convinced myself I was sparing her, aware of a growing sentiment between us."

He said nothing. Convincing myself it mattered little what Kael believed—of me, of the situation—I remained silent as well. Needing validation from anyone besides myself would only lead to disappointment. Besides, what could he say? Immortals and humans did not partner well together. Willingly loving someone, knowing you would experience their death was foolish, in my opinion. I'd met few immortals who didn't, at some point, regret the decision. It wasn't that we never felt the pain of loss. My mother, for example. It was just easier to avoid the situation altogether, if possible. Especially when the human in question was as kind and compassionate as Issa. And the immortal was a corsair who lived on the wrong side of the law.

"I never planned for Mevlida."

As the ship swayed gently from side to side, the water near perfect even without my guidance, I waited for the Gyorian prince to continue. In some ways, he was as rumor suggested. Pragmatic. Direct. But there was a thoughtfulness to him I hadn't expected. Not from a Gyorian, and certainly not from King Balthor's son.

"Sometimes," he explained, "the things we don't plan for are the ones that change us the most."

I thought on his words while Kael headed back down, below deck. As I'd done hundreds, if not thousands of times, my thoughts drifted back to my mother. I hadn't planned to lose her, especially not to drowning. A Thalassarian? An experienced pearl diver? It was unheard of. I hadn't planned to grow up learning that love was something you could drown in, something that could slip beneath the waves and never return.

So aye, I agreed with him, that things we never planned for could change us the most.

* * *

If there was one thing I could rely on during my time at Hawthorne Manor, it was Issa stalking the halls before daybreak, checking in with her commander and steward, ensuring all was well. So when she never appeared on deck to break her fast, I began to worry. Mev and Kael had returned to their cabin after eating so I was loathe to disturb them. But now that I stood in front of the captain's quarters, I reconsidered fetching Mev.

By the tides, Marek. Just knock. Ensure she's well.

I did. No response.

Any number of things could go wrong with humans. I imagined her having fallen from the bed. Or a sudden illness plaguing her in the night. Pushing open the door, I was greeted by darkness. Knowing my way in this space, I moved toward the desk, felt for the moonstone and allowed my energy to flow into it. Whipping it toward the bed, an astonishing sight greeted me.

Issa was sprawled out, one arm above her head, as if cradling it. She was fast asleep; my knock and subsequent entry into the cabin, along with the glowing moonstone, had not disturbed her. For a woman who woke before the sun each day, it was a remarkable display of slumber.

So often, she wore her hair back, off her face. But those wavy tendrils always managed to find a way to escape. Now, however, her hair was loose. Her full lips, slightly parted. Her eyes slowly opened, as if sensing my presence. I expected her to sit up, curse my presence, or at least question it. Instead, she simply looked at me as if I belonged in the cabin, watching her sleep.

Which, of course, I did not.

"I assume there is a reason you're here?"

"You are calmer than I would have expected, to find me hovering over you in your cabin."

"Your cabin," she corrected. Issa pulled the coverlet toward her chin, rolled to face me, but otherwise, remained.

"Not for this voyage." I replaced the moonstone in its wooden holder. "I remembered how early you woke at Hawthorne and became concerned."

"Has the sun risen?"

I laughed. "Some time ago. I broke my fast with Kael and Mev and... decided to ensure you were well. You did not stir when I knocked."

Issa sighed. "I had some difficulty falling asleep last eve. But when I did... I suppose the motion forced me into a deeper sleep than usual, as you are correct. I am an early riser. There is much to be done... normally."

The burden of running a border estate was not lost on me. "You are free here to do as you please. Including sleeping all day, if you'd like."

"I confess, such a thing would not normally tempt me, but there is something about being on your ship..."

Without asking, knowing how she might respond, I pulled out the wooden chair from my desk and sat on it, facing her. "Sailing agrees with you."

"I suppose it might."

She had wanted me to take her sailing, and I'd agreed. Stupidly, I'd agreed and woven tales about all of the places we could go. That was the night before I left. The night I realized what was happening. That I was making future plans with a woman who could never be mine.

"You told me once you wished to sail the whole of Elydor."

We had been sitting before the hearth in Hawthorne's hall, a game of chess underfoot. One that, if I recall, was never finished.

"I did not think to do it like this."

"How did you imagine it?" I wasn't certain if Issa took our "re-introduction" to heart or if she was not awake enough to remember to glare at me this morn, but I was thankful for it.

She tucked the seasilk pillow under her head. "I thought it would be more akin to sleeping under the stars. Beautiful yet uncomfortable."

I smiled. "Are you certain there is not Thalassari in your blood?"

"Quite certain. I am as human as any in Estmere."

Human, and not immortal. The idea of watching Issa growing old, an inevitable illness as age's companion, was enough to make my stomach roil. Against my will, I imagined her in that bed, sickness overcoming her. Watching Issa die. I simply could not do it. And yet...

"I could take you. If I survive the Depths, that is."

"Marek—"

I tossed up my hands in surrender. "Forgive me. Pretend I did not say it."

"Promises you will not keep. Or this death wish that you seem to have. Which shall I forget first?"

"Gods, Issa. You wound me. I do not have a death wish, just a very, very concerning lack of self-preservation."

Thankfully, her smile returned.

"I believe another 'very' may be in order."

"Two are not enough?"

"Where you are concerned? Nay. Besides, even if I wished to, you know well I cannot."

That was wholly untrue. Issa simply believed it to be so. "Will not. There is a difference."

"Hawthorne Manor—"

"Was your parents' dream." I had an uncanny knack for finding ways to make Issa angry with me, even as I began to chip away at her defenses. "Was it not?"

Her eyes narrowed. She could not deny it; the words were her own, given on that very same night an unfinished game of chess led to our first, and only, kiss.

"My parents' dream is my own."

"Nay, yours is to sail Elydor and beyond. Yours is a call to adventure, Isolde."

I was naught if not consistent but my honesty did nothing to improve her mood.

"Sometimes, we sacrifice for those we love. I am certain the concept eludes you, otherwise I would elaborate."

I clutched my chest, as if taking an arrow to the heart. "You wound me, Issa. Neither sacrifice nor love are concepts I am unfamiliar with." I held up a hand to forestall the argument she would make. "I did not say I agree with either, but I am familiar with both."

Rolling her eyes, Issa shook her head as if to dismiss me. But I would not be so easily dismissed.

"A sacrifice implies you are giving something up, does it not?"

"I believe it is time for me to get up."

"Convenient, but as my lady wishes." I stood and replaced the chair. "A meal of bread and cheese awaits you in the tidehall. The sea is cooperating today, if you would like to sail."

"You would allow me to sail your ship?"

I would allow you to do anything you wished, Issa, if it would put a smile back on your face.

Knowing I was the cause of her current state of displeasure did little to erase the memory of the Issa I first met. The one who happily showed me her home, introduced me to her people. The joy I took in her own was a feeling I remembered so distinctly, I could recall it easily.

"Of course. I await my lady's pleasure." I bowed. "If you need anything at all, you know where to find me."

"Marek." She stopped me as I stood and turned to leave.

I closed my eyes before facing her. That voice had haunted my dreams, but this was no dream. Isolde was very, very real. With more very's than my lack of preservation.

"Do not make promises, again, you do not intend to keep. It was that very thing that nearly broke me when you left."

The immediate reply I thought to offer stuck in my throat.

What was worse? Knowing I had done that which she accused me of? Or "nearly breaking" a woman as strong and unbreakable as Isolde?

Both.

The answer was both.

I bowed my head in deference, sighed, and lifted it. "My mother will take me to join her if I do so again, Issa."

This time, when she called my name, I did not turn back.

10

ISSA

My mother take me to join her if I do so.

I ate without tasting, sitting back in the wooden chair, which was secured to the floor beneath it, thinking back to when I'd first met Marek. For days, I had all but neglected my duties, spending every waking moment with him. Walking the castle grounds, with Marek. At first, it had been easy enough to pass off that time as the lady of the manor entertaining a guest. But the more time we spent together, others began to notice it was something more.

We spoke first of the amulet, Marek initially skirting his procurement of it. Eventually, he admitted to dealings that some might question. But we also spoke of our past, Marek's much longer and more interesting than my own. He had risen through the ranks after growing up in port, his father a sailor, his mother a pearl diver.

Eventually, we spoke of our past relationships, his more extensive than my own, of course. I'd admitted to being a virgin still, not having ruled out the need to use my innocence as a bargaining tool one day. Estmere's politics were unstable, at best, even without a brewing war with Gyoria.

But one thing he never discussed was his mother. Aside from mentioning that she, an experienced Thalassarian pearl diver, had drowned. Marek had been willing to share everything about his life, even the sordid parts, but the few times I attempted to learn more about his family, his characteristic grin would falter and Marek changed topics. Every time.

My mother take me to join her if I do so.

I knew without asking his words were more significant than, perhaps, anything Marek had ever said to me before. And yet... this was the same person who had kissed me in a way I'd never been kissed before. He had asked for my permission, and I had given it gladly.

I touched my lip, like I'd done the day he left, and many days afterward, as if able to feel that kiss so many years later. I always wondered how someone could kiss me in that way but then leave without a word. The answer? "That kiss" meant something different to me than it did to him. I still felt foolish for believing otherwise.

And despite telling myself it was Marek's issue, not mine, that could prompt such cruel treatment... a part of me felt foolish still since when I woke and saw him standing there, I imagined him kissing me again.

By the time I tidied up and went above deck, the sun was high, the water calm. There was no sign of Kael and Mev, but Marek was in his usual spot on the quarterdeck behind the ship's wheel. He looked every bit a Navarch, a distinction even humans could appreciate. It meant there were few in all of Elydor who could command the seas as well, an honor typically reserved for thaloran who had been alive for over five hundred years.

He didn't seem to notice me as he stared out to sea. Hesitating, and then reminding myself it would be impossible to avoid him, I made my way across the deck, its floorboards creaking softly under me. The sharp tang of salt air mixed with the scent of oiled wood and rope was oddly comforting. I'd left my cloak below deck, not thinking to need it during the day, but the wind whipped at my tunic. I hesitated again, adjusting my balance to a sudden rolling motion that was both liberating and unsteadying at the same time.

Climbing a narrow and well-worn set of wooden steps, I gripped the railing as the ship lurched slightly with a shift in the current. Once at the top, I sucked in a breath at the sight from this vantage point, the Veiled Sea stretching endlessly around the ship. Even more magnificent? Marek's eyes were now trained on me.

"You've got your sea legs already. Impressive."

"You wouldn't say that if you had seen me creeping across the deck."

His gaze was as appreciative as it had always been when Marek looked at me. Many years of noticing women, no doubt, had honed that particular look.

"I saw you the moment you emerged from below deck, Issa."

I was not worldly when it came to men, but I knew any hint of interest would encourage Marek's natural flirtatious tendencies. And, historically speaking, resisting the captain's flirtations was not one of my strengths. So I made no response.

"Here." He removed his cloak. "On the quarterdeck, the wind will cut through to your bones, even on the balmiest of days."

I tried to ignore the scent of him, a familiar one of faintly spiced, sun-warmed leather and sea, as he wrapped his cloak around my shoulders.

"Come on then," he said, nudging me to take his spot behind the wheel. "You are the captain of *Tidechaser* today."

I stepped forward. My heart raced at the possibility of doing something I'd dreamed of since hearing Marek explain the thrill of attempting to control something as massive and unpredictable as *Tidechaser* at sea.

As my fingers lay on the wooden wheel, worn smooth from years of use, I looked to Marek for guidance. He stood beside me as I reached up to tuck loose strands of hair behind my ear. The wind was stronger up here than it looked.

"It will resist you at first."

I understood immediately what he meant. "I can feel the tension in the ropes," I said, not convinced the ship would listen to my command.

"Just remember, the ocean isn't a still force. It will tug, pushing back like a living thing. Because it is. Respect it, and it will obey." He grinned. "Sometimes."

It was impossible to ignore Marek's easy grin.

"Should I do anything more?"

Marek shook his head. "Not yet. Simply feel the weight of the wheel beneath your hands."

Seemed clear enough. "So, how does one respect the sea?"

Marek's grin deepened, a flash of white against his sun-warmed skin. He stepped closer, resting a calloused hand on the wheel beside mine, his fingers brushing the polished wood.

"You listen to it," he said, voice quieter now, as if sharing a secret. "Feel the wind, watch the waves. The sea speaks, Issa, in whispers and tempests. Ignore it, and it will remind you who is in command."

He nodded toward the horizon, where the water stretched endless and untamed. "Steer too sharp, and she'll throw you off balance. Take her for granted, and she'll drag you under." His gaze flickered back to me, something unreadable in the depths. "But if you learn her moods, earn her trust, she'll carry you farther than you ever thought possible."

"You speak of the ocean as if it is truly alive," I said, becoming more accustomed to the pull of the waves, a constant but unmistakable tug under my fingertips.

The ship rocked beneath us, the rhythmic creak of the hull and the snap of sails filling the quiet space between Marek and me, though his presence was undeniable beside me.

"Respect," I murmured, running my hands over the wheel's worn surface. "Not control."

Marek's lips curled, approval gleaming in his eyes. "Aye, sereia."

My heart skipped a beat, sereia sounding like an endearment. I should chastise him for the intimacy, but instead questioned his choice of words.

"Sereia is a sea spirit, is it not?"

Marek leaned back on the nearby railing, watching me. "Indeed. Do you know the Legend of the Drowned King?"

I shook my head.

"There was once a Thalassarian king who sought to command the seas themselves. He sailed into the heart of a storm, believing he could bend the waves to his will. A sereia appeared to him, her voice woven with the wind and water. She warned him, 'The ocean is no one's to rule, but to honor. Yield, or be claimed by the Depths.' Proud and defiant, the king laughed, and the sea swallowed him whole. Yet, the sereia took pity on his people, for they had not shared his arrogance. She granted them safe passage, whispering the secrets of the tides to the ones who would listen. From them, the first true sailors of Thalassaria were born: those who did not fight the sea, but danced with it."

"They are not real, though, right?"

That was the look.

The one that drew me in.

Gave me hope.

Stole my heart.

This time, I knew better. But it still had an effect on me. I was not Gyorian, made of soil and stone. I was just a human, with only one lifetime to learn. The lessons—ones like "do not let the same person break your heart twice"—offered to a human could only be ignored at one's own peril. Even so, I was not impervious to Marek's charm. The battle between my head and my heart was as real as the one humans fought against their enemies.

"They are real in the sense that, when a Thalassarian uses the term, it means they see something untamed, something powerful. It's not just a name but an acknowledgment of a force that cannot be controlled, only deeply respected."

"Always, you have the right words."

"I have only the truth."

The wheel jerked beneath my hands. In a flash, Marek was behind me, his hands covering my own as a large swell hit the hull unexpectedly, shifting our course.

"Lightly," he said, as we began to turn the wheel to the left. "Into the wave. *Tidechaser* may be reluctant to obey an unfamiliar hand, but she will heed your touch if you do not force her."

He was so damn close. His fingers brushed mine, making it difficult to concentrate on the task at hand. Trying harder, I slowly pulled the wheel at the same speed as Marek. With a creak of the ropes and rigging, *Tidechaser* began to respond.

"She's moving," I said, unsure why the fact surprised me.

"That is, generally, the point," he said. Marek's voice had always affected me by its tone and pitch. Something about the deep, gravelly tone to it made me shiver.

"If you plan to be *Tidechaser*'s new captain on this journey, you'd best dress warm. This time of year, even on the nicest of days, the wind's chill can be felt."

I wasn't cold but didn't mention that fact.

As Marek stepped back, he said, "Keep it steady there."

I was doing it. The ship responded, our course now reset. Every bit of me felt alive, the vastness of the sea before us without compare.

I would not mourn the loss of him pressed against my back, or the feel of his fingers next to mine. Reminding myself of the days after he left when I hadn't wanted to rise from bed in the morn, when near constant thoughts of him intruded, uninvited, I steeled my mind against a different kind of intruding thought.

"This is incredible," I said, breathing in the salt air. "It is... indescribable really."

Crossing his arms, Marek followed my gaze to the horizon. "It's freedom and fury, grace and chaos all at once, but never the same. One moment, the sea is a mirror reflecting the sky, so calm you might believe you could walk across it. The next, it rises up, wild and untamed, reminding you that none truly command it." Marek exhaled slowly. "There's nothing like it. No walls, no borders, just sky above and water below. You can lose yourself, or find yourself, here, if the sea wills it."

"You belong here," I said, his words making me almost forget the pain. "Your passion for the sea is..."

His left brow quirked upward. Everything about Marek was lighthearted and teasing, until it wasn't, and he allowed you to peek into a part of him he kept hidden.

"I'm waiting."

I had no proper word. "I would say 'inspiring' but worry you might—"

Without warning, Marek sprang into action. He scaled down the wooden stairs to the main deck so quickly I would have thought he flew had I not seen his feet touch the steps. Just as Kael and Mev appeared, Marek sped past them to the starboard railing. The reason had become apparent. As we were speaking, a rogue wave came crashing toward *Tidechaser*'s side. It rose unnaturally fast, curling higher than it should have, as if the sea itself had decided to test us.

Marek didn't hesitate. With a flick of his wrist, the water around the ship stilled as he thrust his hands outward. The wave halted mid-rise, its crest suspended in the air, trembling as if caught between forces unseen. Then, with a slow, deliberate motion, Marek twisted his fingers, and the wave unraveled, cascading harmlessly into the sea.

A hush fell over the deck. Even Kael and Mev, who I assumed had seen Marek's abilities before, watched in awe. Noticing he had an audience, Marek winked at me before capturing the droplets and, instead of allowing them to follow the rogue wave into the sea, he raised both arms upward. The droplets paused in mid-air as the sun caught them, turning each into a thousand glistening gems before they, too, vanished into the sea.

Arms now down at his sides, he said something to Mev and Kael, who laughed, and then bounded back up to me as effortlessly as he'd turned away that wave. "You were saying?" he asked, his signature grin firmly in place.

"How... did you do that?"

"You've been to Thalassaria. Surely you've seen water-wielding on a grander scale than that."

I thought back to the tricks he'd shown me at Hawthorne Manor. To the Thalassarians I'd seen in Serenium Square by the fountain and another display on the coast not long after I'd stormed out of The Moonlit Current.

"Not quite like that," I admitted. "What should I be doing here?" I asked, eager not to show Marek I was more impressed with him than I had already.

"Keeping her steady."

"I've seen you up here, not even touching the wheel when the sea is calm. Is this necessary?"

"I can create a channel through the waves that will make it less so. If you'd like."

"No," I said, too quickly. "I would like to learn more."

"Of sailing?"

Of you. Of why you left. But since I was the one to forbid the topic, for good reason, I could not say as much. Besides, he'd answered the question once, and it was unlikely I'd get a different response, even if the first one was less than satisfactory.

"Aye."

He was looking at me oddly. More serious than usual, as if studying me. Then, without warning, he turned away, toward the sea. Reaching out his hands, he turned them slowly, palms facing upward. Ever so slightly, Marek twitched the very tips of his fingers forward while lifting his arms higher. At first, nothing happened. Eventually, as his arms rose, a mist formed across the water. Soon, the entire ship was enveloped in fog. I couldn't even see Mev and Kael, the entire deck below us now covered in a fine mist.

Marek had disappeared too, but a hand on my lower back told me he'd moved next to me.

"Watch," he whispered, lowering his hand. I clung to the wheel, the sensation of his breath in my ear reminding me of our kiss. "Are you watching, Issa?"

Somehow, he knew I had not been.

I looked up, back toward the water.

The mist began to coalesce into a form. It was as if a figure rose from the sea, sculpted of water and light. It was a woman made of thick mist, her eyes sparkling like the water droplet gems, her hair flowing as if she were alive.

"What... who is she?"

"Meet the Spirit of the Tides."

I wanted to reach out and touch her. "I've never heard of her."

The water woman actually looked at me. And then smiled. She actually, truly, smiled.

And then, was gone, as quickly as she'd formed.

The mist cleared, and as usual, Marek was grinning.

"The Spirit of the Tides is an ancient Thalassarian legend... part myth, part warning, part blessing. Some say she is the soul of the sea itself, watching over those who respect its power and punishing those who do not. Others claim she was once a Thalassarian woman, a navigator who defied the gods and was bound to the ocean for eternity."

"And you... summoned her?"

The thing I liked most about Marek's smile? How it always reached his eyes, crinkling at the sides just enough to distinguish him from a human of my age.

"Not truly. That was an echo, a fragment of her presence that only those with an affinity for the sea can call upon."

"So all Thalassarians can do that?"

"No." His chuckle, from Marek's chest, would have made me feel foolish for asking if it were anyone but him. "All Thalassarians have an affinity for the sea, it is true. I should have been more precise. A reverence, more like. And you do not have to be Thalassarian to be deserving of her presence. As for the summoning... it is a rare and, some say, dangerous skill among Thalassarians. Some revere it. Others fear it."

"Why would one fear such a thing of beauty?"

He looked at me for so long, and with such intensity, that it would have become uncomfortable. Except, somehow, it was not.

"That you would ask such a question," he said finally, "is the reason I brought her forth."

11

MAREK

As I tied off the ship with Kael's aid, the women were nowhere to be seen. Though I normally remained on the ship at port, this eve was different. After spending my days teaching Issa how to sail, and my nights mostly sleepless, waiting for her to emerge in the morn, one thing had become clear these past days.

Isolde deserved to see the Spirit of the Tides, a sight typically reserved for those who had given themselves to the sea for many years. Convinced she must have Thalassarian blood somewhere in her ancestry, I was amazed how quickly she had taken to every aspect of sailing. Not a hint of sickness, even yesterday during a brief, but violent, storm.

"If you stare at the deck harder, she's not any more likely to appear."

I *had* been staring. Finishing the knot, I stood beside him, waiting. "They know we are in port, aye?"

As the words left my mouth, the women appeared and made their way toward us. Handing Kael a satchel, Mev took the Gyorian warrior's hand. She was so slight standing beside him, but they partnered well together.

Issa and I would partner just as well.

It was that sort of thinking that prompted me to flee Estmere in the first place. I reached forward to take Issa's satchel as well.

"You don't have to carry it for me."

"I don't not have to carry it either."

Her expression made me smile. It was never difficult to tell what Issa was thinking at any given moment.

As we made our way onto the dock, Mev asked about the port town. At dusk, it was a sight to behold, its weathered, wooden piers, lantern-lit alleys, and harbor filled with ships of questionable allegiances were a unique blend of human construction with Aetherian architecture mixed in.

"Technically, we are in Estmere, but just beyond the town is the northern border of your kingdom, my lady," I said.

"Oh God, no. Please. I get enough of that back home."

"Home? That is the first I've heard you call Aetheria home," Kael commented as we walked down the dock toward town.

"Is it?" she asked.

"Do you miss the human realm?" Issa asked.

"I miss some things about it. But mostly, my friends and my mother. Kael assures me, based on how we believe time between realms work, she won't realize I'm missing yet. But if we don't find a way to open the Gate..." Mev swallowed. "I can't even think about it."

I only caught her eyes welling with tears as we walked past a hanging lantern, one of many at the docks and on the nearby buildings. Stopping, I realized all talk of the Depths' dangers had to cease. I was as guilty as anyone, but me failing meant the mission failed.

"Mev," I said quietly. "I will get the Wind Crystal. When I do, Kael will retrieve the Stone and the Gate will be reopened."

"None have survived it before. I hate that you're even attempting this, Marek."

"I've always been terrible at doing what's expected of me."

Mev let go of Kael's hand and hugged me. Meeting Kael's gaze, the Gyorian wasn't angry, as I expected, knowing the possessiveness of his kind.

When she let me go, I cleared my throat and launched into the history of Valmyr Port. "Like all of Estmere, this was once Aetherian. When your father gifted land to the humans, it was built up to what you see today. The coastal settlement is a smuggler's haven, a trade hub, and political gray zone. Estmerian nobles, Aetherian exiles, and seafarers all mingle, making it... unique in many ways."

"There are exiles from Aetheria?" Mev asked.

Kael responded as we wove through the busy, cobblestone street, beside Issa.

"There are exiles to, and from, every clan. Some leave willingly, but most... do not."

The cobblestone street seemed to narrow as we walked, and for a moment, I could feel the weight of unspoken words between Issa and me.

"Exile isn't just about punishment," Kael added after a beat, his voice lowering. "It's about survival. Sometimes, it's easier to stay away than returning to where you no longer belong."

He was speaking of himself. When Kael had taken Mev to her father, rather than his own, he'd chosen sides.

"If not for the king," I said, having voiced as much once before, "Gyoria would welcome you back."

Kael made a sound of disgust. "If not for the king. My father."

"He is right," Issa added. "Look at us. We forged a friendship. Without his influence of hate, I think many would do the same."

Kael only grunted. I understood his frustration. War was

brewing in Elydor and had been since the Gate's closing, a far cry from the kind of peace we discussed.

"Marek?" Issa's pace slowed.

Immediately, all three of us surrounded her, Issa's expression making it clear something was amiss.

"What is it?"

She held a hand to her heart and closed her eyes.

I looked at Kael, who seemed to understand what was happening.

"She senses something."

I turned to Mev, who shook her head. She could sense both emotion and intentions, both good and bad, but apparently, there was nothing nefarious nearby.

Issa opened her eyes. "An artifact. Stronger than most. Ancient, perhaps."

"Where?" Kael followed Issa's gaze toward a poorly lit alleyway.

"That way. There is a crest above the door."

I pointed to the closest building to us. "They all do here. It is the mark of Valmyr. Each claims an alliance to a house of Estmere. A business or residence marked with a noble house's crest is less likely to be targeted by thieves or rival factions. Merchants and tavern owners align with noble houses to gain favor or a steady flow of customers loyal to that faction. And some use the crest to strengthen false ties, misleading competitors or gaining access to faction-only dealings."

Issa closed her eyes again, her hand still lying gently on her chest.

How many humans had I seen use their abilities, some in ways that continue to amaze me, even after all these years? But there was something about watching Issa do it...

Her eyes whipped open.

"The crest is dark blue. Two crossed swords over a trexan—"

"Gods," I cursed, frowning. "Perhaps we should let it be."

Kael's eyes narrowed. "A powerful magical relic, possibly ancient, and you want to... let it be?"

Of course not. But the owner of that shop would likely have something to say and I would prefer he not.

"It is an antique shop," I said. "You can settle and get a meal while I investigate."

Kael's rare, but not subtle, laughter caught the attention of two sailors walking past us. They looked at him, and then Mev. I could hear their whispers of "the lost princess" as they passed. "We will be coming with you."

"It feels like... something important," Issa said, ensuring they would come along.

Reluctantly, I led our group down the alley. "This way. Issa, stay close."

As I said the words, a group of three men stumbled from a less reputable tavern. Mev's pearl-white hair must have caught the eye of the largest of the three. Without even a glance at Kael, he made a sound of appreciation and took a step toward her.

A flash of steel from the corner of my eye reminded me that Issa had been trained by her father, a ruthless warrior who had defended Hawthorne's borders tirelessly, according to Kael. At the same time, Mev raised her arm, but no magic was needed. He was already being lifted by Kael, the man's friends heading quickly in the opposite direction.

"Kael," Mev said in an even tone. "Let him go."

"I intend to," Kael replied as the man demanded the same. As if he were a leather satchel, Kael tossed him a good distance away. The drunkard grunted but extended his legs.

"He's alive, at least," I said, watching as Issa put away her blade.

"Not for long, unless he disappears quickly," Kael said, loud enough for the man to hear. Somehow, he managed to stand and stumble away toward his friends.

"Gyorians," I muttered, shaking my head.

"You do not agree with his methods?" Issa asked.

My eyes darted to the blade now at her hip. I'd seen her use it once, hunting, and had no doubt it would have been lodged in the man's throat before he was even hit by whatever magic Mev had planned to use on him.

"Sometimes, more finesse is called for."

Issa pursed her lips together to keep from smiling. "And what, precisely, would you have done in the same situation?"

I thought about that one, my pulse quickening at the thought of Issa being mine.

My partner. Mine to hold. To kiss at will. To make love to. Travel the seas of Elydor with, teaching her to sail as we've done these past few days?

A very, very dangerous thought.

"I would use my natural charm to talk our way out of an escalating conflict. Leveraging words is not something a Gyorian would ever consider, I will admit."

"And if that didn't work?" she asked as we stopped in front of Bram's shop.

"I might make a pointed remark to undermine the man's confidence, ensuring he knew I could easily deal with him as a Thalassarian but choose not to."

"We'd call that a psychological advantage in my realm," Mev added from behind.

Kael grunted. I assumed it meant he disagreed with my methods.

"And how would a Thalassarian deal with him, being there is no water nearby?" Issa asked.

This would be fun.

It was a tricky bit of magic that Nerys perfected well before I ever attempted it. Lifting both hands, I first summoned moisture in the air. It was easy enough this close to port. With the mists, I twisted my fingers, creating two deceptively thin ropes. Bound by water, no human could break them. With a final movement, I flicked my hands and sent the ropes coiling around Issa's hands, first separately and then, with a stronger pull to account for her resistance, gently binding them together behind her back.

Grinning, I took a step toward her, grateful to have Kael and Mev as an audience. There was no accounting for what I might attempt otherwise. Kissing Issa again had become a near constant vision in my mind. One "aye" from her and the thing I promised myself not to do—get close to her again—would be a foregone conclusion.

"I could, of course, also summon water from the bay. But this would do just as well."

Issa rolled her eyes. "Are you planning to release me?"

I hesitated long enough for Kael to issue a warning. "Marek," he grumbled.

A curse on meddling Gyorian princes.

Another flick of my wrists and the ropes turned back to mist, evaporating into the air almost immediately. When they did, I stepped past Issa and reached for the door, but not before whispering into her ear.

"A good thing we have witnesses, sereia."

12

ISSA

An antique shop. Its owner was a human. Not surprising since we were still in Estmere. But what did surprise me was his greeting to Marek. He looked as if the Spirit of the Tides had just walked into his shop.

"Uh," he stammered, clearly nervous. The older man moved with the careful precision of one who had spent his life handling delicate and dangerous things. His fingers were smudged with ink.

"Relax, Bram. I'm not here to collect payment."

So the two knew each other. Was that the reason for Marek's hesitancy coming here?

"You're... not?"

"Payment for what?" Kael asked.

"We're here for an item." Marek looked around the dusty shop. Every corner was filled. From books to stopwatches, to tarnished silver goblets and ornate dagger hilts... the artifacts peeked out of wooden crates and crowded the countertops. The scent of old parchment, polished wood, and something faintly metallic filled the space.

"An item," Kael repeated. "Procured legally, I'm certain."

I was equally as certain it was not. The owner stared at Mev, no doubt wondering if the rumors were true, likely having guessed her identity.

"Are you..." Bram began, without finishing.

"Princess Mevlida," she said.

Bram immediately bowed, nearly slamming his head on the counter in his haste. When he stood, his gaze fell on Kael. "Which means you must be Prince Kael of Gyoria?"

"No bow for me?" Kael taunted in his typical, gruff, Gyorian manner.

"Gyorians have not been kind to Valmyr, or Estmere. Your father's policies have made it more difficult to conduct business these past years."

"And precisely what sort of business are you in, Master Bram?"

"Kael," Mev warned.

"You are an antiques dealer." Kael's voice softened, but not by much.

"Bram is *the* antiques dealer. Human or otherwise," I said.

"What can I do for you, captain?" he asked Marek, still wary.

"You've procured an item with extraordinary magical properties."

The man might be an experienced shopkeeper, but he was not as proficient at hiding his true emotions. Eyes wide, he all but announced the truth of Marek's words.

"How do you—"

"It would please me very much, if you might show us the item, good sir."

I had never heard Mev speak so firmly, and eloquently, before. That was a princess's request, and not simply a woman who'd fallen through the Aetherian Gate.

The shopkeeper stood straighter, his shoulders back, head held high. "Of course, your grace. It would be an honor."

I caught Kael's eye roll and nearly giggled.

Disappearing into a back room, Master Bram left the four of us alone.

I had questions.

"The two of you know each other well, it seems?"

"Well enough," Marek said good-naturedly enough, but there was a hesitancy to him not normally evident.

A good thing we have witnesses, sereia.

I wanted to get him alone to ask what Marek had meant by that. Or at least, part of me wanted to know. Part of me knew already. And another part of me wanted nothing to do with the conversation.

I held a hand over my heart, listening, not even needing to block out my surroundings. "It is close."

"Remarkable," Kael said. "I've not seen a human do that before."

"My father had the same ability. And harnessed it in the same way. He is the only other I know who did as much."

The shopkeeper emerged with a water-stained, leather-bound book. "I bought it from a Thalassarian."

"May I?" Mev asked, perhaps sensing he would trust her with the book.

Indeed, he handed it to her without question.

"It doesn't appear magical to me." She began flipping through the pages.

"I thought the same and would have turned him away if it weren't for another patron who sensed its magic."

My ability wasn't rare but neither was it common. I exchanged a glance with Marek, who was likely thinking the same.

"This is why I kept it," he said, reaching forward and opening to a page. Kael looked over Mev's shoulder and read.

"She called upon the sea, but it answered in hunger. Not offering the tide its due. The Depths demand more than courage. They demand a heart willing to break."

At "The Depths," my stomach flipped. The reality of what Marek was attempting to do sometimes felt as if it were just another of his adventures, many of which he had told me about. While dangerous, Marek's command of the sea kept him safe. The Maelstrom Depths were different. There was a real possibility he would not make it out of them alive, and despite everything, I did not want him to die. The thought of it, in fact, left me in a constant state of unsettledness whenever we were faced with the reality of the situation.

"What is this?" Marek demanded, his tone losing all of its typical, teasing qualities.

"Supposedly, a journal kept by a sailor who perished in the Maelstrom Depths. As you can see, there is nothing inherently magical about it. But if it truly has been to the Depths and back..."

"Its magic will be felt," Marek finished. "Comes from the same one that created the Depths in the first place."

"I don't get it." Mev flipped through the book once more. "How is it intact if it was in the water? And what magic created the Maelstrom Depths? I thought it was just a dangerous patch of sea?"

Kael took the book from her and held it under the candlelight on the counter in front of us. Master Bram looked as if he wanted to take it back from him, but the shopkeeper didn't dare.

"The legend varies, depending on who's telling it." Marek exhaled, looking at the journal intently. "Some say the Depths were born from the anger of a god. Others, that a sorcerer sought to control the winds and failed, drowning the sea itself in cursed magic. But the oldest story—the one that was whispered long before the clans of Elydor carved their names into maps—speaks of a living force that does not forget. Does not forgive."

I leaned forward, as if understanding the words in the journal I was looking at, which I did not.

"Doesn't forget what? What does it want?" I asked.

It was Bram who answered. "Balance. Not unlike Elydor itself."

"They say nothing taken from the sea is truly free," Marek said. "It must be earned or returned. If not, the Depths will claim their due."

Mev frowned. "A soul for a soul."

"Or worse," Bram muttered, "a fate for a fate."

I looked up. "You know much about the Depths for a human living so far away from them?"

The shopkeeper was hiding something. I had the sense that, beneath his affable demeanor was an astute mind, one that weighed every word and every deal.

Master Bram coughed, apparently not willing to respond. It was as if... as if he deferred to Marek. My eyes narrowed. There was much more to this journal than appeared on the surface.

"I will take it," Marek said. "And consider my debt paid."

Though Master Bram appeared anything but pleased, he did not argue.

* * *

It wasn't until later, when we were seated at The Drowned Oath, an inn and tavern where we would spend the evening, that I called out Marek on the deal he'd made.

"What did you not tell us back there?"

Kael had escorted Mev to the privy chamber, despite her insistence on being able to do so alone. I understood his concern. When we'd asked Marek where we would stay the night, he'd said, "A place where the ale is strong, the card games cut-throat and rumors whispered in dark corners often prove more valuable than gold."

"I don't know what you—"

"Please, stop."

Marek's hand froze halfway to his mouth. Placing his ale back down, he watched me.

"I was angry when you left. And even angrier when I saw you in that tavern because I realized in that moment how much I'd truly allowed you to affect me all these years. I had finally begun to let it all go, until you showed up at Hawthorne. When you suggested we begin again, I told myself... this is for the best. Holding onto those feelings has done me no favors. But understand, Marek..." I said his name forcefully, channeling my mother, who had never doubted her authority. "For that to happen, you need to be more honest with me than before."

He blinked. "Honest," he repeated, as if the word was foreign to him.

"Honest. I cannot be myself with someone who I do not trust." I could tell that hurt him, but there was no hope for it. "You know more about me, the true me, than most. Please do not abuse that knowledge by lying to me."

I had opened myself up to him in a way I had not any other. A difficult lesson, but one I would not repeat. I picked up my own ale, confirmed Kael and Mev were still nowhere in sight, and turned back to Marek.

When he wasn't smiling, Marek actually appeared quite fierce. His jawline defined and set, clothing denoting him very much a sailor, he fit in quite well with The Drowned Oath's clientele.

He glanced up, over my shoulder, Marek's back to the wall, and focused once again on me.

"Bram secured that journal for me. I have been coming to Valmyr Port for many years as it is a known smuggler's haven. The antiques dealer is one of a very few who know the truth about the reason behind my less than above-board activities."

He stopped as Kael and Mev sat down, Mev immediately launched into a story about a conversation she had overheard between the innkeeper and a patron who apparently refused to pay the coin owed for his meal because it was "unseasoned."

It seemed I would have to wait for the rest of his story. One I didn't expect to hear, even after asking him to be honest with me.

The reason behind my less than above-board activities.

What could that possibly mean?

"Tell them what else we heard," Kael said, taking a bite of one of the meat pies that had been brought to the table. He, apparently, would have done so himself but Gyorians were a hungry clan. It was well known, they ate more than most Elydorians, more akin to humans.

Was I imagining it, or did Mev seem nervous as she watched me take a tentative bite of pie? It was surprisingly good.

"There was apparently a skirmish in the northern borders," Mev said, concerned. "The humans barely held off a band of Gyorian raiders with Aetherian aid."

"It's only a matter of time before it escalates," I said, having experienced the same along the southern border for some time. "Before we left, I heard the Gyorian War Council is eyeing new alliances."

Marek stiffened. "With whom?" He shot a look at Kael.

"I haven't been home since before Mev came. Don't look to me for answers."

"There must be someone you trust to temper your father's appetite for vengeance?"

"My men, those I can trust, are working with Adren to help us secure the remaining artifacts. Reopening the Gate has taken precedence."

"Understandable." I came to Marek's aid, my thinking similar to his own. "But there won't be any humans left when it does reopen if things continue to escalate."

Mev sighed. "The war could spill over into every clan, dragging Aetherians, Elydorians, and humans into a full-blown conflict. I think me coming through didn't do Elydor any favors."

Kael set down his mug. "You coming through was the catalyst we needed to put an end to it, Mev. You didn't start this. My father did." He looked at me. "There's more."

"Why do I sense this has something to do with Issa?" Marek asked.

"Because it does. Mev and I lingered, none seeming to care either of us overheard."

"This is the place to come to hear rumors, and to spread them. But we'd best keep our own voices down." Marek sat back, waiting.

Our table was in the only window, isolated but... his words were wise. I looked out onto the docks, still bustling despite the hour, and then turned back to see all three of them watching me.

"What is it?" I asked, having dismissed Marek's concern. There would be no talk of *me* here, surely?

"A human sailor suggested Lord Draven is feeding intelligence to both sides, ensuring that the tension between Gyorians and humans reaches a boiling point," Mev said.

I startled, surely mishearing. "Draven? My Lord Draven?"

Kael all but growled. "Aye, your Lord Draven. I, for one, am not surprised. He positions himself to take on a greater role among humans, starting with Hawthorne Manor."

I refused to have this same argument again. "I've told you, so many times—"

"I agree with him," Mev whispered.

My head whipped in the princess's direction. Surely, I misheard her.

"Kael had asked I not interfere, given your history with him as your father's friend and right-hand man. But if there is any hint of truth to these whispers..." She frowned. "When we first met at Hawthorne, I had a feeling about him. It was before I knew about, well, all of it. My Aetherian father. My magic. I know now I was sensing his ill intentions."

"No," I said. I refused to believe another who I trusted could be so complicit. If it were true, I would never trust my own instincts again. "He served my father well for many years."

"Your own commander doesn't trust him," Marek added. "We spoke of him. Sir Warren told me of an incident—"

"The two have never gotten along," I admitted.

"With good reason, to my thinking," Marek said.

"I concur," Kael added.

Mev said nothing, but her expression did. Had I been wrong to leave Hawthorne in his hands? I looked to Kael. "He and my father," I said meekly.

"Were friends, aye. But even friends can be blinded by loyalty. That does not mean he's the same man your father trusted."

I swallowed hard. The weight of my decision to leave Hawthorne in his care suddenly felt heavier.

Marek bounded from his seat. Without a word, he left us and headed directly toward the men, apparently, Kael and Mev had overheard. How had he even noticed that? We'd been in the midst of our own conversation. One I was very much anxious to finish.

"What's he doing?" Mev asked.

Kael smiled. "What he does best."

As the couple focused on their meals, I continued to watch Marek. He moved from man to man, smiling. Talking. Gesturing. He clasped one on the shoulder, as if they were long-lost friends. This was his element. Marek, among his people, even if they were human, though I would not be surprised if there were a Thalassarian mixed in with that group. You could find a Thalassarian at every port in Elydor, it was said. Unlike Gyorians and Aetherians, the Thalassari could pass for humans. Although often, they had a *look*. One difficult to describe, but unique to a southern climate where it never cooled.

I watched as he sauntered back to us. When he made eye contact with me, I had some difficulty not feeling as if I had won some sort of prize, to be the object of his attention. His obvious approval at what he saw.

I wouldn't pretend he had lost his appeal because... it would be a lie of epic proportions.

He sat, leaning forward. "The whispers in Valmyr aren't just rumors, Isolde." It was as if he used my given name to emphasize that he was serious. "Draven's been moving pieces on the board for longer than we realized. I will learn more, but I suspect Mev and Kael's overheard conversation is the start of it."

I felt ill. Pushing away my meal, no longer hungry, I stood. "Pardon me."

Needing air, I made my way out of the tavern and ran toward the dock. No ships were coming or going now, but all were swaying gently with the breeze.

What had I done?

I whipped around as a hand lay on my shoulder.

"Put the dagger away, sereia."

Every time he called me that, I had difficulty breathing normally. It was like a lover's touch, soft and gentle. And all-knowing.

"Come with me."

Marek guided me away from the lantern-lit docks, past warehouses stacked with crates. The night air was thick with salt and the distant scent of fish, but as we moved deeper into the port's underbelly, the scent shifted. Woodsmoke, damp stone, and something faintly metallic, like rust or old blood.

He led me through a narrow alleyway between two looming buildings, the ground beneath us uneven, cobbled but worn down by time and foot traffic. A single torch flickered ahead, illuminating a heavy, iron door set into the stone wall of an aging structure.

We didn't speak.

Marek rapped twice on the aged, wooden door, then once more, in a distinct pattern. A moment later, the door opened, but the darkness within revealed no one. Inside, the air was tinged with pipe smoke and the sour scent of spilled ale. We walked into a dimly lit room, a handful of oil lamps casting long, flickering shadows over rough-hewn tables and mismatched chairs. A few men and women, lingered in the corners, their conversations hushed as they cast wary glances toward us.

"A smuggler's den," Marek whispered, tilting his head toward the farthest table, where an older man with storm-gray hair watched us as we approached. "Are you ready for the truth?"

"Yours," I asked, "or Draven's?"

"Mine can wait. Draven's cannot."

"I want both," I said, realizing it was true.

Marek looked me deep into my eyes. "And you'll get both, before the night is through."

13

MAREK

Cormac watched us carefully as we sat. His eyes that never missed a detail were as cold and calculating as ever, but when he looked at Issa, something softened in them. He knew who she was already.

Not surprising.

He knew everything that happened in Valmyr. The moment we stepped onto the dock, his spies would have been watching.

"We're seeking information about Lord Draven of—"

"You know better than to ask without an offer, Marek."

Of course I did. But a man like Cormac, his rugged, weathered face and silver-streaked hair evidence of his age and many years of these type of deals, thrived on leverage, always ensuring he had the upper hand. I would take it from him where I could.

"Have I forgotten that bit?" I asked, his eyes narrowing at my cheekiness. It was a delicate balance with a man like him. I wanted information, but he would never give it to any who cowered in his presence.

"Aye, and you know it well."

Enough games. I pulled a piece of parchment from my pocket and slapped it on the table.

"This," I said, voice low, "is a ledger of Thalassari supply shipments set to dock in Valmyr over the next month. Goods marked for inspection, patrol rotations, and which captains can be bribed to look the other way."

His eyes widened. Leaning forward, Cormac inspected the information, slid the parchment toward him, folding it and hiding it away inside the folds of his worn, leather jerkin.

"Start talking," I said.

Cormac turned to Issa, who had been watching the exchange with more than a measure of incredulity that couldn't be helped. I'd seen her expression as Mev and Kael relayed the conversation they'd overheard. Issa needed the truth. She needed to come to terms with any guilt she might harbor for having trusted Draven.

"Lady Isolde," he began, Cormac lucky he used her title and was giving Issa the respect she deserved.

"How do you know me?"

Cormac simply smiled. "Lord Draven has been making moves for years. Forging alliances. And looking for... something."

Isolde crossed her arms. "Alliances with whom? What is he looking for?"

"With human nobles. He's looking for something your father hid from him."

A chill crept up my spine. Cormac's knowledge might be more than we bargained for, but it was too late to hold him back now.

"My father?"

"It's not a well-kept secret that Draven has always wanted Hawthorne Manor."

By Issa's expression, it was clear that particular secret was not one she was a part of keeping. I didn't know Cormac's sources but didn't need to. This, taken with what Issa's commander had told me, confirmed her allegiance to Draven was ill-advised.

"Draven," Cormac continued, "has been asking about blood-lines, about the first humans who crossed into Elydor."

That got my attention. "The Harrows?"

In response, Cormac simply raised a brow. One. Not two. It was an uncanny ability of his. There had been rumors about the Harrow family since they'd arrived. I didn't give them much credence, but I was curious about how this tied to Draven.

"Aye, the Harrows." He gave his attention back to Issa. "Your father knew something connected to that first family. Connected to the Aetherian Gate. Whatever your father kept from him, lass... it is keeping Draven from everything he's ever wanted."

Riddles. As usual. "Speak plainly," I said, impatient. "She is more confused than when we came."

Cormac shot me a look and sat back, crossing his arms. As usual, none in the dimly lit room paid us any mind. If they did, Cormac would have already shuttled them.

"Lord Draven positions himself to become Lord Protector of Estmere. He will use control of Hawthorne Manor and the southern borders, and his brokering of power with midland border nobles, as evidence of his influence."

Damn. It was worse than I'd imagined.

"Lord..." Issa stuttered, clearly shocked. "We have no Lord Protector of Estmere. Humans have rejected a king since they came through in favor of sovereign lords governing their own lands," she finished, her voice shaky.

Cormac nodded. "Aye, and Draven means to change that. With the right alliances, enough coin, and a firm enough grip on the borders, he'll make himself indispensable. And once he's indispensable..." He trailed off, letting the implication settle.

Issa's hands curled into fists on the table. "He wouldn't dare."

Cormac arched a brow. "Wouldn't he? He's been moving pieces for years, laying the groundwork. After your father passed, he continued looking for answers, but it seems whatever secret your father held in connection to the Harrow family died with him. He's shifted to finding something to push the nobles to rally behind him."

Issa looked at me, clearly panicked. "And I gave that to him."

I would kill the man before I allowed him to take Hawthorne from Issa. But I didn't say that. Instead, I shook my head. "No, you did not. You gave him your trust."

"Stupidly."

I had no wish for Cormac to hear Issa berate herself. Standing, I pulled her up with me. It was time to go.

"Until next time," I said to the hardened smuggler. One I dealt with out of need and not desire. He was as unsavory as they came, but to his credit, Cormac had delivered.

"Good luck," he said to Issa, pulling out my parchment, holding it up in gratitude that I took no pleasure in receiving. Willing myself to keep a smile plastered to my face, I nodded and led Issa from the room back out onto the street.

We walked back toward the dock, Issa silent.

It wasn't until we stood in an abandoned spot with a view of *Tidechaser* and the sea beyond her in front of us, the tavern we'd return to at our backs, that Issa finally spoke.

Or tried to.

She lifted her gaze to me with such a look of despair, I acted without thinking. Pulling Issa into me, I wrapped my arms around her. It only occurred to me to be surprised she allowed it as Issa wiggled in closer, her arms going tentatively around my waist.

We'd held each other this way only once before, after our only kiss.

She felt better than I remembered. Too good, in fact.

With Issa's head settled on my chest, I had to resist kissing the top of her head. Resist lifting her chin up and claiming those full lips once again. Familiar dockside sounds of water lapping against the pilings and the distant creak of ships at anchor filled the silence between us.

"Is it all true?"

If only I could confirm it wasn't. That Cormac was full of shit and Hawthorne Manor was safe from Lord Draven's designs. Unfortunately, the opposite seemed to be the case.

I pulled back to look at her, kicking myself immediately as Issa, seeming to realize for the first time she was actually in my arms, stepped back. I felt the loss of her body heat immediately. Maybe it was for the best.

"In all the years I've traded information with Cormac, I've never known him to be false. There are few ports, few people, in Elydor with more knowledge than him."

She shook her head, as if still disbelieving.

"But... how?"

"How does he get such information?"

"That. And how... if it's true... how could I have been so blind? Warren tried to tell me. Edric never liked him. Even Kael tried to tell me that Draven couldn't be trusted. But... my father."

"Was fallible too. We all are, Issa, especially with those closest to us."

She looked so miserable. Draven was lucky he was so many miles from us. For now.

"I am not good at discerning men's true nature."

"Because you trusted a man your father clearly trusted too?"

"He wasn't the only one I misjudged."

She was talking about me. And she wasn't wrong.

Biting back my long-held fear of vulnerability, the one that had kept me from letting anyone too close, I exhaled slowly. "Come with me."

Leading Issa to a winding stone staircase not far from The Drowned Oath, we climbed it to my favorite view of port, a secluded outcropping of rock with a weathered wooden bench beneath it. We sat, the soothing sound of waves crashing below.

"All Thalassari have an affinity to water. Some prefer the gentle lapping of the tides along shore. Others, the trickle of a fountain. For me, it's the crash of waves against the rocks. No matter how fierce the storm, the waves always return, steady and unyielding. It reminds me that some truths can be buried, but never washed away."

I'd sat here many times, Valmyr one of the ports that elicited the most information in all of Elydor. Remembering the last time I'd sat on this bench, after leaving Hawthorne Manor, it was hard to believe Issa sat beside me now. Convinced she would never speak to me again, and not willing to risk finding out, I had instead attempted to forget her.

A fool's endeavor.

She looked out to sea while I watched her. Even anguished, she was perfection. Some believed the slow aging of native Elydorians perfect, faint lines appearing only after hundreds of years. I disagreed. Everything about humans, with their urgency to live and experience as much as possible in a way only mortality could elicit, was beautiful to me. And none more so than the woman sitting beside me.

"I criticized him once," she said. "I'd seen, perhaps, ten summers. It was nothing more than a look, but something about the way Draven watched my father as he received petitions unsettled me. When I told my mother this, she advised me to hold my tongue. 'You must not criticize the lord of Hawthorne Manor publicly, Isolde. He holds no power over our people except that which they give him freely.' I felt foolish for thinking ill of my father's friend. For saying as much aloud." Issa looked at me. "I loved my mother dearly, but never agreed with her ways. She was too deferential to my father. I always wished she would be more like a native Elydorian woman... I should not speak ill of her."

"Your instincts were true," I said. "It is also true even those we love are flawed. My mother..." I stopped. It was unnatural for me to speak of this aloud. But I had promised Issa, and it was the reason I brought her here. "When she was alive, I thought my mother could do no wrong. She was perfect in every way. An expert diver, fearless beneath the sea."

Issa's brown eyes were fixed on me, pulling me in as surely as a strong tide. I swallowed, trusting her, even knowing I did not deserve that same trust in return.

"You speak of your inability to judge character as though it is a flaw. My mother... she lived over three centuries and yet, even she trusted those she should not have. Some are simply more inclined to trust than others, but that does not make them weaker. It only makes them more open... and sometimes, that comes at a great cost. But there is a high cost for trusting no one, as I do. None of us come out unscathed, Issa."

"What happened to your mother?" she asked softly.

I looked out to the sea, trying to find the words for a story I had never told.

"She was the best pearl diver in Thalassaria. So much so that others sought her counsel. One, a man named Olivar, a respected sailor and diver, was well-known for his deep knowledge of the sea. He and my mother completed many dives together throughout the years, and she trusted him as a friend." My jaw clenched as I envisioned his face, one that haunted me in my dreams. "He convinced my mother to dive in an area well-known for its turbulent waters. Some say, tainted by dark magic, an ancient one older than the tides itself."

"Marek," she said, her voice full of concern.

I turned toward the sound, oddly comforted in a way I'd never allowed myself to be with anyone. Even Nerys.

"It was rumored to contain pink pearls."

Her eyes widened. Even humans knew that pink pearls were rare and highly coveted for their ability to bring good fate to their owners.

"My father tried to talk her out of the dive, but Olivar convinced her, with the proper precautions, they would be safe. I was on an expedition to Aethralis and only learned of her death upon my return. The moment we ported, I knew something was wrong. My father was there, which was exceedingly odd. If either of them would be standing on the docks waiting for my safe return, it would be my mother."

"Do you know what happened?"

I shook my head. "Her body washed up on the shore days later after my father led a fruitless search."

"I do not think... for a Thalassarian to drown—"

"She was not just any Thalassarian, Issa. There were few more skilled at diving than my mother. And aye, it is extremely rare for a Thalassari to drown."

"And Olivar?"

Drown him to the Depths. "Was never found."

Her big brown eyes widened. "Did he... do you think he drowned too?"

I reached into the folds of my breeches where a small, leather pouch was tucked away. Pulling it out, I loosened the drawstring and tipped it into my palm: a single, luminous, pink pearl, unlike any found in common waters.

Issa gasped.

"This," I said, rolling it between my fingers, "was found on her when they pulled her from the sea. So I began searching. Asking questions. First among pearl divers, then traders, then those who dealt in rare things. Eventually, my questions led me to men who asked their own price for answers. Smugglers. Thieves. Black-market dealers." I met Issa's gaze again. "One thing led to another, and I found I had a talent for trade. For moving things others could not. At first, it was only a way to uncover the truth. But the truth is slow, and survival demands coin. And so... I became what I am."

"All for answers about your mother's death?"

I turned the pearl in my fingers, watching how the dim light of the lanterns behind us caught its strange, otherworldly shimmer. "I have never stopped looking. And I do not intend to."

"Why... You told me your mother had died, but not... this."

I replaced the pearl my father had given me after he discovered it preparing my mother's body for her final voyage at sea.

"I haven't told this to anyone," I said, matter of factly.

Clearly, Issa didn't believe me. "Anyone? Surely, in all these years..."

"My father knows, of course."

"Nerys?"

I shook my head. "No one." Then, qualifying my statement, I said, "Some know more than others about the information I seek. Bram, for instance, secured that ledger for me because he knows I pay handsomely for any information tied to the Maelstrom Depths."

Issa's brows drew together. Anticipating her question, I added, "Some believe the same dark magic that tainted the waters in which my mother dove also made the Maelstrom Depths so dangerous, even for water-wielders. Like other unexplained phenomena in Elydor, the belief is that an ancient ritual, tied to a time when magic in Elydor was unbound to the elements, was used for personal gain. For power. And when someone, or something, is too powerful—"

"Elydor seeks a balance."

"Always."

Issa was now properly horrified. "And yet, believing they may be tied to each other, you are prepared to descend into the same Depths whose dark magic may have claimed your mother?"

"Who else should retrieve the Crystal than someone with a command of water, who has spent his life seeking the truth of such waters?"

"A truth you've not fully grasped."

I could not argue that. "There is no help for that unfortunate fact."

"Why, Marek?"

"I've told you, Nerys and Mev—"

"No. That is not what I ask. Why did you tell me about your mother?"

Why, indeed?

"Because I promised you I would. And I don't intend to break a promise to you again, Issa. Not even an unspoken one."

She could push back. Press me as to the real reason. But, as difficult as it was to tell the story of my mother's death, and my inability, after so many years, to piece together a puzzle that would haunt me forever... telling her the true reason I opened up to her unlike I had with anyone before?

Some truths were better left buried at the bottom of the sea.

14

ISSA

"I'm not surprised," Mev said as we walked toward the docks. I recounted the smuggler's conversation from last eve, pushing Marek's revelation to the back of my mind. The confession, and subsequent promise, was too much to consider at the moment.

When we returned to The Drowned Oath, Kael and Mev were already abed. After a fitful sleep, my dreams filled with visions of Lord Draven standing at the gatehouse, denying me entry to my home, I woke to Mev at my door. Apparently, Marek had left already, so a quick change and breaking our fast in the ale-scented hall of the inn saw us following Kael back to the docks.

"That the same man I left in charge of Hawthorne Manor is making a play to become Lord Protector of Estmere."

"Well," Mev said, her presence in Valmyr Port seemingly no longer a secret. Some stared openly, others bowed as she walked by, but one thing was clear: Mev was no ordinary human. "Maybe not all of that. No shade to you at all, Issa. If you knew how many men I dated whose glaring red flags... Never mind. Bad analogy."

I had no sense of what she spoke about.

"Sorry. I forget sometimes, especially in Estmere, that I'm not just in some medieval town in England. That this is real."

It was hard to imagine being transported, without warning, to a place you didn't know existed and then taken by the son of your enemy. "I am sorry I didn't help you," I said, not for the first time.

"No worries. I get it, friend code and all. If it had been Clara, I'd have done the same and protected her at all costs. Anyway, what I meant to say was... don't beat yourself up about not seeing Draven for who he really is. The guy's obviously pretty crafty, and from what you've told me, has been keeping his cards close to his chest for a long time."

That one, I could understand, even if I'd never heard the expression before.

"Maybe even since when my father was alive."

"Most likely. When we get to Aethralis, we will speak to the king. He's been a champion of Estmere since its inception and will not take kindly to the type of power play Draven is attempting."

"I could not ask him for aid. With tensions as they are, Aetherian involvement in Estmere could be the excuse Gyoria needs to declare all-out war."

"We will find a way to stop him, Issa."

"I just feel so... helpless. I know this mission is bigger than me, bigger than Hawthorne, but..." I sighed as one particular woman got too close to Mev. Kael stepped between them, but she stopped him. She was weathered, as if the docks were more than her home but the woman's identity. She fell to Mev's feet and began to cry.

With a stern glance at Kael to stay away, Mev squatted down, placing her hand on the woman's back. Mev said nothing as a crowd began to gather.

"Mevlida." Kael's voice held a warning that Mev didn't heed.

"My son," the woman said finally, looking up to Mev with an expression so filled with anguish that I instinctively moved closer, as if to comfort her. She had seen, perhaps, fifty or so years. A human, for certain. "He was just two years old when I came through... It was my first time away from him since he'd been born. A friend and I took a train to York overnight. It was supposed to be a lark, the whispers about The Crooked Key." She shook her head. "They were not just rumor. They were real."

"You were separated from your son when the Gate closed."

Tears streamed down the woman's face. Mev took her by the hands and they stood together. Mev whispered something to the woman, who gasped in response, as if attempting to breathe normally from an old wound reopened. Mev pulled her close, allowing the woman to drench her tunic as she cried inconsolably.

I peered at Kael. Not once had I seen such an expression on his face. His typical mask of strength, bordering indifference, had been cracked. No matter it was his father that had separated this woman from her two-year-old son. For years, I had attempted to sway him to the human cause, to no avail. Mev had done what I could not, and he would never be the same.

When the woman finally pulled away, her expression had changed. Her eyes, still glistening with tears, held something more now.

Hope.

She stood back, allowing Mev to drop her hands, but not before squeezing them and nodding. The woman smiled, tears still streaming down her face, as she turned without a word and edged her way through the gathered crowd and sped away.

Springing into action, Kael cleared the crowd, allowing Mev and I to move forward. He said nothing more as the docks appeared before us.

"Your role as Princess of Aetheria suits you, Mev," I said softly. "Though I am sorry you were thrust into it rather than choosing it for yourself."

"I still can't..." She made a sound of frustration. "I don't see myself as a princess. Sometimes, in the early morning, before I'm fully awake, when I completely forget... I'm surprised to wake up, not in my bed in Boston but"—she shrugged—"here. A princess whose father is a king. Whose partner is a prince. It's still so surreal. But encounters like that— there've only been a handful since I haven't spent a lot of time among humans yet— are a stark reminder that I'm not the only one at risk of being separated from my family forever. I've never been a mother, but I am the daughter of one who was never shy about sharing her love for me and can only imagine the anguish that mother has felt. Doesn't matter it's almost thirty years. I'm pretty sure that kind of pain never goes away."

I could not internalize the kind of anguish that mother had been feeling, being torn away from her young child.

"What did you whisper to her?" I asked, curiosity making me toss decorum to the side. "Of course, you do not have to—"

"I told her that I would not rest until the Gate is reopened so that she could reunite with her son. And that us being here was tied to that very mission."

She began walking once again, and I followed, expecting to see Marek already on the ship, preparing her to continue our journey. Instead, he was talking to a woman. A comely one at that. When they embraced, I stiffened.

"You were gone a long time last night," Mev teased.

I raised my chin, continuing forward and pretending Marek's philandering didn't affect me. I knew his reputation with women because he had told me about it himself. Just one of many clues to his character that I ignored.

"It's so easy to forget," I admitted.

They finally disentangled, the woman blowing Marek a kiss as she turned toward us. He didn't even see Mev and me before boarding the ship.

I avoided looking at her as she walked past. She appeared to be either a human, or perhaps a Thalassari, her sun-kissed skin and effervescent beauty bordering unnatural.

"Forget what?" she asked.

He spotted us then.

Marek grinned as if he hadn't a care in the world. As if he'd not just been embracing a woman who looked as if she'd just climbed up onto the docks from her previous post as a siren of the seas. A vision of that morning, the one after he left, when I'd jumped from my bed, excited to begin the day. Excited to see him. Hopeful that something might actually be budding between us that wasn't fleeting.

"Forget that he has the ability to break my heart. Again."

15

MAREK

Issa hadn't looked at me all day. She never came up to the quarterdeck for lessons and, when I joined the others for a midday meal, she left without a word.

Fitting, I supposed.

Immortality had many benefits, and one of those was the ability to understand situations because, most likely, you'd been in one similar before. As I thought on it, I couldn't help smiling now, certain my assessment was correct.

She was not angry with me when I walked her to her room at the inn. Having no idea I'd slept in the hallway in front of her door, not leaving her safety to chance in a place like Valmyr Port, Issa had come to the docks with Mev and Kael, only moments after I spoke with Cassandra. Since then, she'd kept her distance.

Issa was jealous.

And if that were the case, it meant she still had lingering feelings for me that were not all entirely murderous. Except... my vast experience with women lent very little to helping me navigate this particular situation.

Issa was not like the others. I'd known that almost from the start. It was the reason I left. Remaining at Hawthorne any longer would have led to a bond that would have been even more difficult to break. One that would have led to me eventually losing her to an inevitable human's death. That still mattered. And yet...

Start by making her smile.

It was the advice my mother gave me the first time I confessed my feelings toward a young Thalassari girl in my training pod. Sound advice, to my thinking.

Letting go of the wheel, I first steadied the ship by creating a channel of calming water in front of us for as far as the eye could see. Kael looked up from his position beside Mev, who was in a deep conversation with Issa.

Next, I lifted my hands, twisting them as water lifted all around the ship in ribbons, sunlight catching her in angles and encasing *Tidechaser* in a celebratory display. All three turned in circles, watching as the ribbons twisted in place even as our ship continued forward. Releasing them, I brought my hands back down to my sides, all evidence of the display now back in the sea.

Mev's hands reached into the air, and as we watched, the wind began to swirl around us. At first, it seemed as if the air patterns were random, but soon the spiraling gusts began to take shape. First, as her hands twirled flingwing fitches as they flew around the ship. Next, the fitches converged into a giant silver-winged deer that pranced beside us before evaporating back into the sky.

It had worked.

Issa was smiling from ear to ear.

Again, lifting my hands, I took Mev's cue and formed a school of marisol that leaped from the sea into the air beside us as they once again descended into its depth.

Smiling, but not at me.

I waited to see if Mev would counter. Instead, it was Kael who lifted his hands into the air. Looking toward the small island off our port side, assuming that was what he would manipulate, I wasn't surprised to see a massive rock outcropping begin to move. Shifting the rock's position took more skill than most Gyorians could manage, Kael showing once again the depths of his magic. As we watched, the rock moved into the shape of... was that... a heart?

Mev's arms were around him the moment Kael had dropped his arms.

King Balthor's son. A romantic. I was certain no one would believe me if I told them this tale.

Issa turned toward me.

I beckoned her to come up, not expecting she would. When she took a tentative step toward me, my heart raced. Seeing her bound up the stairs to the quarterdeck, her sea legs firm beneath her, I could not help but be proud even though my contribution had been minimal.

"I've seen Thalassari make their way with less ease around *Tidechaser*."

I stepped back and gestured for her to take the wheel.

Issa seemed to feel comfortable in the spot, and there was something extremely sexy about seeing here there too. Her tunic and breeches— Issa's practical clothing serving her well on this journey— tightly fitted, it took every bit of effort on my part not to stare.

As her hands lay on the wheel, she continued. "I will admit, it strangely feels... comforting to me, in a way I'd never have expected, having spent so little time near the sea."

I let Issa take the lead, waiting for her to speak.

"Did you sleep well?" she asked finally.

"Well enough," I said. "You?"

The corner of her mouth lifted, as if confused. "Not as well as I expected, despite the size of the bed compared to yours."

Hearing "bed" and "yours" in the same sentence did little to keep me focused.

"I dreamed of Draven," she said, hesitant. "That he refused to allow me entry to my own home."

The tides curse Draven and his ambitions.

"As luck, or Thalassa, would have it, my half-sister arrived in port this morn."

Her head whipped toward me, Issa not bothering to hide her surprise. I was careful not to smile.

"Cassandra? The woman on the docks... that was your sister?"

Do. Not. Smile. Marek.

"It was."

Cassandra was raised on the opposite coast of Thalassaria where her mother lived. I told Issa about her at Hawthorne when we'd spoken of our families but still was amazed she remembered.

Perhaps I should not be.

Willing my expression to remain neutral, I told her of our conversation. "She is headed south and will port at Valewood Bay and track the movements of mercenaries arriving by sea, identifying which ships are loyal to Draven. She will also keep an ear to the ground for whispers of supply lines, bribes, or weaknesses we can exploit."

Issa's mouth dropped.

"You were... she... she is helping me?"

"Cassandra is family and would do anything I asked of her, as I would do the same."

"But... I thought..."

Finally, I broke, unable to resist the small smile. "What did you think, Issa?"

"I thought she..." Her eyes narrowed. "Marek?"

"Aye, sereia?"

So much for the smile. "You knew?"

Never would I admit as much. "I know very little compared to what I do not know."

"Riddles," she murmured. "Always riddles."

I crossed my arms and leaned back against the railing.

"Thank you," she said begrudgingly. "For speaking to her on my behalf."

"You are most welcome. Issa?"

"Aye?" she asked as I gestured for her to steer us slightly to port. She did, expertly.

"We will not allow Draven to take Estmere. Or become Lord Protector of Estmere, for that matter."

Her chin raised defiantly. "No," she said. "We will not. Though I do appreciate your assistance."

"My network may be unsavory, at times, but it is vast and connected."

"I'm learning the truth of those words." She sighed, looking up to the sky, as if content. At least, more so than when we first began to talk. I knew she was worried about Hawthorne Manor and her people. She'd admitted more than once that she felt it was her duty to ensure her parents' legacy endured. They had committed themselves to keeping the southern border of Estmere safe from Gyorians who had no wish to live so close to humans, a feat that would be much easier if King Balthor were not so openly hostile to her kind.

But... it was not Issa's calling. A duty? Aye. But not her dream.

"I have a question for you."

"Just one?" I asked.

She laughed. "Many, in fact. But one I thought of this morn as I woke."

"You thought of me as you woke? Interesting."

"Marek," she chastised, her eyes not matching her tone. They were teasing, bordering preciously close to flirting. So close, in fact, that I did not hold back my own appreciation of her. One that was always simmering beneath the surface. In fact, I let my gaze wander at will, paying the price when it lifted to once again meet hers.

"Aye, sereia?"

"Why do you call me that?" she said, her voice barely above a whisper.

"You know why, Issa. Now, was that your question?"

"No. My question was, why did you have those trade routes written down, as if knowing you would need them?"

Not what I was expecting, but perhaps I should have. Issa was observant.

"I expected to use them in some capacity," I admitted, "though not precisely as it happened. I've been trading in information for many years, and would find it difficult not to think in such ways, even if I suddenly had all of the answers I sought."

"Do you worry, with Nerys as queen, that you will compromise her position? With your 'unsavory' practices, as they are."

A good question.

"No more than I've always worried about how my dealings might negatively impact those I care about. Thankfully, the list is small and thus far, I've avoided any lasting consequences. My turn."

"To ask a question?"

"Aye."

If Issa was wary, it was with good reason. If I were more cautious, I'd ask her about any number of things... except this.

"If you despise me so, not that I blame you for leaving as I did," I began.

Issa's head slowly spun toward me, her soulful eyes narrowing.

"Why were you jealous of Cassandra?"

Issa looked as if she would throttle me.

Instead, she jerked her hands from the wheel and clasped her chest. Something was wrong.

Very wrong.

16

ISSA

I'd never felt magic like this before.

Squeezing my eyes shut, I felt the beat of my heart beneath my chest. Marek was beside me, either having taken over the wheel or ensuring I remained safe, I wasn't sure.

It wasn't just powerful; that was not the most unusual thing about this magic. Typically, when magic was close, it cascaded through my senses, but not this. This was like a crash, sudden and... unnatural.

How to describe it?

I opened my eyes. Marek was so close, I could hear his breath, even over the wind that had suddenly picked up.

"Issa, what is it? What's wrong?"

"This magic is so sudden, as if it were dormant and then just..."

I looked out to the sea. Nothing seemed amiss. But it was.

"You sense magic near?" Marek asked. "Maybe a pelagor? I've not seen one but—"

"No." I shook my head. "I can differentiate between different... types of magic. It is unlike any other I've ever sensed before.

As if something..." I tried to grasp it once again, but the feeling was gone. "Awoke."

It was the only way I could describe it.

Marek took the wheel. He could have used magic to steer the ship, but I understood why he did not. There was something comforting about it. A false sense of control, perhaps?

Moments ago, I'd have shoved him off the side of the ship, if I could have managed it, if for no other reason than verbalizing the truth. I had been jealous, unreasonably so. But it was uncharitable of him to say it, not that proper decorum was high on Marek's list of attributes.

But now, the way he looked at me, his eyes full of concern... I could easily fall back into his arms, and that was precisely the problem.

"Mev," I whispered.

Marek saw her at the same time as me, racing toward us with Kael on her heels. They scrambled up to the quarterdeck, which became quickly crowded.

"Lyra," she blurted, "just whispered to me."

"Out here?" I asked. Though skilled Aetherian whisperers could communicate the length of Elydor, it was still a surprise their whispers could travel across the sea.

She cupped both hands over her mouth, as if still processing what had happened. Moving them to her cheeks, Mev appeared as surprised as I was at the communication.

"Lyra was the first one to teach me how to whisper," she said, dropping her hands. "Maybe that's the reason... I don't know."

"Tell them," Kael prompted.

"Rowan sent word to her, hoping she could get to me. He had a vision."

I didn't believe in coincidences. Though the feeling of a powerful, dormant, magic was gone, it must have been related.

"It was disjointed," she said, lifting her hand into the air, as if not even realizing she was doing it. With one flick of her wrist, the sails caught a stronger wind and *Tidechaser* moved more quickly through the water.

Marek and I exchanged a glance, likely thinking the same thing. Mev manipulated the air as if she'd been born in Elydor, raised to wield it.

"Mev... the Depths... they remember. Not safe. Not meant to be disturbed. Tell them."

Kael cleared his throat. "I believe you left something out?"

She stared blankly at him, as if trying to remember. "Oh, yes." Mev made a face, as if it were painful to repeat the next words. "A sacrifice must be made..."

She looked at Marek. We all did.

He shrugged. "I've no notion of what that means."

"I felt something," I said. "Just before you came up here. A magical presence unlike anything I've felt before."

"Unlike anything?" Kael asked. "How so? Stronger?"

"Maybe," I admitted, unsure how to put it into words. "But more than that. The awareness of it began differently. It was as if something... awoke from a slumber. It slammed into me, making its presence known, and as quickly as it came, it was gone."

"A sea animal, perhaps?"

"I said the same," Marek admitted as I shook my head.

"Wait." Mev leaned against the rail, into Kael's side. It was still strange to see him, my friend but always the stalwart Gyorian prince, this way. She had changed him. In a good way.

"Technically, everything in Elydor is imbued with magic. So every animal... actually, every Elydorian... do you sense them all?"

"No, not any longer. Before I was trained, aye. To an extent. Maybe like when you sense another's intention—"

"Ahh, I get it. I only feel it when I open myself up to receiving it. Or when it's so strong, I have no choice but to notice. It's been like that from the start."

"Without training?"

"Right. No training. My mother is a psychic. It's what led her to The Crooked Key in the first place, I assume: whisperings of a secret portal among the magical community. But me? Nothing. Nada. At least, not until I came here. It came on gradually but, no. There was never any training involved. At least, not with my human abilities. Anyway, tell us more about what you felt."

"It was dark," I blurted, realizing I had not mentioned that.

"Dark magic?" Marek asked.

"I'm not sure. I've never sensed dark magic, that I know of."

"Not surprising," Kael explained to Mev, "it's extremely rare."

Unfortunately, I had nothing else to offer.

I began to pace, thinking back to Rowan's vision, or what we had of it, at least. "The Depths remember. Not safe. Not meant to be disturbed. A sacrifice must be made. Do you think... could the magic I felt be the Depths themselves, somehow? The two must be related."

"You said there are all sorts of stories about the Maelstrom Depths," Mev said to Marek. "But that the most likely spoke of a living force that does not forget. Does not forgive. Isn't that what you said?"

"Oldest story, but perhaps most likely too." Marek nodded toward the ship's wheel, stepping aside.

I took it, thankful to have something useful to do.

"So that tracks with Rowan's message," Mev said.

All three of us looked at her, confused.

"Sorry. That... makes sense. You felt as if something, maybe dark, came alive. And legend speaks of the Depths as if they are alive. 'They remember. They require a sacrifice.' It must all be related."

"Marek," I said quietly, knowing what I did about his mother's death. "Where does one learn more about them?"

His brows arched. "Sailors' journals, like the one we acquired. Oral history. I've asked Nerys to research The Deep Archives for information on the Depths and other underwater disturbances like it. But thus far, very little information has been useful."

Our group fell silent.

Marek's mission was dangerous before. But this? He would not survive those Depths. Of that I had no doubt. We couldn't let him go into them. Not like this.

Mev straightened, her gaze sharpening with realization. "Then we need more than old sailors' journals and fragmented myths. Kael and I will scour The Luminara for information. We need to figure this out before you retrieve the Wind Crystal, Marek."

Kael nodded, his expression thoughtful. "Those vaults house the oldest records in Aetheria. If there's any written account of what dwells in the Maelstrom Depths, it would be there."

Marek rolled his eyes playfully, bringing a much-needed lightness back to the conversation. "Aetherians and their books."

"I agree," I said, running my fingers along the wheel's smooth, time-worn wood. The ship swayed beneath me, steady despite the storm of uncertainty brewing in my mind. My grip tightened... not to steer, but to ground myself.

"Then it is settled." Mev pushed off the rail and headed back down to the main deck, Kael falling in step beside her.

"Where are you going?" I asked, curious.

Mev tossed a grin over her shoulder. "To make sure we don't all starve. Unless you'd rather survive on Marek's questionable stash of dried fish?"

They were gone before he could reply.

Marek moved toward me, his presence solid and sure. I breathed in his scent of salt and sun-warmed leather. He didn't speak at first, just rested a hand on the wheel beside mine, his fingers brushing my knuckles as he adjusted our course.

"The wind's shifting," he murmured near my ear. "Feel that?"

I did. A subtle but distinct change in pressure, the sails catching at a different angle. I nodded as his other hand came to rest at the small of my back.

"Steady," he said, his voice a shade rougher now. "You're compensating too much."

I hadn't realized I was. The ship's movement was instinctive to him, but to me, it still felt like an untamed thing, responding too easily to my slightest shift.

He exhaled, a near-silent chuckle. "You're fighting her."

I tipped my chin up at him, half in challenge. "Then show me how not to."

His fingers curled over mine on the wheel, adjusting my grip. The touch was jolting, but not in the least undesirable, despite the fact that this was Marek, a man I'd been cursing most days for years.

"Don't force her, sereia. Let the ship tell you where she wants to go, then guide her there. Not too much, not too little. Just enough."

His words were low, deliberate, sending a different kind of awareness curling through me.

I swallowed. "Like this?"

His chest brushed my back as we moved with the ship's subtle sway. "Better. Now, what were we talking about before that strange turn of events? Ahh, yes. I remember now. Us."

Us. Me being jealous of Cassandra. My tumultuous thoughts that ranged from anger to gratitude to bitterness to desire.

"I'd prefer to talk about something else."

He waited until I locked eyes with him before responding. "I'd prefer not to talk at all."

His meaning was clear. But instead of scolding him, as I should, my gaze fell to his lips, remembering. His lips parted, inviting.

Damn him to the Depths. After everything, I still wanted to kiss him.

17

MAREK

This was too deep, even for me.

The pressure crushed my chest, but that pink glow still beckoned. Swimming toward it, I finally saw her. My mother's hair flowing behind her like seaweed. I couldn't see her face but knew it was her. Bubbles floated upward from her mouth. She was alive! Just as I reached out to grab her, something pushed me down from above. I struggled to break free, but an unseen force dragged me deeper into the darkness.

The harder I fought, the deeper I sank. The water around me like tar. My vision blurred and lungs burned. I couldn't move. Couldn't breathe.

"Marek."

A soft voice. Hand on my arm.

"Wake up."

I woke with a gasp. Sweating, I looked around, orienting myself. I was not in the ocean's depths but slumbering against a coil of rope.

Issa squatted down beside me.

Sitting up, I looked around. It was still dark, not yet morning.

I saw Issa but couldn't fully appreciate her features. I still saw my mother's hair, floating behind her. Felt the pressure of diving so deep against my chest.

"A nightmare?" she asked, sitting beside me, her back against the rope.

Looking at her, the terror of knowing I couldn't save my mother still fresh, I couldn't yet speak.

Issa lay her head on my shoulder, the small comfort enough to remind me to breathe. I wasn't underwater. My mother, long gone.

It had been some time since that particular nightmare had plagued me.

The fog of my dream finally lifting, I was hesitant to move, wanting Issa to remain exactly where she was.

"It's early for you to be awake."

"You didn't feel the ship lurch?" she asked, lifting her head, unfortunately.

"I didn't," I said, standing. Before I dozed off, the sea was eerily calm. If not for magic, we'd have struggled to travel north efficiently with the lack of strong winds on this journey. Looking out to the sea, assessing it, I sat back down. "All seems well enough. Although a storm is coming."

We were so close, and yet, if I tried to touch her... it was too soon. Issa did not yet trust me, and perhaps that was a good thing. It would be wise to keep my distance, however...

"It wasn't the waves, Marek. It was something else. Like a pull beneath us. And then it stopped."

"Do you think it's related to what happened earlier? With you and Mev?"

"I don't know," she said, her voice low and soft. "Do you have them often?"

I sighed, thinking to brush off her question and discuss what woke her instead. But the way she looked at me...

"It seems to come and go."

"It? The same dream?"

"Every time. I'm underwater, deeper than is safe, but a pink light beckons me. That's when I see my mother, floating, her body still and only her hair moving in the water. Before I can get to her, I'm pulled under by an unseen force. Unable to move, or even breathe."

Without warning, she reached up, Issa's hand cupping my cheek. I laid my own over hers, closing my eyes.

No words were needed.

Pulling her hand away, Issa laid her head against my shoulder again. The sound of her steady breathing, along with the feel of her so close beside me, lulled me back to sleep.

It wasn't until the sun rose over the horizon that I woke once again with Issa slumbering in the same position she'd been in when we had fallen asleep.

I didn't dare move, even as Kael's head rose above the quarterdeck. I held a finger to my lips, and even though he didn't speak, Issa woke, moving quickly away from me and stood up.

"There was a disturbance," she said, speaking quickly. "I woke and came here to find Marek—"

"You owe no explanation, Issa."

Standing, I made my way to the ship's wheel. The natural winds were picking up, our calm waters about to be at an end.

She sighed as I remembered Issa telling me once her father had told her not to explain, or apologize, when she had done nothing wrong, but that Issa found the directive difficult. I thought back to our time together, back to that conversation in particular, pulling the words from my memory.

"There is no need to explain yourself to anyone who truly

knows you." I adjusted the wheel, my gaze on the horizon. "And to those who don't? No explanation will ever be enough."

Watching her to see if I got the words right, as her eyes widened, I was fairly certain I was close.

"You remembered..."

As we stared at each other, Kael slipped back down, leaving us alone once again on the quarterdeck.

"I remember all of it, Issa."

She turned away, moving toward the railing. As always, her hair was braided. Only once, at Hawthorne, had I seen her dress in a gown. More often, Issa was dressed as if prepared to ride, or hunt or... chase down Gyorian raiders.

I was still watching when she turned back to face me.

She was so beautiful.

Trained as a warrior, forced to become Lady of Hawthorne Manor too young, she had sacrificed everything—her life, her own happiness—for the sake of her people.

The ship lurched, the sky now darkened as if it was not morn.

Issa grabbed the railing to steady herself.

I reached out a hand. "Come. I'll show you how to ride the storm."

She took my hand, her grip just as firm as I remembered it. Pulling her in front of me as the deck pitched beneath our feet, I guided her hands to rest beside mine.

The sea roared around us, waves cresting high as the ship fought to stay its course.

Her fingers curled white-knuckled around the wood. "It feels alive," she murmured.

"It is." I reached over, adjusting her stance, steadying her hands. "You don't fight the storm. You move with it. Feel the wind, the pull of the current."

"It feels as if the sea will swallow us whole."

I grinned. "Then we make it work for us."

Another wave slammed into the hull, sending a spray of seawater over the deck. Issa gasped but held firm. She was a fighter. Always had been. And standing here while the storm raged around us, I realized she was meant for this life more than she knew.

The wind howled, tearing through the rigging as the ship surged forward. Lightning split the sky but Issa continued to stand her ground, hands firm on the wheel, her breath steady now.

Then, through the mist and driving rain, a break in the storm.

Beyond the endless waves, dark cliffs rose from the water, wreathed in mist. Issa stiffened beneath my touch.

"Welcome to Aetheria," I murmured as another roll of thunder echoed behind us.

18

ISSA

I'd been to Aetheria before, but never from the sea. And the only time my father and I travelled as far north as Aethralis, we'd seen the palace from a distance. But as our party stepped onto the docks, the palace rising high above us, seemingly into the clouds, I wondered how we would get there.

The sea had been ruthless, but now, the storm seemed to die behind us. Aetheria rose ahead, wreathed in low-hanging clouds, its ethereal glow casting the cliffs in an otherworldly shimmer.

From this vantage point, the city was unlike anything I had ever seen. Waterfalls spilled from floating isles above, cascading down and vanishing into the mist before they reached the sea. The blue glow of enchanted stones pulsed faintly along the cliff-side, embedded into the rock itself, as if Aetheria had been carved from magic rather than stone. And high above, the palace of Aethralis loomed. Its gleaming white towers pierced the sky, their intricate carvings barely visible through the haze.

"This is very different from Valmyr Port," I said, glad to have taken a cloak with me. It was barely spring and though never bitterly cold anywhere in Elydor, there was a chill in the Aetherian air that Estmere lacked this time of year.

"When I first got here," Mev said, in step beside me, "after I realized it wasn't a dream, I couldn't understand the perpetual perfect climate. Back home, you could drive twenty-four hours and go from freezing cold to almost tropical."

"I've heard of your cars. And planes. I don't believe I would ever trust such a thing to take me through the sky that way."

Mev laughed. "At least there's a reason why it works. This"— she flicked her wrist, sending a blast of wind upward in a spiral— "not so much. Lyra tried to explain it to me. My father made sure I was taught Elydor's history. But by our technological standards" —she shook her head—"it still doesn't make logical sense."

"A ship that flies through the sky?" Marek added as he and Kael caught up to us. "Sounds like the kind of tale a drunken sailor spins after too much rum. At least with magic, I can feel the wind shift, the tide answer. Your planes? What stops them from simply falling?"

"You're ridiculous," Mev said. "They aren't ships. But physics wasn't my strong suit, so I'm not sure I can explain how they fly with any accuracy."

"He's jesting," I said. "Elydorians have studied human technology since they first arrived. It's all chronicled in the Luminara. We have our own version of it in Estmere, but Aetherians, as you probably know, excel at preserving history."

"How did I not know about this?" Mev asked Kael, who smiled mischievously. "You have chronicles of our technology?"

"You've been... otherwise occupied."

"Ugh," she said, in mock indignation. "You're impossible."

We'd arrived at the far end of the docks, in the opposite direction of where the others seemed to be going. It was always difficult for me not to stare in Aetheria, the striking beauty of their shades of white and silver hair making them the most distinguishable among all Elydorians. Though it was usually fairly easy to spot a Gyorian as well—their size and usually dark hair coupled with a sternness that stemmed from countless years of physical training—those that lived among the clouds had always been the most striking to me.

Marek's arm brushed mine as he walked past me to talk to Kael.

The jolt of awareness when he was close wasn't new. The shift that had happened these past few days was, and it concerned me. Marek was still the roguish ship captain who strolled into my life, made me feel things I had never before and then callously left without even a goodbye.

But he was also someone deeply affected by his mother's death, enough so to have altered his life's course because of it. The terror I saw in his eyes when he woke was real. And I wasn't immune to it.

"Here we are," Mev announced proudly.

Two Aetherian sentinels stood on either side of a white marble arch, much like the ones at the Temple where the Aetherian Gate was housed. None were allowed inside, but my father had taken me to it once, to show me where my ancestors had come from their realm into Elydor, some believing it would be a temporary stay, others, happy to leave permanently for a new beginning.

Aetherians often greeted each other with a slight bow of the head, but these guards bent theirs deeply, looking down to the ground. It was easy to forget Mev was the king's daughter, an Aetherian princess. But their greeting was a reminder she was no ordinary woman.

The guards stood to the side, allowing our party admittance

into a mist that hid whatever was beyond the arches. As we passed beneath them, the air shimmered and I realized, with a jolt, that the path ahead wasn't a path at all.

It was floating.

"Uh, Mev," I said, unable to see anyone.

"It's fine," she said. "We're almost there."

It was like being caught in an updraft, the wind cradling me, lifting me higher. The mist began to clear. Below, the docks shrank, the sea stretching endlessly beyond them.

Then, just as suddenly as it started, we were weightless no more. My boots met solid ground... a floating platform of smooth white stone, suspended high above the cliffs. Ahead, an ornate bridge stretched toward Aethralis, gleaming in the glow of the enchanted city.

Mev smiled. "Welcome to the Ascension."

Of course. I should have realized. All knew of it, but few traveled through it.

"That was... different," Marek said as we began to walk toward the palace.

"You've never used the Ascension before?"

Marek's laugh was immediate. "The company I keep doesn't usually involve royalty and special treatment."

"Yet here you are." Mev smiled. "Maybe the company you keep is shifting. You're never too old, or young, to reinvent yourself." With that, she bound ahead, clearly happy to be home. Or at least, her home for now. What would happen when the Gate opened?

"How are you feeling?"

Marek's voice pulled me from my thoughts. "From that ascent?"

"That. The storm. Hawthorne. I know it bothers you still."

As we passed buildings that seemed to float on islands of

clouds with waterfalls cascading onto more clouds below them, I marveled at how different it was than Estmere.

"I feel so... powerless. But the storm? Oddly, navigating through it made me feel just the opposite."

"Not odd at all, Issa. You belong on a ship."

I could argue with him, tell Marek I belonged in Estmere, at Hawthorne, but something stayed my tongue. Perhaps because there was some truth to his words?

Hawthorne was your parents' dream.

I had never spoken the words aloud, but somehow, from that short time we'd been together, Marek had guessed what no one else in my life knew.

Guilt welled in my chest, a vision of my parents in the great hall, sitting on the dais as they'd done each day until they left this world too soon, replaced by the one of me standing behind the wheel of *Tidechaser*.

"I belong at Hawthorne Manor."

Marek had no chance to respond as we approached another archway, its sentinels greeting Mev as the other two had done. The Aetherian palace in Aethralis was an awe-inspiring place of gleaming white stone with lush gardens in every direction. As we climbed the marble stairs, the sea beyond beckoned.

I stopped to stare.

"I didn't realize how high up we were until now."

Marek stopped with me, taking in the sight. "It calls to you."

It wasn't just the sea that called to me.

"Marek?" I turned to face him.

"Aye, Issa?"

I hesitated, then asked the question I never thought I'd let myself voice.

"Did you ever regret it? Leaving Hawthorne that way?"

Our eyes locked.

"Every damn day, sereia."

It was something, I supposed.

I took a step when Marek reached for my hand, stopping me. Though he let me go immediately, the effect of his touch lingered.

"I regret leaving at all, Issa."

19

MAREK

"You almost look respectable," Kael said as we walked toward the Celestial Hall. I'd been given directions but still managed to lose myself in the vast corridors of the palace.

"I brought it." I gestured toward my high-collared naval coat that every officer in the Thalassari fleet wore. Its fitted tunic was adorned with silver embroidery reminiscent of cresting waves and a sash bore the Tidebreaker Fleet's insignia. "For this meeting alone. It's not every day you find yourself in the Aetherian palace about to meet with a king." And then it occurred to me. "You, on the other hand, are the son of such a king. I forget the fact, oft-times."

As we passed gleaming white columns that soared above us, Kael frowned. "My father is a very different king than Galfrid."

"Meaning?"

He shot me a look, for pressing him, no doubt. "I was blinded by the fact that he was my father for too long."

It was as much of a concession that Galfrid was the better king than Kael was likely to offer. That he served here, and no longer for his father and his own men, told me more than Kael's words ever would.

"Too long, but not forever. I admire your courage. It could not have been an easy decision."

Kael did not take compliments well. "One I'd not have made if it weren't for Mev."

Fair enough.

"As for women showing us the right path..." His sidelong gaze was not subtle. I thought back to what I'd said to Issa and would not regret it, even if speaking the words aloud did little to simplify our relationship.

We slowed, the hall where we were to meet the king apparently in front of us as evidenced by two guards standing in front of the tall doors where there were none at any other corridor.

"I'm not certain she will ever fully forgive me," I said finally.

"Do you want her to?"

"Of course I—"

"Don't answer too quickly, Marek. If she forgives you, there is naught standing between you." His eyes narrowed. "And Issa is no man's paramour."

Though it was an insult, it was well-deserved. I would think the same of anyone with my reputation.

"No," I said. "She is not. As for what stands between us? Everything. Her mortality. The fact that this mission has never been attempted successfully. Most importantly..."

His brows lifted. "More important than her mortality and you facing your own? Do go on."

I was about to brush off his question when Kael looked me in the eyes, dared me to dismiss him. I sometimes forgot he knew Issa, perhaps better than I did. They were friends and had been for some years. She was the only human he truly cared for, before Mev.

"I am in love with her," I said, knowing it was no true revelation. "I've loved her almost from the moment we met."

Kael didn't laugh, as I expected him to, but he did study me at length before speaking. "You've risked your life for your clan, for information, for gold. And yet, the one thing that makes all that worth it, the one thing that might make you whole, you would turn away from out of fear?" His lips pressed into a thin line. "You're braver than that."

Was I? If I closed my eyes, I could see my mother's hair floating in the water. If I reached out, I could feel it. Humans were braver than any immortal. They experienced the pain of losing loved ones and still carried on. I'd prefer to lose my own life than experience that again.

With those words, he gestured for the guard to open the doors.

The chamber was a breathtaking combination of elegance and power, a space that seemed suspended between the heavens and the earth. Towering columns of smooth, iridescent stone framed the vast room, their surfaces laced with glowing veins of Aetherian magic.

Above, the vaulted ceiling was open in places, revealing glimpses of swirling clouds and cascading waterfalls. A long, curved, white marble table stretched across the center of the chamber with cushioned chairs, embroidered with sigils of noble houses and ancient lineages.

The most striking of all... Issa.

She sat beside Mev, a vision in a gown clearly borrowed from her friend, the princess. Sky blue with billowing sleeves that turned to white near the edges, the bodice of her gown fit snugly enough that I needed no imagination to conjure what was beneath.

Most surprising of all? Her hair was down, in waves behind

her back. She looked entirely different, just as beautiful as before, but... different. Staring at her, I nearly forgot to bow to the king. Thankfully, I remembered my manners and did so, King Galfrid bidding me to stand immediately.

His long white hair and blue eyes were not unique to Aetherian men, but Galfrid's presence was very much so. He struck equal measure of fear and awe in most who met him, a true leader of a proud people.

"Captain Marek of Thalassaria." The king gestured for me to sit beside Issa as Kael sat on her other side, next to Mev. "It is my pleasure to introduce Lyra of Aetheria, a former member of the Gate Council and advisor to myself and my daughter."

"My lady," I said, knowing she was also of noble birth, her parents a preeminent family in Aetheria. Her eyes were as piercing a blue as the king's, her long silver hair and graceful movements not surprising given her station. She inclined her head as the king turned to the one beside him.

"And this is Commander Eirion, a former general of the Aetherian forces, once the Council's enforcer and now my closest advisor."

A brilliant mind and fierce warrior, all in Elydor knew of Eirion, who also inclined his head, though less deeply than Lyra. He mistrusted me, and I could not blame him. We might both serve our clans, but the commander and I were as nearly different as a native Elydorian and a human.

"It is my pleasure to meet you both."

"The pleasure is ours," the king replied, gesturing for the cup bearer to fill the goblet before me before he left the chamber. "I understand you have volunteered to retrieve our most sacred artifact from the Maelstrom Depths, if indeed Balthor has somehow managed to hide it there."

"I have, your majesty."

"Why?"

His bluntness didn't surprise me, the king's reputation preceding him.

"Queen Nerys is a friend," I said. "And now my liege."

"He is a most skilled Navarch," Mev cut in. "Nerys believes Marek is uniquely qualified to enter the Depths and survive them."

The king remained skeptical. "Yet you still volunteered for this mission."

He knew as much already, the king's statement less a question than a thought spoken aloud. I wanted to drain the goblet in front of me but didn't dare touch it before King Galfrid took a sip of his own. My mother may have unknowingly raised a smuggler, but she'd taught me proper decorum too.

"So you risk your immortal life because Queen Nerys... is a friend?"

I respected that the king would have me doing this for the right reasons, but I would not lie to him. "I believe in the human cause, in their rights as Elydorians. I believe the Gate should not have trapped some here unwittingly. I also wish for Mev to be reunited with her mother. But aye, your majesty, my primary reason is because Nerys wished it and, as I said, she is a good friend of mine. Has been for many years."

The king sat back, as if taking it all in. I chanced a glance at Issa, who sat wide-eyed beside me. By the tides, the woman was lovely.

"You are a loyal friend, Captain Marek."

"I like to believe so, your majesty."

"We are lucky it is so as there are few, if any, who would dare such a feat. A toast, to the bravery of Captain Marek of Thalassar," he said, using the more ancient term for my clan.

You're braver than that.

I lifted my goblet along with the others, Kael's words coming back to me.

Drinking deeply, I considered them, knowing he was right. If I could face death for the sake of a friend, could I not face the inevitable loss that would come with loving Issa?

I looked at her, wondered what she was thinking.

Wondering, after everything, if I did survive... would she even have me?

20

"We have a plan," the king said, our dinner meeting with him seemingly at a close.

After being trussed up by Mev, who seemed to take great delight in my "makeover," I'd been forced to confront Marek, still thinking of what he'd said to me in front of the palace.

I regret leaving at all.

His words played through my mind all eve, but now was not the time to dwell on them. Or how good he looked in his formal attire. Or the way he glanced at me throughout the meal.

Take care of them.

My father's final words, uttered repeatedly as he lay on his deathbed, my mother newly gone and buried. It was my duty to Hawthorne Manor that needed my attention, and Mev had promised to raise that very topic at this meeting.

"A solid plan," Mev responded. "We will discover the meaning behind Rowan's warning and send word to you at The Siren's Rest."

"I will recruit every scholar and mage and the Committee of

Elders," the king said. "Do not," he added to Marek, "attempt to enter the Depths before we can fully understand them."

"I'm not certain we will ever truly understand the Maelstrom Depths," Marek said, but at the king's stern glare, he conceded. "I will wait for word, your majesty."

"I should go," Kael said, not for the first time. "It's my clan, my land. Adren—"

"Will meet up with Marek and Issa," Mev concluded. "You will bring too much attention, returning home, as it were. Attention Marek does not need."

Kael's scowl deepened.

"Trust Adren," she said. "He discovered the Crystal's location and will take care of Marek and Issa."

"I trust him with my life, but Gyoria and its people are..."

He stopped.

We waited.

I understood his frustration, feeling helpless to protect people you loved.

"Your father's and Terran's responsibility."

That, from the king.

"He is poisoning their minds," Kael said in response.

"King Balthor," Lyra asked, "or Prince Terran?"

"Both." Kael crossed his arms over his chest, clearly agitated.

"We've another matter to discuss." Mev looked pointedly at me. Perhaps it was to distract Kael from what was, I agreed, a bad idea. "In joining our mission, it seems we've made things complicated for Lady Isolde."

Though Marek and Kael knew of Draven's plans already, the others were clearly confused.

"In Valmyr Port, she and Marek learned," Mev said to her father, "a noble named Lord Draven may be making a play for Hawthorne Manor. He has apparently been lobbying for support to use his status at Hawthorne, and as a border lord, to be named Estmere's first Lord Protector. And in coming with us, Hawthorne Manor is more vulnerable to his machinations."

King Galfrid was clearly displeased at such news.

"I take full responsibility," I added, "for leaving him in command. He was a trusted ally of my father's, and I had no cause to mistrust him. But it seems, I was naïve to place such trust in him."

"Draven," Galfrid murmured. "I've heard the name but know little of him."

"I sensed ill intent," Mev said, "the first time we met, when Kael took me to Hawthorne before I knew of my abilities."

"After he kidnapped you." Lyra's secret smile nearly made me laugh, despite the seriousness of the situation. It seemed she was not ready to allow Kael to forget the circumstances of his and Mev's first meeting any time soon.

"Aye, Lyra," Kael said, his voice making Lyra outright smile. Mev joined her. "Many thanks for reminding the king of the circumstances of his daughter's arrival in Elydor."

"I need no reminding," the king said, making Lyra and Mev burst into laughter at Kael's expression. I glanced at Marek, and not surprisingly, he smiled too.

After the laughter at Kael's expense died down, I addressed the king myself. "My fear is that he will use my absence to seize control of Hawthorne."

"I will not allow it." The king turned to Commander Eirion. "Send a contingency to secure Hawthorne in Lady Isolde's absence."

I worried he might say as much. "I am grateful, your majesty. Though I fear the presence of an Aetherian force so close to the border may agitate the Gyorian raiders, who have increasingly sought reasons to engage with us unlawfully. I would not wish my personal circumstance to push us into a full-scale war."

The king sat back and glanced around the table. He rested his eyes on Kael, as if to convey something privately to him before speaking. The hairs on my neck stood straight, though I could not give a reason why, if forced to name it, at the look that passed between them.

It was not contention. Nor mistrust, as their past disagreements ran deep.

Something else. A shared resolve, perhaps, that I wanted to be a part of.

"War has been brewing for nearly thirty years," he said finally. "If it comes now, so be it. We've all known this storm was coming. We've seen the signs in the shifting tides, felt the tremors beneath our feet. Those around this table who risk all to unite our lands are the echoes of those who came before us, the embers of a fire that has never truly died since I first opened the Aetherian Gate. Those who fight for a just cause, for more than their own personal gain and for those weaker than us," he said, a clear nod to the humans, "do not yield. We do not bow."

I understood their look now.

Kael had not just taken a stand with Mev when they partnered. If it came to war, he would be fighting against his people. His family. The king had been asking for Kael's silent permission and Kael had given it.

I had no wish to be the catalyst for war. And yet, it seemed there was little other choice.

"Thank you, your majesty," were the only words left I could offer.

He nodded, and stood, an indication the meeting was over.

"I would speak with you," Marek said before I rose in my seat.

"On the morrow?" I asked, knowing we sailed out in the morn.

"No," he said, his eyes holding mine.

He was asking permission to seek me out this eve.

My mouth dry and apparently unable to form a response, I instead found myself nodding.

"I will find you."

* * *

Mev brought me back to my chamber, easily the most beautiful one I'd ever seen. Its pale, stone walls were etched with delicate silver filigree. A four-poster bed, draped in silk the color of twilight, sat in the middle of the room, its plush, celestial, embroidered pillows stacked as if they were rarely touched.

My favorite feature, though, was a large, arched window with a latticed balcony that overlooked the sea. The full moon's glow lit the room with a soft luminescence as I entered.

"I had a night rail brought," Mev said, entering with me. "Please keep it, and the gown too."

"I cannot—"

"Issa," she said, sitting on the edge of the bed. "Please take them. You're sacrificing so much to be here."

I sat beside her, watching as the gossamer drapes billowed inside from the sea breeze. Some said the beauty and magic of Aetheria was unmatched anywhere else in Elydor, and at that moment, I tended to agree.

"What we're doing," I said, having realized as much this eve, "is bigger than me. Than Hawthorne, even. There are so many like you, and your father, who have been separated from their loved ones for far too long. If there is a chance the Gate can be reopened, I am happy to be a part of making that happen."

"My father will protect your lands, Issa. Together, we'll make sure Draven's ambitions remain nothing more than a pipe dream."

Mev said the strangest things. "Pipe dream?"

She laughed. "An expression. Honestly, I have no idea where it comes from. Basically, he can go fuck himself."

That I understood.

"I've never told anyone this before," I blurted before thinking it through, but trusting Mev completely. "I love my people. Many of them are like family to me but." I swallowed, feeling as if I were a traitor to my parents' memory. "It was never my dream to remain there. As an only child, it was, of course, my duty to inherit. And I knew that, but... I begged my father for any opportunity to travel outside Estmere. And then they got sick."

I stopped, remembering. Wishing I could forget.

"Tell me, what is it you plan to do with your one wild and precious life?"

Her question snapped me back to the present.

"Not my quote. Mary Oliver, but still a good question."

My one wild and precious life?

"I... I do not know. There is only what I should do and what I wish to do."

"Okay then, what do you wish to do?"

That was easier. "See all of Elydor, and beyond."

"Could someone else inherit Hawthorne Manor?"

"Draven?" I asked, appalled.

"No, someone worthy. And competent."

"Sir Warren Calder," I said, without having to think on it. "He was my father's commander and has served Hawthorne well. He is respected by all but it is customary for a family member to inherit. And I'm not certain he would want the position. But also, what would I do? Where would I go? Hawthorne is my home. Has always been my home."

"Boston was mine," Mev said softly. "I never imagined being anything but a museum curator, or living anywhere else. But here I am. In Elydor. An Aetherian princess. Go figure."

She smiled; a look of understanding, and sympathy, passed between us.

"You are always welcome here."

"Thank you," I said. "Although I will admit to a more pressing problem than my future."

"What could be more pressing than that?"

I glanced at the door, knowing the knock would come at any moment. "Marek."

"Ahh, I see." She followed my gaze. "He is coming here?"

I nodded. "He asked to speak with me about something."

"That couldn't wait until tomorrow?"

"My thoughts precisely."

Mev stood. "I'm probably not one to give relationship advice, being I'm married... or partnered or whatever... to a guy who kidnapped me. Literally. And I don't blame you for being cautious. What Marek did was really shitty. But..."

"But?" I asked, anxious to hear what she had to say.

"Sometimes, people make mistakes."

I sighed. "I swore never to let myself get hurt like that again. Especially by the same person who did it the first time."

"I get it. But I also see the way he looks at you. There's something there, Issa."

I didn't deny it.

But whatever else she might have added would have to wait. A knock meant our time was up. I stood, heart racing, and walked Mev to the door.

"There always has been with us," I admitted, "which is the problem."

"Only if you let it be one," she said, pulling the door open. "Oh look. Marek. Who would have guessed?"

Laughing at her own jest, Mev pushed past him, waving a hand in the air and calling out, "Goodnight," leaving me standing there alone.

With Marek.

Against my better judgment, I stepped aside, gesturing for him to enter. We'd been in closer quarters than this, and would be again tomorrow. But somehow, him being here felt... different. More meaningful.

"You wanted to talk?"

He took my lead, came into the chamber and closed the door behind him, smiling.

"Among other things."

21

MAREK

I had nothing to tell her.

Truth was, I didn't want to wait until tomorrow to see her again.

"Pardon me?"

I swept past her, assessing her chamber and its balcony. Striding toward it, I gestured outside.

"I'm jesting, of course," I said. "May I?"

She didn't believe me, likely because I was not jesting at all.

When she followed me, I took that as a yes and stepped past the billowing curtains into the warm breeze. Though not as warm as it would have been in the south, it was unusually so for Aetheria this time of year.

Taking a deep breath, my shoulders immediately relaxed. We were too far away to hear the sea, the moon hardly enough to illuminate much of its dark expanse, but that smell...

"I grew up in a small home in Corvi. My father, the head of the Navigator's Guild there."

"What is that?" Issa asked, joining me. She wrapped her

hands around the marble rail, looking down to the palace lights below.

"A training center for seafarers and mapmakers. It was not extravagant, our home, but I could step outside and onto the shore. This smell, the sound of the sea... I find it difficult to be away from it for long."

"I can understand that. I wasn't raised near it but feel the same. There's a calmness, a peace that is indescribable at sea. Or even here."

"Do you know why?"

"Sure."

I considered explaining the rhythm of the waves being in tune with the natural world of Elydor or how the origins of its magic were tied to the sea.

But I didn't.

Turning to her, I offered Issa a bigger truth.

"It's a reminder that there is a world beyond duty and expectation, a place where you could be something more than what was dictated for you. I also believe you may even have an ancient connection to the water, deep within your soul."

Her laugh was hesitant, as if Issa recognized the truth of my words but would never admit it.

"I doubt that," she said, dismissing me. "I am destined to be landlocked, unfortunately."

No, you're not.

I didn't argue the point, though.

"How do you feel, after the meeting?"

"Uneasy," she admitted. "I'm grateful for the king's aid, but know those borders well. It will be seen as a threat to Gyoria and my fear that it could spark a war is not hyperbole."

"No, I don't imagine it is. But war has been brewing for some time. Unless the Gate is reopened, I fear it's inevitable."

"And if it is reopened?" Her body's movement underscored her words. "You believe King Balthor will simply shrug his shoulders and accept it?"

"When we met," I ventured, knowing the subject of our first meeting was a sore one, "it was that passion of yours that first captivated me."

"Marek—"

"Issa," I countered. "Pretending those days never happened isn't the answer."

Her eyes flashed, angry and ready to battle.

"I hurt you," I continued, "in order to protect myself. Immortality, the long life I've enjoyed thus far, hadn't prepared me to meet someone like you. I don't try to escape blame for what I did, but to better explain my reasons."

She sighed, as if defeated. I hated seeing her that way. Hated that I was the cause.

"What do you want from me, Marek? Why did you come here tonight?"

I didn't trust myself to answer the first question. Loving Issa wasn't enough. The second one was easier.

"Because I am drawn to you, as I've always been."

She opened her mouth to answer, but then closed it. It was foolish of me to have inserted myself back in her life. But did I regret it? I was selfish enough not to, even knowing I wasn't enough for her.

"I shouldn't have come."

Her hand on my arm as I took a step away was like an anchor, snagging me even as the tide attempted to pull me away.

"Marek."

I should have walked away. But I didn't.

The permission I needed was in the way she looked at me, more trusting than it should be after all the pain I caused her.

"Sereia," I murmured, reaching for the back of her head, weaving my fingers into her hair. Groaning at the feel of her, at the look in her eyes that told me not to stop, I took the step that closed any remaining distance between us.

Pulling her toward me, I covered her mouth with mine. I drew her in, reminding her of the first kiss, parting her lips with my tongue. Hesitant, inexperienced, Issa touched her tongue to mine as she had the first time.

I pulled her head into me, giving no quarter and ensuring Issa would not want to pull away. I drew her in deeper, and deeper, the kiss a long time coming. When her other hand joined the first, now both tentatively lying on my arms, I gave into the kiss completely.

Pressing against her, our bodies touching at every point, I drank from the innocence she offered, Issa's head tilting to give me better access. When she murmured, low in her throat, the shred of control I hung onto evaporated.

Though the gown she wore placed layers of material between us, its bodice begged to be explored. Slipping my hand from her hair, I moved it between us, edging upward until the embroidered threads ended and the curve of her breasts began. My thumb explored and dipped below the material, emboldened by her response.

"Issa," I murmured, breaking our kiss, moving to her neck, surprised when she tossed her head back to allow me better access. It was the same as when she'd taken control of the ship. Issa did nothing in half-measures, and now unleashed, her passion was on full display.

I moved lower, and lower, kissing the top of each breast and moments away from tearing the gown from her body when her words from before came back to me.

I am a virgin.

Still, I lifted my head and looked into her eyes.

"Are you... When last we met, you were an innocent still."

Her lips were swollen from our kiss. Her breath came quickly, Issa as caught up in the moment as me.

"I have saved myself, in case the need arose for me to be wed."

It was the same answer she gave before.

"You would use your virginity as a bargaining chip?"

Her head rose. "If I must. To save Hawthorne. There are noblemen who—"

I could not hear anymore. The thought of Issa being with one of those so-called nobles who hung onto the old ways made my stomach turn.

Issa is no man's paramour.

"We cannot do this."

As difficult as it was, I stood back. Dropped my hands and cursed the small bit of honor still remaining within me. "There is no turning back if we continue."

"I may not have been with many men, but even I know there are ways to find pleasure while leaving my innocence intact."

The thought of having my head buried between Issa's legs, then watching her face as I brought her that pleasure, was nearly my undoing.

But then I thought of another man doing it. "You know this from experience?"

It was the wrong thing to say.

"You, of all people, would ask such a question?"

She was right, of course, but the thought of Issa being with another man sent a white-hot need to blast them into the depths of the sea coursing through my body.

"I have no right to the answer," I admitted.

"No," she agreed. "You don't."

"This was a mistake."

"On that," she said, striding into the chamber, "we can agree."

She didn't stop until she was at her door. I couldn't leave this way.

"You are the last woman alive I would wish to disrespect. Just the opposite, in fact."

"I wish I could believe that, Marek."

I wish there was a way to prove it to you.

The only thing I could think of was to leave her be.

"Good eve, Issa." I pulled the words from me like the heaviest of anchors.

"And to you." But her parting was stiff. The walls that had briefly come down between us were once again erected. As I left her chamber and made my way through the corridor, I wondered if the damage I'd done, both at Hawthorne and this eve, was irreparable.

And if I'd already lost her, why did it feel like I was still drowning?

22

ISSA

The sight of the king of Aetheria standing on the dock waving to me—to us—was never one I'd imagined in my lifetime. Then again, I'd never imagined kissing Marek again, so there was that unfortunate fact.

Not surprisingly, I could not get that kiss out of my mind.

When we broke our fast, I thought of it. As we said goodbye to the others, I could have closed my eyes and felt his lips still, if I'd wished. Every waking moment since last eve, I'd vacillated between chastising myself for encouraging it and wanting to feel that way again.

"Will you steer?" Marek asked as we cleared the bay, and I climbed up to the quarterdeck. "I'd like to trim the sails for open water."

It was the first thing he'd said to me all day. Marek skipped the morning meal, as did Kael, so I assumed the two of them had been together.

"Trim the sails?"

"Adjusting them to optimize our speed based on wind direction. We trim sails by tightening or loosening lines to ensure they catch the wind properly."

"Is that necessary if you channel the water?" I asked, taking the wheel, being careful to avoid physically touching him.

"Not necessarily, but it's best not to rely on magic alone. The sea is unpredictable."

He moved past me, saying nothing more. I watched as Marek worked, moving around the ship effortlessly. Not surprisingly, my mind wandered to last eve.

I had been unnecessarily harsh on Marek's question about my innocence, as I thought about it later, one he'd asked out of respect. His comment about my experience, was from jealousy. One I had no right to judge after the incident with Cassandra. But I'd been angry enough at myself for that kiss to lash out at him and told him as much when he returned.

"I should not have reacted as I did," I said as Marek leaned against the railing, looking out to sea. Aetherian ships were a sight to behold.

His smirk nearly made me regret the apology.

"Why are you smiling?"

"I like to smile."

"Marek, I am not jesting."

"Neither am I. But if you'd like me to, I am happy to accommodate the activity you mentioned last eve."

He was impossible. But at least I was spared from further explanation. Telling him I was angry at myself for giving in after promising never to fall for Marek's charm again was not something I relished doing.

"Thank you, but I will kindly pass on your offer."

"When living on a ship," he said, shifting his weight from one foot to another, "tempers often run high. It does little good to dwell on such things."

"You are saying I am temperamental."

His eyes widened. "I did not mean—"

Smiling, I waited for him to realize I had been jesting myself. When he did, Marek shook his head and turned toward the bow. Whatever he was about to say would have to wait. I'd seen that look on his face before and though there was no storm on the horizon that I could see, either one was brewing or something was amiss.

"What is it?"

"Close your eyes," he said.

I did, waiting.

"What do you feel?"

I assumed he meant a change in the wind direction, but it wasn't that. "Nothing?"

"Is there a breeze?"

I tried to sense for one.

"Not really."

"Now, take a deep breath. What do you smell?"

I did that too. "The sea air?"

"Anything else?"

"Salt and brine and..." I could not place the other scent.

"Something faintly metallic?"

I nodded my head. "Aye."

"Open your eyes."

When I did, Marek was watching me closely. I tried not to look at his lips.

"Look up. What don't you see?"

"No sun?" I guessed.

"It hasn't been sunny all day. What's missing that was in the sky earlier?"

Of course. "Gulls. In fact, there are no birds whatsoever."

The way Marek smiled, as if he was proud of me for guessing

correctly, should not have made me feel as if I had single-handedly somehow saved Hawthorne myself.

"A storm is brewing," he said. "Though the signs are subtle. Hold the wheel while I prepare."

He was off again, and while I watched him, as the sky darkened, I realized I had no trepidation being alone here at the helm. Perhaps I should, having such little experience. But instead, a sense of power and fearlessness settled over me.

Also settling over me was a deluge of rain. It came so suddenly, I had no time to prepare, not that I could have done so anyway. Marek returned, telling me to head below deck, but I refused, wanting to navigate the storm, which we did, together.

As *Tidechaser* swayed from side to side, we sailed through increasingly large waves. Some, Marek dampened with magic. Others, he did not. I realized at some point he was playing with the sea, and we were never in any real danger. Even so, as day wore into night, I refused to budge, enjoying every moment, laughing as Marek harnessed the rain, making droplets appear as if they were racing each other.

It wasn't until the storm began to abate and my human needs reminded me I wasn't immortal that I finally relented. I had dried off, changed, and eaten, and now sat in my cabin— Marek's cabin —wondering if I should go back above when a knock at the door startled me enough that I bound off the bed.

When I opened it, Marek stood there, drenched.

"I accidentally left my satchel on deck," he said, nodding to the trunk in the corner of his quarters. "I will be quick to fetch dry clothing."

I handed him a drying cloth and watched as Marek bent down to open the trunk.

"You did well up there. Remarkably well."

"Thank you," I said as he pulled out dry clothing and stood.

When our eyes met, the question that had run through my mind all eve, and most of the days, accidentally popped out of my mouth.

"What if... we had not stopped."

Marek's smile deepened. "If we'd not stopped, Issa, your virginity might no longer be a bargaining chip."

Say it. Say what you've been thinking.

"But the... other things?" I could not continue. "Never mind," I said, hurrying to the door. "As you said, last eve was a mistake. I should not—"

I was spun around so quickly, it took me a moment to regain my footing.

"It would be an even bigger mistake to let you go."

And with that, Marek's mouth slammed down on mine.

It was nothing like the other two kisses. This one was raw and untamed, like the sea itself. He was still wet, but as our bodies pressed against each other, I didn't care about that. Or the repercussions of our past. As his mouth slanted across mine, Marek's tongue tangling with my own, I took his cues.

Leaning into his hands as they explored, I tentatively did the same. How often had I watched him about the ship and wondered what it would feel like to touch his arms as he swung from the rigging?

One moment, he was kissing me. The next, Marek had pulled away and was unbuttoning his shirt, now plastered to his body.

"What are you doing?"

His roguish smile was so very... *Marek.*

"I'm getting you wet," he said, peeling his shirt from his body.

I sucked in a breath, seeing him this way for the first time. Marek was so perfectly formed, I couldn't not help but stare.

"Have you touched a man like this before?" he asked, taking my hand and placing it on his chest.

I shook my head, unable to speak. He took my other hand and did the same, never breaking eye contact.

"Do you remember when you said there were other ways to find pleasure?"

Oh god, the feel of him. The sound of his voice, deep and suggestive...

"I do."

"Do you know what those ways are, Issa?"

"Not precisely."

He closed the distance between us, his devilish smile irresistible. "Let me show you."

With that, he kissed me again, but this time, my fingers brushed his bare shoulders as Marek's kiss began as a soft touch to quickly intensify into a raging inferno. His hands explored, as mine did, tugging my shirt from its breeches. Sliding his hand up to find the laces at my neckline and loosening them with one hand, his fingers grazed my skin.

As the kiss deepened, he pushed the linen shirt off my shoulders, letting it slip down my arms. Only a thin chemise separated our bodies as he pressed closer. A murmur escaped from deep within me, and something seemed to snap in him at the sound.

"Issa," he said against my mouth, the slow, deliberate movements of his hands becoming impatient as he tore off my wide, leather belt and worked open the laces of my breeches. Before I knew what he was about, Marek's hand slipped between us to the most intimate part of my body.

With no time for shock, his tongue working magic and making my head spin, his finger was there.

"Marek," I gasped as he slipped it inside me.

"I'm not the only one wet in this cabin," he said, as if his hand was not... there!

"What are you—"

My words were cut off by his slow movement, in and out, a second finger now joining the first. My eyes widened as he moved, a knowing smile plastered on his face.

I'd never felt anything remotely like it before. Shoving away the embarrassment that threatened to dampen the experience, I let myself go, just as I'd done above deck in the storm. Marek had a way of making me forget all of the constraints of normal society, and maybe I would regret it later.

But not now.

"That's my sereia," he whispered, capturing me in an all-consuming kiss. His tongue flicked against mine as his fingers mimicked the same movements below. Suddenly, the scandalousness of what was happening flooded me all at once, but oddly, I was no longer embarrassed. What was so wrong about finding pleasure?

And what he was doing was very pleasurable.

I held onto his bare arms, feeling his muscles twitching as his hand moved. A building inside me, unlike anything I'd ever experienced, threatened to drown every other sensation. I moaned, the sound not at all familiar, even to my own ears.

In response, he circled his thumb against me while continuing the deliciously tortuous ministrations until I could not possibly hold on any longer. With a flick of his tongue, and his thumb, everything inside me began to tense and coil like the ropes I'd found him asleep on.

And then, it exploded. I couldn't even continue our kiss, pulling away and throbbing against his fingers. It was as if there were too many pleasurable sensations at once, if such a thing were possible.

He wasn't smiling now.

Marek stared deep into my eyes, his lips parted... watching.

I breathed heavily, as if I'd just run through the woods,

unable to continue. His fingers were still there, inside me as I pulsed against him. Then, ever so slowly, he pulled them from me and did something even more shocking.

Taking one finger to his lips, he licked it, that ever-present smile returning.

I blinked, trying to process all that was happening.

"Tastes as sweet as I expected," he said. "Now how about I do that one more time? With my tongue."

As I dressed, my mind replayed all that had happened. Thankfully, I'd been spared a response when he mentioned his tongue—not that I could have come up with a proper one—when *Tidechaser* had lurched, telling Marek that the water channel he'd created had been disrupted.

With a wink, he'd raced from the cabin, leaving me to stare at the door and wonder what in Elydor had just happened. Sitting, even though my shirt and breeches were still wet from being pressed against him, I attempted to gather my thoughts.

As if such a thing were possible.

My world was crumbling around me. Betrayed by Hawthorne. Days away from potentially losing Marek. And what had just happened? I had difficulty forming a complete thought except, I wanted it again. And what he'd said before he left?

The cabin was suddenly getting much too cramped, and hot. I finished dressing and I was about to leave when I realized Marek had never changed his clothing and was still soaked. I made my way to the trunk, hardly even needing the moonstone, having learned the cabin well.

I reached for it to look inside, wondering which pieces Marek might need. Thalassari clothing was resistant to water, especially their boots, but they were not completely impervious. I took out a shirt when a deep-blue handkerchief caught my eye. I knew that piece of fabric, its gold trim woven by my mother. Pulling it out, I turned it over. Sure enough, the Hawthorne crest stared back at me as my mind was brought back to the day I'd given this to him.

We had been about to ride out of the manor house when Edric had stopped us. He'd handed Marek a small, glass bottle, asking him to carry it to the village. He'd received word the midwife needed its contents to concoct some sort of remedy and asked us to take it to her. I gave him the handkerchief to wrap around the bottle to keep it safe on the journey.

And he'd kept it.

Why? Perhaps he had forgotten he had it? Or had there been another reason?

Knowing it was likely the first, I quickly grabbed it, along with clothing for Marek, and hurried above deck. The rain had long stopped, and darkness, fallen. Though the sea was fairly calm, I spied Marek behind the wheel.

When he noticed me, he smiled.

That smile would have me forgetting the duty I held to my parents. My people.

That smile would be my undoing.

Climbing up the ladder, I didn't give him a chance to speak but thrust the handkerchief in front of him.

"I brought you dry clothing, and found this."

He looked at it and then up at me.

"Why did you keep it?"

Marek reached out, and taking the slip of cloth from me, he brought it to his face, inhaling deeply. "It smelled like you. But no longer. I'm unsure when it lost your scent, but that was probably around the same time I lost hope to ever see you again."

"You could have seen me any time, Marek."

"I know. But what would I have said?"

"The truth?"

"That you deserved more than I was back then? More than I am now?"

"You don't believe you're... worthy of me?"

"I know I am not, Issa." He glanced down at the clothing. "Are those for me?"

Not knowing what else to say, I handed them to him. Marek took them and immediately began to undress.

"What are you... You cannot undress here."

He waved an arm around to the open sea. There were no vessels within sight.

I cleared my throat. "I believe you are ignoring one person who can see you very clearly," I said as he removed his boots completely.

"The very same person who is still watching," he said cheekily.

"Ugh." I immediately spun around to his chuckle, trying not to imagine what was happening behind me. Instead, I made my way to the railing, the only light from a dim moon partially covered by clouds. The sea at night was both a peaceful, and terrifying, thing.

"Sure you don't want a peek?"

I didn't give him the pleasure of a response. A flash of Marek's bare chest and arms in his cabin came back to me.

"All finished."

Still, I didn't turn.

"Don't trust me?"

That was a question I wasn't prepared to answer. Instead, I

waited a few moments longer and spun around. He was, indeed, dressed once again.

"You look more like a pirate than a Navarch again," I said.

"Perhaps you like me this way? It was you, after all, who chose my clothing."

"Ugh," I uttered again. "You are impossible."

In response, he held out a hand. I looked at it for a moment, and then threw caution overboard into the sea where all sorts of unknown creatures lurked. Stepping forward, I took it. Marek pulled me in front of him but didn't move away. He stood at my back as my fingers circled the now-familiar wheel.

Placing his hands beside mine, for once, Marek didn't tease me. Instead, he simply stood at my back, the heat of his body warming me in a way no cloak could ever do. Together, we navigated the dark waters ahead, each thinking our own thoughts both knowing the most difficult days were just ahead.

* * *

Making my way above deck, the morning sun bright, I attempted to reconcile the tumbling mess of thoughts in my head. Last eve, as I nearly fell asleep on my feet, the soft sway of the waves and comfort of Marek at my back, he finally urged me below deck. I touched my lips now, remembering. As I turned from the wheel, he'd reached for my face, cupped my cheeks, and kissed me.

It was soft, almost reverent. A very different kind of kiss than in the cabin, but no less heady. Then without a word, Marek released me as I stumbled below deck in a half-asleep state of euphoria.

Sanity returned this morning as I dressed, but the anger I'd felt for Marek for so long never followed. I'd seen too much of a side of Marek that contrasted deeply with the villain I'd made him out to be. Was I still angry at how effortlessly he'd broken my heart? Aye. But I could not hate a man who had devoted his life to finding out the truth about his mother's death, at the expense of himself.

That did not mean Marek was good for me. And I was fairly certain what happened in his cabin was clouding my judgment, but a part of me no longer cared. I had sacrificed myself for Hawthorne, and what good had it done? I may be powerless to stop Draven myself, but I still had control of one thing.

Myself.

"You look refreshed," Marek said as I climbed up to the quarterdeck.

"I slept well. Why don't you let me take over so you can get some rest?"

"I rested well enough up here," he said. "The waters were calm overnight."

Hesitant, I was about to move to the rail when Marek reached for me. Pulling me into him, he kissed me, and I allowed it. Wanted it. Craved the way his lips moved over mine. He tasted minty, smelled like the sea and before long, I was deeply under his spell.

A lurch of the ship pulled us apart. Without warning, the same feeling as the day Lyra whispered to Mev washed over me.

"Issa?"

Marek held my arm as I closed my eyes, attempting to reconcile the magic that was nearby.

"It's the same as that day," I whispered, blocking out everything but the sensation of magic. "Precisely the same."

When I opened my eyes, Marek was at the railing. He made a circle of the quarterdeck just as the wind picked up, as it had done that day.

"Nothing is amiss that I can see," he said finally, coming back to me. "What do you feel now?"

It was gone. Just like the last time, it came and went with the same unusual abruptness. "Nothing. Which is unusual. It just feels... different. Like a foreboding or emptiness. Magic typically feels..." I tried to capture its essence. "Not quite like that."

While he waited, Marek approached me and tucked an errant strand of hair behind my ear. The feather-light touch of his finger was somehow almost as intimate as his kisses, as if he had the right to reach out and do that. Which he did, I supposed, since I hadn't stopped him.

Nor did I want to stop him.

He grinned. "Does it feel like my fingers bringing you to climax?"

"Marek!"

"Issa," he countered, his chuckle a sound I could become accustomed to hearing.

"You are a rogue."

"I've never claimed otherwise."

"And ungentlemanly to say such a thing aloud."

"Also never claimed to be a gentleman either."

It was true, of course. And part of Marek's appeal.

"No," I said, "it does not feel that way at all. That was..."

Oh, that grin. He already knew it was divine. Incredible. I would not confirm it.

"Fine."

His laugh startled a gull that had been about to land on the railing. It thought better of such a plan and flew away.

"It was more than fine, sereia. And will be if you allow me to do it again."

My core clenched at the very thought of such a thing. Marek

had a way of turning the conversation to his advantage, every time.

"That is, perhaps, something we should discuss," I said, giving up the idea of attempting to describe the feeling of nearby magic as it was difficult to put into words.

"Ease the helm to starboard just a touch. Feel the current shift beneath us." I did as he said, easily able to feel the current shift as he mentioned. "Good, just like that. Hold steady there."

"A ship," I said, spying a dot in the distance.

Marek looked up and headed to the railing, cursing under his breath. "Gyorian," he said.

"How can you tell from so far away?"

"The sails," he said, eyes narrowing. "Gyorians favor a square rig with black trim... efficient for speed, but distinct."

"You can see all of that, from here?"

"Look carefully at the way she moves. What do you see?"

It still appeared like a dot in the horizon, but it seemed to be moving quickly. "Is it fast?"

His eye lit up. "Well done. Their hulls are sleeker, built for cutting through the waves like a blade."

"Do you think there's something on that ship that carries a special kind of magic?"

Before I even finished, Marek was shaking his head. "They are a band of Gyorian smugglers; the only special magic they can manage is moving goods under the nose of unsuspecting Aetherian watchmen."

"Are they dangerous?"

"The only danger you're in at the moment is falling under my spell, especially if you keep staring at my mouth like that."

The gall. "I was not—"

He jested with me.

"You are attempting to distract me from my earlier question."

Marek reached for my arm, pulled me toward him, and kissed me so thoroughly, I did forget what I meant to ask him. But then it came to me.

Pulling away reluctantly, I remained in his arms, looking up at him.

"I agree," he said. "We should discuss this."

"So you didn't forget."

"I forget nothing where you are concerned, Issa."

"I don't want to fall under your spell," I said. "Not again."

He sighed, as if torn. "Do you want me to release you?"

"No," I said, being honest.

"Do you want me not to kiss you again?"

"No, I don't."

"Then it seems we are at an impasse. One which the Depths may very likely solve for us." Marek's wink matched his smile, and yet, there was something to his tone that told me he wasn't entirely jesting.

"I suppose we are," I admitted. "And perhaps, that is not such a bad thing?"

It was a lie, and I knew it. I was setting myself up for devastation, again. But when this was over, my days would be filled with wresting control of Hawthorne back from Draven and calming tensions with increasingly emboldened Gyorian reivers. I would take, if nothing else, these brief memories of a budding passion I knew nothing of before this journey.

"Not a bad thing at all," he said, just before Marek lowered his head.

24

MAREK

She was a true sailor now.

As the sun began to rise, I alternated between watching our course as we approached the rocky cliffs of the Gyorian coast and watching my slumbering companion. Sailing well into the night together, after talking much like we had when I first came to Hawthorne Manor all those years ago, I'd encouraged Issa below deck. But with the turbulent waters, I couldn't join her so she opted instead to rest "for a moment" against the ropes where she promptly fell asleep.

I'd considered waking her but couldn't bring myself to do it. There was a comfort having her up here with me. How often had I sailed alone, never once wishing for a companion? After managing a crew as Navarch of the Tidebreaker Fleet, when not on mission for the crown, I preferred to be alone.

Until last eve.

"I fell asleep."

"You did indeed," I said, gesturing, as Issa rubbed her eyes, to have her join me at the wheel. "And just in time."

"Oh my!"

I watched her expression change from sleepiness to pure wonder. It was like seeing the sun rise over the magnificent Gyorian cliffs for the first time.

"Spectacular, is it not?"

"When you said we were sailing into a stone city, I didn't realize how serious you were."

"Grimharbor is unlike any other port. Unlike most coastal settlements, it was built into the rock itself, its tunnels, terraces, and massive stone arches forming a unique infrastructure. It's a crucial hub for Gyorian trade, particularly in minerals and gemstones. As you can see, its natural barriers make it difficult to approach undetected."

"It will be safe, for us?"

"Safe enough. We'll be going in through the Black Docks which are only accessible at this time of day. Oftentimes, we're forced to anchor and wait for morn for entry."

"What are the Black Docks?"

"I assume they're named from the black-sand beaches, but it's a tricky bit of winding inlet carved into the cliffs, favoring... discreet travelers looking to avoid unwanted attention."

"Discreet travelers." Issa chuckled. "You have more names for smugglers than a human with a Gyorian bounty on their head."

"An apt analogy," I said sardonically as Issa headed below deck. "Gather as many of your belongings as you can. I have little notion how long we'll be docked here until Kael and Mev send word."

Issa saluted me—more like a mock salute—as she disappeared from view. By the time she rejoined me, *Tidechaser* had entered the inlet, towering cliffs rising on both sides. She was quiet, watching me, gasping more than once, until the docks came into view ahead.

"I thought we would surely crash into the mountains," she said as I navigated the ship to dock. "Why didn't you use magic?"

"Gyorians have little respect for Thalassari sailors who are unable to navigate these cliffs using magic alone."

Issa had changed, re-braided her hair, and looked every bit like the human warrior I had first met. I'd wanted to kiss her all morn, but it wasn't until the ship was docked and I gathered my belongings that I gave into the urge. Emerging from below deck, she was waiting for me, leather satchel in hand, staring at the harbor. It was quite a sight, I would admit. As elsewhere in Gyoria, many were dressed in deep greens and browns, often embroidered with patterns of vines and stone. Buildings with intricate stone carvings that told stories of past battles and legendary warriors surrounded us. The scent of earth and damp stone filled the air, mingling with the occasional waft of roasted meats and spiced ale from nearby taverns.

"We're no longer in Aetheria, aye?"

She spun around at the sound of my voice.

"I've only been along the human Gyorian border, in the midlands. This is... incredible. But scary too."

I reached out and took Issa's satchel. "You are safe with me." Leaning forward, I was pleased Issa did not rebuff my kiss. Each time she allowed me close, it felt as if I'd been given a gift. One I had no intention of wasting. Her lips were soft and welcoming, like coming home after a long journey.

"I would say this is unusual for you Marek, but..."

Groaning inwardly at the words, if not the voice, I broke the kiss and stood back from Issa. Not surprising, she gave me a look of disappointment. Encouraged that she cared, but cursing the interruption, I introduced the two.

"Ilyas, meet Lady Isolde of Hawthorne Manor. Issa, this is Ilyas Rho."

With a fist over his heart in greeting, Ilyas was clearly surprised. Admittedly, Issa was not typical of the women who could be found in this port, or any like it. Even for a human.

"A noblewoman," he said as Issa greeted him in kind, a sign of respect in Gyoria.

"You evidently received my message?" I asked, picking up my satchel and carrying both off the ship as Issa followed. The dock-workers had secured the gangplank we walked across, and not surprisingly, we were eyed with suspicion. It had been some time since I'd visited this port, and though a network existed for me here, it was less used than most others.

I preferred to avoid Gyoria whenever possible, as most Elydo-rians had begun to do these past years.

"I did. And have alerted Adren to your arrival."

I watched as Issa look upward in awe at the massive fortress built partially into the mountain.

"The Warden's Hold," Ilyas told her. "Local leaders and their families live there."

"Wardens," she murmured. "They enforce Gyorian law."

"And oversee trade here." His eyes narrowed on her. Though I trusted Ilyas with my life, having saved his once, he was Gyorian. And always had an ulterior motive.

"What is that?" she asked, indicating the market's entrance to our right.

"The Veiled Market," Ilyas responded.

With his classic Gyorian traits, dark hair and deep-green eyes, he was unusual in this clan for the approachable warmth in his gaze. Smaller than most Gyorians, he was wily and strong, but not overly intimidating, with exception of the battle scars etched along his arms.

"It continues underground. Rare minerals, magical stones, and earth-infused weapons, among other things, are traded there. Marek can take you but I'd not venture into the market-place alone. It would not be entirely safe for a human."

Issa's grimace was warranted.

"Don't take offense," I said. "The Veiled Market isn't a safe place for any Elydorian not accustomed to its more... unusual dealings."

Issa opened her mouth but I stopped her, knowing every word we spoke was being overheard. Gyorian smugglers were notorious for their ability to blend with a crowd while gathering information. "I will explain later."

Gyorians were not normally a talkative bunch, but Ilyas was an exception. Born into a noble family, he was less war-mongering than his parents and thus an outcast to them. Prefer-ring to operate on the fringes of society, he had lived more than two hundred years learning, over time, to navigate the tricky business of being a friend to all despite the growing anti-human, and Aetherian, sentiment.

As we walked, he explained the origins of the port to Issa, who seemed equally enthralled and a bit in awe of the town built into a mountainside. When she stopped to inspect a patch of flowers growing from the side of the cliff, with a wave of his hand, Ilyas doubled the number of flowers, an easy trick for a Gyorian, but one Issa seemed to enjoy.

"Here we are," he announced as our unusual group that had garnered more than a few sets of stares arrived at our temporary new resting place. If not for Issa, I'd have remained on the ship, but she deserved a real meal, bath, and a bed.

"Virdelan's Rest," she read on the wooden sign hanging from the inn nestled into the side of the cliff overlooking the sea below. "A strange name."

Made from dark stone, with heavy, wooden doors and narrow

windows that let in little light, it was set apart from the port town, as private as we could get in Grimharbor.

"It was named after an ancient Gyorian hero," Ilyas said. "Known for his diplomatic efforts between the Gyorian clans and humans, he helped to establish safe passage routes fostering rare moments of peace and mutual respect during a tumultuous time. This location was said to have been one of his final stops. After his death, a fading he had long desired after so many years of war, this became a haven for non-Gyorian travelers of a certain... breed."

"I understand," Issa said with a glance toward me. She didn't seem to judge, though. It was a mere statement of fact, as if the friends and network I'd made throughout the years weren't as appalling to her as they perhaps should be.

We stepped inside, the air smelling of salt and iron. Dimly lit sconces cast flickering shadows across the walls. The floors were worn stone, the furniture sturdy but unadorned. Its main room featured a large hearth and was filled with quiet conversations in hushed tones.

"I leave you here," Ilyas said. "To await your guest. It was a pleasure to make your acquaintance, Lady Isolde."

"And yours," she replied genuinely as the proprietor, a woman said to be a descendant of Virdelan himself, greeted Issa.

"Ilyas," I said stopping him, whispering a request into his ear.

With a nod, he left us to settle, as comfortably as was possible for a human and Thalassari deep in Gyorian territory.

25

ISSA

Gems of every color and size. Obsidian shards. Stonecap mushrooms. Gauntlets and daggers. I didn't know where to look first, the Veiled Market unlike anything I'd seen before in my life. I'd had to quiet my senses, there was so much magic. It reminded me of when I had first learned how to harness my intuitive abilities and became easily overwhelmed, or when we'd used the Ascension in Aetheria and first entered the palace.

After securing a room at the inn—one room for us both, after a brief discussion that still made me blush thinking of it—and assurances from Marek he had already sent inquiries regarding Draven's movements, we set out for the market. With naught to do but wait for word from Mev and Kael, and for Adren's arrival, I attempted to shake off the guilt that plagued me. While I galivanted about the port with Marek, what was happening at Hawthorne? Had Lord Draven made a play to take command? I had no doubt Sir Warren could keep the Gyorian reivers at bay in my stead, but never would I have imagined Draven as a threat to Hawthorne Manor or its people.

"If you'd hadn't joined us, we may not have learned of Draven's duplicity," Marek said beside me.

I hadn't realized I'd stopped and was staring at what appeared to be a broken piece of black glass, its seller eyeing me warily.

"I thought the same," I admitted.

Marek stepped toward the seller with a wink to me.

"May I?" he asked.

The seller, a gruff-looking Gyorian nearly as large as Kael, gestured for Marek to help himself. Picking up the black shard, he inspected it.

"A fine piece of obsidian." He placed it back down. "And unfortunately, a fake."

The ground suddenly rumbled beneath our feet. I hadn't even seen the seller use his hands to make it happen, but watching closely, I noticed the seller's fingers twisting at his sides.

"No need to get angry," Marek said easily. "I'm trying to help you out. That piece is from Cretnor, aye?"

The ground stilled. The seller's brows knitted together in confusion. "It is."

Marek shook his head, as if sympathizing with him. "He sold me a fake bit of stonecap. If you see him, give him my regards." Marek placed a fist to his heart.

The seller hesitated, and then returned the gesture. "He is a dead man."

"Hmm, best of luck with that. Cretnor is a slippery one."

We moved away from the table.

"How did you know it was fake?"

"The obsidian? I've seen a real one. Its edges are smoother, shinier. I also happen to know the dealer well. He's been peddling fake 'dark magic' objects all over Elydor for years. Someday, it will catch up to him."

We walked through the marketplace, which reminded me of an earthier, more dubious Valmyr Port. I asked about some of the items for sale, things I'd never seen before. Marek introduced me to at least two of the dealers, neither of whom seemed surprised to find a human in their midst. Along the border, near Hawthorne, such a thing would be unheard of. Marek laughed off my observation.

"The people of Grimharbor care little about the politics of their regions. The battles of their kings and queens have hardly affected them. They operate in the underbelly of society where survival is paramount, the squabbles of their leaders secondary to eating, drinking, and whoring, in that order. Apologies," he said immediately. "I didn't mean to—"

"I may be innocent in some ways," I said, cutting him off, "but have spent enough time with my own warriors to have heard much worse. No apologies are necessary with me."

I doubted the wisdom of my words when the glint in Marek's eyes told me he was about to say something that would likely remind me of that night in the cabin. Or he would have, at least, if a voice from behind hadn't interrupted him.

"Marek. This way."

I turned to face an imposing, dark haired—though with strands of gray—Gyorian warrior. His striking green eyes and rugged face seemed familiar.

Since Marek followed, I assumed he was friend, and not foe.

"Adren," Marek whispered as we wove through the stands, the pace one I could hardly keep up with. How did he know? Marek had never met Adren before.

He seemed familiar because I had met him once, many years ago when I'd traveled from Hawthorne to the capital of Gyoria to plead with the king for the minerals that would potentially save my parents' lives. The king denied my request, but Kael followed me from the palace and tried to help, against his father's wishes. It had been the beginning of our friendship, and Adren had been with him that day.

In the years afterward, Kael's right-hand man had never traveled with him to Hawthorne, but I'd heard of Adren many times. Fiercely loyal, he was as intelligent as he was pragmatic. According to Kael, he was also ruthless in battle and had earned the respect of their men.

Following Adren to what looked like the entrance to a cave, once inside, we continued through the side of the mountain in which Grimharbor was built. Wall sconces lit the way, and neither man spoke until we came to a wooden door which Adren opened without touching. Some sort of Gyorian magic, though I had no notion of how he'd done it.

"A tavern?" I said, not realizing I'd done so aloud.

There were patrons, though very few of them. Wine barrels with slabs of wood for tables and candles on each one. We sat at the far end of the strange room, a server immediately appearing at our table.

"Mead and trexan ribs for my friends and me. Unless you'd rather stonefire stew?" Adren asked me, apparently not caring if Marek had a preference.

What *was* this place?

"Ribs will do," I said, trying not to stare.

"How did you know each other?" I asked. "If you'd never met before."

"A Thalassarian sailor and human woman," Adren said. "An odd combination, even in Grimharbor."

Fair enough. "But you knew him too?" I asked Marek.

"Kael told me of his scar."

Adren reached up to touch his chin. "A skirmish along our northern borders, courtesy of an Aetherian wind whip."

When he dropped his hand as the mead was served, I squinted but could hardly see it. How Marek noticed such things, and so quickly, amazed me.

"Welcome to Gyoria," Adren said, lifting his mug. I took a sip, unprepared for the heavy, spiced drink. It would take more than a sip or two to become accustomed to its strong taste. "It has been many years," he said to me, obviously remembering our first meeting. "My sympathies for your parents' passing."

"Thank you," I said. "Much has happened since then."

Adren sighed heavily. "You are safe enough here," he said. "But I will admit, I was surprised to learn you were accompanying Marek on this mission."

"She will not be entering the Depths," Marek said. "But will only verify the crystal's presence, if she's able to do so from a safe distance."

"You can sense magic?" Adren asked.

It was odd, admitting my ability to a Gyorian, even knowing I could trust him. "Aye," I said.

"So tell us what you know." Marek took a deep swing of mead. I must have stared at the way his lips curved over the mug for a bit too long and earned a wink for it. Glancing away quickly, I pushed this morning's kiss, one that hadn't lasted long but somehow felt more intimate for its casualness, from my mind.

"Years ago, during a mission for Kael, I interrogated an old sailor who lives on the outskirts of Gyoria. He was half-mad and obsessed with the sea. I got little information from him, but he muttered, 'The wind sleeps beneath the tide,' over and over again." Adren took a sip of mead so I did the same, attempting not to grimace. "I'd forgotten the incident, but as I searched for the Wind Crystal, his words came back to me. I remembered he was a navigator in Balthor's fleet. I paid him a visit, and he was as mad as ever. But every lead kept pointing to the sea, so I asked him directly if he knew anything about the Crystal. He didn't confirm it, not with his words, at least, but he continued to babble about lost ships and swallowed secrets."

"How did you connect him to the Crystal in the first place?" Marek asked.

"I found a set of cryptic records disguised as naval logistics reports. Movements of ships and resources that made no sense. The same captains ventured out time and time again. On one of those missions, a ship and its crew vanished completely. I tracked down a witness who had worked the docks that day, and though he couldn't confirm where it was headed, all clues lead to the Maelstrom Depths. I dug deeper into the archives and found a reference to the 'king's greatest treasure' in connection to the missing ship. That's when I realized, it wasn't our king but Aetheria's."

"So that's how he got the Crystal into the Depths," I asked, having wondered that all along. "By sacrificing its crew?"

Adren shrugged. "Maybe they thought they could get out alive. More likely, they knew it was their last mission. Balthor can be persuasive, and ruthless, but sacrificing his own men is callous, even for him." Adren grimaced, shaking his head. "Hate has consumed him."

"Hate for humans," I said, disgusted. "For my kind."

Adren turned to me. I looked into his eyes, seeing none of the anger Gyorians so often harbored for us.

"I do not hate you, or your people, Lady Isolde."

I had not realized my tone was so bitter. "You are an exception."

"I'm not as rare among Gyorians as you might think," he said. "There are others like me."

There was something about the way Adren was looking at me that felt... odd. Marek seemed to pick up on it too.

"Adren?" he asked. "You are among friends."

Adren drained his mug, sat back, and crossed his tree trunks of arms.

"Not just friends," he said, looking pointedly at me, "but relatives."

26

MAREK

"Another, please?" I ordered a mug of mead, my instincts telling me I would need one. "Three, actually," I added, seeing Issa's expression.

Unless I was mistaken, Adren had directed that comment toward her.

"Pardon me?" she asked, the epitome of politeness.

I was more direct.

"What in the tides are you talking about, Adren?"

He pressed his finger to his lips, nodding to the serving girl who was already on her way back to us. "Thank you," he said as the mead was delivered. Issa didn't seem pleased, and I couldn't say I blamed her. The heavily spiced drink took some getting accustomed to.

"Have you heard of Lady Evelyne Hawthorne?" Adren asked Issa.

"No, I haven't."

"She was a noblewoman of Hawthorne Manor, trained in diplomacy and healing and known for her intelligence and unwavering sense of duty."

"I know my family lineage." Issa seemed puzzled. "How is her name not familiar to me?"

Adren took a swing of his mead and settled in to share his tale. "She was also known for her curiosity with Gyorians. This was well before the Gate had closed, but even then, as you know, there were tensions between our two clans."

"Which began when King Galfrid opened it in the first place," I said.

"Aye," he agreed. "With permission from the other clans. Permission, we now know, that included the use of their most revered artifacts."

"A recent revelation." I glanced around to be certain we could not be overheard, but all looked to be Gyorian. There were few places private enough to escape Aetherian whispers.

"Mmm." Adren's grunt sounded familiar. It was a sound Kael often made. "Against her family's wishes," he continued, "Evelyne fell in love with a Gyorian warrior, a warden of the borderlands. Their relationship was seen as a betrayal of humanity, and when she became pregnant, she was given a choice: abandon the child or be exiled. She chose exile."

A shiver ran up my spine, the story beginning to make sense. I watched Issa for a hint of understanding but she was concentrating on Adren's next words.

"Evelyne was taken in by her lover's people, though many never truly accepted her. She became a healer, learning to use earth-based remedies and magic. She raised her son among these warriors, ensuring he was strong, disciplined, and prepared for a world that would never fully accept him."

"How could I not know this?" Issa whispered.

"The Hawthorne family erased her from their records, calling her disappearance a tragic accident rather than acknowledging that she had chosen a Gyorian over a human. In time, tales of those history wishes to erase are lost."

"Who was she?" I asked bluntly.

"Lady Evelyne's son was my father."

Issa's jaw fell. "She, Lady Evelyne, was your grandmother? How did... but... Kael never told me."

"Kael doesn't know."

"Why?" I asked, knowing how close the two were.

"My mother, Serapha, was a half-human and half-Gyorian healer. As you know, such unions were taboo, even more so then. Revealing it would have put Serapha in danger from both clans. While researching Balthor's movements in connection to the Wind Crystal, I came across an old record from a Hawthorne steward in the archives detailing my grandmother's life. My mother was not demi-immortal and died before sharing her past. Or perhaps she never would have told me."

When Elydorians partnered and bore children, they could be demi-immortal, enjoying a longer lifespan than a full human, or not. That's when it occurred to me.

"You are not thaloran?"

When I first noticed Adren's gray hair and slight wrinkles, I assumed he had seen more than five hundred years. But he could not be thaloran based on his tale.

"Nay, I am not. My aging is due to a partial human ancestry, but few dare ask for specifics."

"Is your father still alive?" Issa asked the question I'd been about to.

Adren's sad smile was the answer as he glanced between us, as if wondering about something himself. "No," he said. "My mother returned to her ancestors' realm to find a human solution to her illness, and my father chose to go with her."

It was not a common occurrence, but one with precedent.

When an immortal left Elydor, they eventually would become mortal. Adren's father had chosen to die with his mother. Which is when I understood the unasked question in Adren's eyes.

Were Issa and I together?

It was the age-old problem for any Elydorian and human couple. Chances were, Mev would prove to be demi-immortal, so it was not a problem Kael would face for many years if they chose to remain in Elydor. Nerys and Rowan, on the other hand, were not so lucky with Rowan being fully human.

Like Issa.

How Nerys so easily resolved herself to the thought of the inevitability of losing Rowan, I couldn't grasp.

"Adren," Issa said, the mead seemingly going down easier now, "we are related."

He reached to his belt, opened the pouch at his side, and slid a gold pendant toward Issa. "It seems we are," he said. "This was my mother's. She gave it to me just before she passed through the Gate with my father. Turn it over. The crest is faded but..."

Issa gasped. "Hawthorne."

"I assume so. It is no Gyorian house I know. My mother was a healer, not a noblewoman. Or so I thought. So I never imagined it would be a noble house of Estmere."

Adren and Issa looked at one another as if seeing the other for the first time. She handed back the pendant.

"I'm sorry her name was erased from our records. If Hawthorne survives, we will rectify that, if you wish it."

Adren's nostrils flared. "I am not ashamed of my human blood, Lady Isolde."

"Issa," she said. "We are family."

"If you had not searched for the Crystal..." I stopped, our food having arrived.

Adren reached for a rib, but his hand froze midway. "If Hawthorne survives?"

Issa sighed. "Lord Draven. Lyra's whispers. Dark magic... We have much to tell you."

Adren turned the pendant over, looking at it one last time before returning it to the pouch on his belt. "I'm listening."

* * *

"How long will you wait?"

We stood in front of Virdelan's Rest, Issa having gone inside. Giving her privacy for the hot bath she'd arranged, Adren and I continued the discussion we began many meads ago. Dusk had fallen, lights dotting the mountain behind us where caverns and dwellings had been carved into it by skilled Gyorian stone-wielders. In front of us, the sea in all its wild and untamed glory. A storm was coming, one that I'd have enjoyed navigating.

How long would I wait? It was a question I'd been asking myself.

"There is no guarantee Mev and Kael will learn anything. I've been hunting for information on the Depths, and phenomena like it, for many years to no avail."

"That isn't an answer."

Gyorians. Their bluntness was universal.

"A few days, perhaps."

"Days? Marek, that seems ill-advised."

"Issa needs to get back. She worries for Hawthorne Manor, and I have few words of comfort for her. I've sent a man to inquire as to Draven's standing since we last made port, but I fear the worst."

"He will have more than Galfrid's men to worry about if he aims too high."

Having heard his story, now knowing Adren's ties to Hawthorne, I wasn't surprised to hear him say as much. "When I leave..." I swallowed, knowing my second question was inevitable but wishing it didn't have to be asked. "You will stay here to watch over her?"

"Of course."

"And if I don't return—"

"I will see her back safely."

I nodded, assuming as much but wanting to be certain.

"There are others that are nearly as skilled as I am. Nerys will know who to send next, who to trust with the information."

"Nearly?"

"I said what I said."

And then pulling my mother's pearl from my belt, I handed it to him. "You are not the only one who carries a token of your mother's. Give this to Issa."

He took the pearl. "I've never seen a pink pearl before."

"They're extremely rare."

He lifted it, and it took everything inside me not to snatch it back. She had died for that pearl, and now someone I hardly knew held it in his hands.

Trusting did not come easily, or naturally, to me. But I had little choice.

"Why not give it to her yourself?"

"She won't accept it," I said simply.

He opened his mouth to argue, but stopped. An understanding passed between us as Adren put it in his leather pouch. Accepting the pearl was an acknowledgment I may not make it back from the Depths.

"When will you take Issa to verify the Crystal's presence?"

"Depending on this storm," I said, "tomorrow or the

following day. I see no reason to wait. When we return, if there's not been word from Kael and Mev..."

"You should wait for them."

I thought of all the leads I'd followed, all of those I'd spoken with about tainted waters like the Depths... Would the Luminara hold its secrets when the Hidden Depths, the records of all great Thalassarian divers and sailors throughout Elydor's history, provided little in the way of answers?

Likely not.

"Are you staying here?" I asked.

"No. Given what I've learned today, I have some business to attend to, but I will be back in a few days. If you have need of me before then—"

"That will do," I told him. "It'll take a full day to get close enough for Issa to sense the Crystal's magic and a full day to return." As we spoke, the winds signaled the storm was coming more quickly than I expected. "And it seems as if tomorrow will not be ideal for sailing."

Adren laid a fist on his chest.

I mimicked the gesture, marveling, as Adren walked away, at today's turn of events.

Hoping enough time had passed for Issa to finish her bath, but also hoping it had not, I made my way inside the inn, putting all thoughts of my conversation with Adren behind me.

Our days together were coming to an end, but tonight? It was time for me to make good on my promise to Isolde.

27

ISSA

I sat on the edge of the bed, my hair still damp from a glorious bath. I hadn't expected anything more than a wooden tub and was surprised when the innkeeper led me to a sunken stone basin, its waters scented with crushed nightbloom petals and warmed from beneath by hidden embers. She had locked the door behind me, another clue, as if I needed one, that I was in Grimharbor and not back home in Hawthorne Manor.

Above me, thick, dark beams gave the room a cavernous feel, while the lanterns flickered with an eerie orange/yellow light, fueled by the region's peculiar firevine oil. It smelled of spice and damp earth, a distinctly Gyorian scent.

That I would find myself here, in enemy territory, welcomed by both the innkeeper and Adren, was wholly unexpected.

Adren. Was it more than coincidence that Kael had befriended me, his right-hand man a relative the entire time? And that I should find my way here, working with him to restore the portal to my ancestor's realm? There was a saying in Elydor: the threads of fate are woven long before we see the pattern.

I had never put much stock in such things, yet here I was,

entangled in a history I hadn't known was mine, in a land that should have been hostile, with a man who should have been my enemy.

And then there was Marek.

He was acting strangely today. I'd seen the look that passed between him and Adren when speaking of the Depths. For all of Marek's bravado, and skill, he knew deep down what I did. What everyone who spoke of the Maelstrom Depths knew. What Adren had uncovered about how King Balthor was able to hide the Wind Crystal in them: by sacrificing those who carried it to their watery graves.

There was little chance he would make it out alive.

I closed my eyes, imagining myself standing on the dock, waiting for him to return just as I stood on the battlements back home, scanning the horizon in the hope that he had simply gone for a morning ride and would come back at any moment. This time, I'd not find him in The Moonlit Current. He would be gone, forever.

If only I had fallen for someone easier to love. A human who could help me secure Hawthorne. One without years of scars from a search for answers. One whose endless smiles didn't mask a pain that ran deeper than I could have imagined but one I knew all too well. The pain of the loss of a loved one. The kind of pain from which you never truly heal but only learn to live with, some days better than others.

There were times I woke up and didn't think about my parents immediately, even getting dressed and beginning my day without a memory intruding. But there were others—a comment about them, a vision of them sitting on the dais together in the hall—the smallest thing could trigger a sadness that welled inside me, having to live without them and their guidance.

When the door opened, a decidedly damp Marek stepped inside.

"You've been to the stone basin?" I asked as he tossed his satchel beside the bed and locked the door.

"I have, though I'll admit my first thought on seeing it was that I wished you were still there."

"You are wicked," I said, my heart racing at the sight of him.

Marek ran his hand through his hair and then, as if realizing he'd slicked it back, shook his head. That unkept look was part of his appeal.

"I'll not deny it."

Every step he took toward me was predatory, and with each one, I had to remind myself to breathe. Without warning, he lifted me, carrying me to the bed. Just as quickly, he placed me on it and climbed up, positioning himself at my feet.

"Uh, Marek. What are you doing?"

I should stop him. Knowing it and being motivated to do it were two different things. It was unlikely I would ever have a chance to do this, certainly not with Marek, again.

"I might be wicked," he said, pushing the camisole Mev had given me upward with both hands. "And a slew of other bad things." Just as the urge to cover myself grew too strong, Marek stopped the camisole's progress, took my hands, and placed them on the bed, silently telling me not to hinder his movements. He then grabbed the inside of both knees and spread my legs wide. "But I never. Ever..." Marek lay both hands on me, his thumbs opening me wide. It took everything inside me not to move, to cover myself. "Break my word. When I make a promise, sereia, I fulfill it."

With that, Marek grinned and lowered his head between my legs. At the first touch of his tongue, I nearly came off the bed. It was such an odd sensation, I had no notion of whether it was good or bad. The sight of him like that... I grabbed the coverlet between my fists to keep them immobile.

At the second touch of his tongue, becoming accustomed to the sensation, I nearly jolted off the bed for an entirely different reason. With each lick, Marek's tongue swirling and teasing as his fingers had done, I struggled to breathe. To think. It was the singular most pleasurable thing I'd ever experienced, and apparently, he wasn't finished. Groaning, as if he too enjoyed it, Marek did not let up.

I grabbed the back of his head, holding on as if he were the quarterdeck railing and a strong storm threatened to toss me overboard.

"Marek," I murmured, no other words forming in my mind. "Please," I begged, not wanting him to stop. "Please."

In response, as if knowing what I asked for, he increased the intensity. With the flick of his tongue, I tightened my grip, belatedly realizing I was clenching his hair between my fingers. He didn't seem to care. Whatever he was doing, how he'd learned that, I didn't care.

Nothing mattered.

Nothing except, "That," I said. "Just that way, please."

My entire body shuddered, clenched. Released in a wave of sensation that was unlike even the last time Marek had made me feel this way. I gasped, wanting to pull him back toward me as Marek lifted his head. He watched as I struggled to compose my thoughts, the tumbling mess that made little sense.

Nothing did.

That was...

"Incredible."

"A promise is a promise," he said, as I collapsed on the bed. He said nothing for a moment, but when he joined me, I realized it was because he had removed his shirt. He wore nothing but loose, linen trousers, suitable for sleep. Lying beside me, propped up on his elbow, Marek was also grinning from ear to ear.

"You seem... pleased with yourself."

"I'm pleased you are," he said, leaning forward for a lingering kiss. I turned toward him, Marek pulling me into his bare chest. Another strange, but enjoyable, sensation. We stayed that way, wrapped in each other's arms, until I heard his steading breathing. Peeking up, I realized he was asleep.

I allowed my hand to lay on his chest, the warm skin beneath my fingers oddly comforting. Not knowing what tomorrow would bring, I closed my eyes and tried not to think on it. The Depths. Hawthorne Manor. Draven. The Gate. I attempted to let all of it slip away, pretending, for just this moment, my growing affection —once again—for him was not going to likely be my undoing.

And yet, as I lay in his arms, I could not shake a vision of Marek at the helm as a storm raged around him. No one knew precisely what the Depths were like since none had survived them, but my imagination conjured an image anyway. I saw him attempting to tame unnamable waters, both Marek and *Tidechaser* losing the battle.

I did not want Marek to die.

Pressing myself closer to him, I wanted to wake him up and beg him not to do it. Find another way. Instead, I contented myself in this moment, knowing such a plea was futile, but also knowing there was a real possibility we would share very few moments like this again.

28

MAREK

"Shall I bring my belongings?"

When dawn broke, the storm having already passed, I reluctantly woke Issa to let her know we would sail out. It was the best night of sleep I had ever had. A dreamless and peaceful slumber, punctuated only once when Issa moved away. I pulled her back and promptly fell back to sleep, waking before dawn in search of a window to the outside world.

I shook my head. "I've arranged to keep this room, and we should return before tomorrow."

My gaze fell to the stretch of Issa's tunic across her breasts. Despite our intimacies, I'd not seen her fully naked. Not felt their fullness beneath my fingers, even though I'd ached to do so when I woke this morn. I'd not taken her nipples into my mouth or driven into the sweetness I'd tasted last eve. I knew her more intimately now, but not nearly enough.

I wanted all of her.

"Marek?"

Shaking off the thought, I turned, knowing if I touched her

now, we would not sail out this morn. "Come," I said, "let's get this done."

Thankfully, we made our way back to *Tidechaser* without incident. Ilyas was nowhere to be found, and since he was most often at the docks, I could only assume he'd not yet returned to port. Watching as Issa untied us, I marveled at how far she'd come since that first day.

"Why are you smiling?" she asked, joining me.

"Do you remember when I gave you a tour of the ship?"

She laughed. "I could hardly walk without feeling as if I would stumble at any moment."

"And now, look at you."

We finished preparations, sailing out without the use of magic. That is, until we were away from port, when I reached for the currents beneath us, guiding the ship forward with Issa at the wheel.

Lying out the map on a barrel beside me, I traced out the route. "The waters turn treacherous here, so we'll avoid the southern pass and keep to the eastern current. I'm not expecting to see any other ships today, not in this area. Most avoid it altogether, and so if you do sense magic, we can assume it's the Crystal."

"I've wondered since the start what it might feel like, to be in the presence of magic so strong?"

"How does it differ? When you sense something like me, for instance, as opposed to an ancient artifact."

"You are entirely different," she said, a twinkle in her eyes. "When you're near, I feel as if I can hear my heartbeat in my ears. I feel warm, suddenly—"

I laughed, interrupting her. "Cheeky human. You know that's not what I meant."

"Oh," she said, trying not to laugh. "You were speaking of your magic?"

I couldn't resist. Holding the map down with one hand, I kissed her on the cheek. When Issa playfully swatted me away, saying she was attempting to concentrate, a vision of Mev doing the same to Kael on the lower deck came to me.

At the time, I'd thought their easy banter was not something I would have for myself, knowing it came with strings I had never been interested in tying.

"Issa—" I started.

"Um, Marek. Didn't you say an unnatural stillness in the water could be a sign of an impending storm?"

She was right.

I headed to the railing, watching the horizon. Our steady, rhythmic rocking had abated.

"The glassy calmness of the water and lack of temperature shifts lead me to think it may be an anomaly." I returned to Issa. "Our proximity to the Depths may be the cause. Many have reported such things, though I'd not have thought we were close enough to see any effects. Anything yet?"

Issa closed her eyes, her hands steady on the wheel. She took a few deep breaths, and then opened them once again. "Nothing."

We sailed in companionable silence for some time, changing places, then talking and observing. If we were not headed toward arguably the most dangerous place in all of Elydor, it would have felt natural. And more than a little enjoyable, sailing with someone curious about every movement, willing to learn how to navigate the seas.

Someone as intelligent and passionate as Issa. Her response to me... It took every bit of restraint that I'd learned in my long lifetime to lie with her all night and not touch every curve. I hadn't dreamed of the Depths, navigating what would be waters so treacherous it would take skill beyond, possibly, even my capabilities.

I dreamed of her.

Making love to Isolde. Sailing with Isolde. Life... with Isolde.

When I agreed to this mission, I could never have imagined there would be more at stake than myself. If I died in service to Nerys, to Elydor... it would be an honorable ending to a life well lived. But suddenly, there was a possibility of more. I was no longer risking just myself but a glimmer of hope that Issa had suddenly given me.

"Issa," I said, looking to the sky. "Do you feel that?"

Confused, she shook her head. "Feel what?"

"The temperature dropped."

"It did?"

"You were right. A storm is brewing."

No sooner had the words left my mouth than a gust of wind hit the sails forcefully, yanking the rigging hard. The gentle ripple of the water suddenly became churning waves.

"Issa," I yelled, the wind beginning to howl as ominous clouds churned above. "Hold her steady. Keep the bow into the waves. Don't fight the current, just ride it until I can break it."

I could admire Issa's calm later as she agreed. For now, I whipped off my boots for a better grip and ran to the stern. Lifting my hands, I began to manipulate the water, reaching into it with magic, feeling the currents like threads in my palms.

"It's pulling us toward the Depths," I yelled. "Issa, turn her around. Now!"

I struggled to counter the pull, redirecting the force below the water as the sky opened on us.

"Issa," I yelled to her again. "The current isn't right. We're being dragged. Turn. Her. Around."

She wasn't listening.

Abandoning my post, I ran back to her. Terrified, she white-knuckled the wheel, staring straight ahead. For a moment, I thought she'd panicked. Frozen. But Issa looked me straight in the eyes and said, "I feel it, Marek. It's there. I feel it."

"Good. I will come back. But right now, you need to turn the ship around. There is an unnatural pull that I need to counter." I reached for the wheel to do it myself but she held steady.

"Let me help you."

I could hardly hear her over the wind. She would not relinquish the wheel.

"Issa," I said, thinking she did not understand. "The storm is pulling us toward the Maelstrom Depths. None in Elydor's history has ever made it out of those Depths alive. We need to turn around, now. I need you to turn the wheel so I can counter the unnatural pull that is dragging us to our deaths."

I knew before I'd even finished, she wouldn't do it. "It's there, Marek. I've never felt magic this strong before. It's the Wind Crystal." Her chin raised defiantly. "None made it out alive, but you will. *We* will. You told me the sea bends to your will. So bend it."

She could not do this. "Issa—"

"Marek," she said, raising her voice to me for the first time since we'd met. "I may not be immortal, or have lived as long as you, but I am not a child. This is my decision, and I've made it. Stabilize us as best you can, and I will steer us toward the Crystal. I can sense it easily and know its location."

My hands shook with indecision. Every bit of me wanted to grab that wheel and turn us around. Bring Issa to safety. I could not turn us and fight the current at the same time, and every moment that passed, we were being dragged closer and closer to the Depths.

I saw my mother, floating, dead, in my dreams. I couldn't do it. I would not see Issa face the same fate.

Issa's hands gripped my face. She had let go of the wheel.

"What are you—"

"Marek. I love you. And if you love me too, you will listen to me. We are going into the Depths to retrieve the Wind Crystal. Together."

I love you. Together.

It had been my mother's decision to dive that day. I always thought, if I'd been there, I could have talked her out of it. But maybe not.

"I love you, Issa," I said, kissing her and making my decision. As if I had any other choice.

Running back to the bow, I reached back into the sea and attempted to steady the ship. But we were barreling forward in a way that was not natural to the sea I knew so well. It was why none before us had ever returned. The maps were wrong. I'd calculated our approach, planned to keep us at the edge. But the Depths had drawn us in.

"There was never a chance to turn back," I murmured, the truth sinking in like a stone. We'd crossed the threshold long ago. This wasn't a storm, not in the natural sense.

We weren't on the edges of the Depths. We were in them.

Now the only way out... was through.

29

ISSA

I hadn't planned to die today.

But as I watched Marek wave his arms furiously, clearly struggling to do what usually came so easily to him... as the ship's wheel stopped responding in the way Marek had shown me, it was clear we were losing control.

Yet as we got closer, the Crystal's magic hummed in my chest. It was the opposite of the feeling I had when Lyra whispered to Mev, and later again when I'd been alone with Marek. That had felt... off. As if it were wrong. Unnatural. But this?

I had to be here with him. Somehow, I knew, without me, Marek would not be able to find the Crystal. Or maybe he could find it, but not retrieve it. Or not get out alive. I wasn't sure how I knew this, but telling Marek I was staying had been a surprisingly easy decision.

The only decision.

"The water feels wrong. This isn't just a storm. It's the sea itself rejecting us," Marek yelled to me.

I understood what he was saying. Though not an experienced

sailor like him, or a Thalassari whose lifeblood was tied to the water, I understood.

Why was the magic so welcoming but the sea, just the opposite?

The magic was the Wind Crystal. Powerful, all-encompassing, welcoming.

The sea was just as powerful but it was angry and very much unwelcoming.

And then it hit me.

"The Crystal doesn't belong there. It's a curse," I called to Marek. "A wound that won't heal until it's removed. It *wants* to be removed. The sea is rejecting it."

I struggled to keep the wheel steady. Struggled to listen to Marek's advice. But the waves, the wind... everything was fighting against me. Against him.

"We'll never survive the Depths if we don't retrieve it. But if we stay too long..."

"I cannot hear you," he yelled.

I turned to watch.

Marek's eyes were closed, his hands were raised, palms facing the water. For a moment, the storm seemed to pause, the waves shifting as if responding to him. But they didn't calm. The waves writhed beneath us, defiant and alive with the magic of the Depths.

"It's rejecting us," I whispered to myself, feeling the truth of it in my bones. "The sea knows the Crystal doesn't belong here," I yelled to him.

The winds howled, and the ship groaned beneath us as if the wood was being torn apart by the storm's fury. We were going to die here. Draven would take Hawthorne. My people would suffer. The Gate would remain closed.

No.

I shook my head.

No. This cannot be happening.

I struggled to remain standing, the force of the waves wanting to rip the wheel from my fingers. I thought of Marek's early instructions to me.

"Don't fight it, Marek," I called over the roar. "We need to listen. Let it guide us."

Marek's gaze shifted to me, his jaw clenched, the strain of holding back the water visible in his face. "I won't let it take you," he said, his voice low and dangerous.

The ship shuddered.

"If we fight it, we lose."

He was silent for a long moment, the only sound the deafening crash of waves against the hull. Then, with a harsh exhale, Marek stepped forward. "Hold fast," he said, his voice steady.

I twisted the wheel, steering us in the direction of the Crystal.

"That way," I called, pointing.

The water buckled beneath us. Marek was at the railing beside me now. His hand shot out, manipulating the waves around us, parting them like a curtain. The space between us and the Crystal grew smaller, but the closer we got, the stronger the pull became.

And then, through the blackness of the storm, I saw it. The Wind Crystal. A bright blue-and-white beacon, bouncing up and down with each wave, but never sinking or even moving positions, as if it were anchored from below.

Its glow cast an eerie light through the murk of the Maelstrom. The air around it hummed with a magic so strong it consumed me. I could hardly concentrate on steering, the intensity of the Crystal was so extreme. Remembering my training, I separated myself from my own senses. Breathed deeply. Pretended it was nothing more than a regular artifact.

"We're almost there," I said, my heart pounding as Marek continued to steady us but no longer battling back the natural currents. It must be difficult for him, not to guide us in the way he knew but instead to allow *Tidechaser* to be pulled closer and closer to the center of the storm.

"Ready yourself, Issa. This will not be easy."

The ship lurched violently as we crossed into the epicenter of the storm, waves crashing higher, the winds screaming. At the heart of it all, the Crystal remained. Unyielding.

Marek reached out in his first attempt to retrieve the Crystal. He encapsulated the water around it, but as soon as he did, it dropped back into the sea. Again and again he tried, and failed.

My arms were getting tired. My hands raw with the pressure of *Tidechaser*'s wheel constantly pulling against me. I could tell Marek was getting tired too. But this was no time to give up.

The Crystal's magic was almost oppressive. I battled not just the wheel but the energy it exuded, as if warning me to stay away. Or maybe that wasn't the Crystal at all but the Depths surrounding it.

"We need to be closer," I said, realizing Marek's last attempt could have seen him retrieve the Crystal if the ship was nearer. Turning the wheel and angling us into the waves, I watched as Marek tried again. This time, the Crystal's glow came closer and closer as the water surrounding it, like a clear, liquid box, held steady. Bringing it toward him, Marek maneuvered the Crystal until he reached out and grabbed it, its water container falling to the deck below.

"Got it," he yelled, securing it into the pouch at his side, the one that held his mother's pearl. "Hold the wheel steady, Issa. Keep us aligned with the current. Don't fight it."

I did as he instructed, the ship gliding in the direction the

Crystal had been. We were going through the Depths, and not back out of them. Trusting Marek's decision, I did as he told me.

"Hold on," he called, running back to the bow. "I'm clearing the path ahead. Just stay on course, Issa."

Perhaps it was because we had the Crystal. Or because we had learned to navigate the Depths without fighting them. Whatever the reason, despite my exhaustion—and I assumed Marek felt the same—our path out was difficult, but not impossible.

"Keep your eyes on the horizon," Marek yelled. "Adjust as the waves come."

We sailed, the oppressive magic no longer encapsulating *Tidechaser* as if it were to swallow us whole, and little by little, the waves calmed. The winds began to die down and eventually, the skies cleared.

Somehow, we had done it.

Together, Marek and I had retrieved the Wind Crystal and survived the Maelstrom Depths. But... as a distant shore appeared on the horizon, one that appeared desolate, abandoned, Marek still seemed uneasy.

"What is that?" I asked. "Where are we?"

Marek's expression was not reassuring.

"Unfortunately, I don't know."

30

MAREK

Perhaps, after facing down death once today, I should not take us ashore. But as a navigator, I simply had to know more. What was this place? I had sailed the whole of Elydor, many times, and was certain this was not any of the islands off its coast. For starters, the air was different here, thick with an unspoken magic I couldn't quite place.

"Do you sense anything?"

I could already tell she did.

"Aye. But it's..."

"Different than usual?"

Issa nodded.

Despite assuring me she was fine, I could tell she was anything but. Remembering my first violent storm, and magnifying that to account for her humanness, in addition to the Depths being much more than any ordinary storm, and I could empathize. Going back through the Maelstrom Depths was not an option. Not one that I relished, at least.

I love you.

We hadn't discussed it yet. Or the fact that Issa had put her life at risk to help me. There was no doubt, without her, had I fetched the Crystal alone, I would not have made it out alive.

"I feel it too," I said, looking back at the map. "There are no markings, no maps that account for this stretch of land. Take the wheel?"

Issa slid seamlessly to it as I descended to the lower deck. "Where to?" she called.

I pointed to the shore, realizing belatedly Issa had never docked this way. Popping my head back up, I grinned. "Just keep her steady forward. I'll do the rest."

"But—"

With a wink, I positioned myself toward the shore, its sandy coastline clear of any rocks, and waited until we neared. As we did, I lifted my arms and pulled on the calm water beneath the surface, coaxing it forth. Mist thickened around me, eventually solidifying. With a sharp crack, the mist condensed, water freezing beneath its weight. Ice formed in jagged, uneven patches which I smoothed, stretching outward toward us.

A dock. Not perfect, but it would do.

I rejoined Issa, who was staring wide-eyed at me. "I've never seen... that is... you made a dock of ice."

"I did. Would you like to learn how to bring us in? There are no other ships"—I waved my arms—"to concern ourselves with."

"Uh..." Issa was staring at my dock. Though I pretended it was of little significance, that particular piece of magic was tricky. I knew few, and only one who was of a similar age as myself—Nerys—who could manage it. "Aye," she said finally.

Taking the excuse to stand behind her, I guided Issa and *Tide-chaser* to shore. Forgetting, apparently, that she'd worried earlier about what we might find on this particular stretch of undiscovered land, Issa raced down to inspect my ice dock.

Pleased she enjoyed it, pleased to be alive... I joined her, carefully leading us ashore.

"There," she said, pointing to a rocky ridge close by. "If we climb it, perhaps we can see more."

I'd been thinking the same. From the ship, we could see the island wasn't mountainous. It was rocky, though, similar to Gyorian's terrain. But its trees were more like the ones in Thalassari, not surprising since the climate was as temperate here as my home.

"What do you see?" I asked her, Issa in front of me, just in case she slipped. It was steep, made more so by the fact that Issa must have been exhausted after our ordeal.

"Nothing. No homes. No people. No animals that I can see."

She was right. It was sparse, though much larger than I first assumed. An unmarked, abandoned island. Nothing more.

As we made our way back, I looked for food, berries maybe, but there was nothing to be found. We couldn't stay here for long.

"We will rest," I said. "And then start back. There is nothing here in the way of sustenance. Thankfully, we have plenty of fresh water aboard and some provisions."

"Marek?"

We'd nearly reached *Tidechaser*.

"Issa?"

"How are we getting back?"

A fine question. We stopped before reaching the dock. Both Issa and I were soaked still. As the waves lapped gently in front of us, I pulled Issa into me.

"I will find a way that isn't through the Depths."

Her relief was immediate. She sagged against me and began to shake. It was the after-effects of what we'd been through, now that the danger had passed and the island proved not to be a threat. I held her, an idea forming.

"We'll take off our clothes—"

"Marek," she scolded, pushing off my chest.

I laughed. "And lay them out to dry. Would you prefer to sail home like this or in dry clothing? Besides, I would prefer to navigate at first light."

"We will remain docked tonight?"

"Aye," I said. "And return home at sunrise."

"Home," she murmured.

Issa longed to return to Hawthorne. I cupped her cheek, wanting to hear the words again, but knowing it would be more difficult to leave if I did.

"I meant what I said back there." I nodded toward the open sea. "I love you, Issa. I've always loved you. It's the true reason I left the way I did. Loving a human..." My words were not coming out as I intended.

"I know," she said. "I figured it out, the night you were having the dream, I think."

"You know?" I teased. "That is all you have to say?"

"That and... I meant it too. I love you, Marek. And if you think loving a human is difficult, try loving a Thalassari smuggler—"

"Navarch."

"Sure."

I kissed her.

We were alive, and so I kissed her, our lips melding together more familiarly now. It was a kiss of longing, but of joy and relief too. It quickly spiraled, though, into something more. I couldn't remove her clothing quickly enough, and Issa evidently felt the same. She tugged on the clasp of my leather belt, and I was all too happy to accommodate.

Pulling away, I released it, placing it carefully on the sand.

"There is something in there," I teased as Issa tugged off her boots, "we would do well not to lose."

As I pulled off my own, Issa paused. She might have let me pleasure her, twice, but Issa was still innocent. She was embarrassed.

"Take off your clothing," I said, turning around. "And lay it on the sand. I will join you in the water."

I turned, and waited. Heart pounding, as if I'd never been with a woman before, I stopped thinking about what this meant. How much of herself Issa would be willing to give me, knowing I wanted all of her. Body, heart, soul. I wanted to sail Elydor with her by my side.

She is human.

Issa will never leave Hawthorne Manor.

"Marek... I..."

The sound of water splashing punctuated the steady flow of the tide. I pulled off my shirt. The hesitancy in her voice... She was scared. I never undressed so fast in all my days.

Turning to face her, Issa submerged now to her shoulders, I strode toward the water, relishing in her expression. If Issa liked what she saw, her admiration was only a fraction of my own for her.

"You took out your braid."

"You... are quite nude."

Laughing, I reached for her, and there was no turning back. Our bodies pressed against each other, my hands roaming downward as the warm, gentle waves rose and fell around us. As my hands covered her breasts, I flicked my thumbs against her nipples, Issa pressing deliciously against my hands.

As our tongues tangled and Issa's own hands explored, I encouraged them to roam, to learn my body as I was learning hers. When she pulled from our kiss, and looked down between us, the blue-green water crystal clear, I couldn't resist a small chuckle.

I laid my hands on her shoulders, waiting until she looked at me.

"Talk to me, sereia. Tell me what you want."

"I want you," she said simply. "I've saved myself for a stranger, and for what reason? Draven threatens to take Hawthorne—"

"He will not have it, Issa. I promise you."

"I want you to be my first, Marek."

First, and last. But that discussion could come later.

"You are certain?"

"As certain as I was"—she shivered, nodding to the sea—"out there."

The full weight of what Issa had done, what she'd been willing to sacrifice, washed over me. I pulled her close once again, kissing her with all that I was. Reaching between us, I caressed her breasts, her stomach, her outer thigh, and then moved inward. Memorizing every curve, I finally reached my goal. Slipping a finger, and then two, inside, I couldn't resist a smile.

"Already so wet for me," I murmured against her lips.

"Mmm, I like how that feels."

"Do you?" I winked since it seemed to bring a smile to her face every time. And I loved it when Issa smiled.

"Aye, I do."

"Issa," I said, when I thought she was ready. "This will hurt, but not for long."

"I know," she said. "I'm ready."

What a gift she was giving me. Spreading my legs apart and positioning myself between her, I prayed for her not to experience too much pain. I wasn't in the habit of bedding virgins, but knew all too well the first time was not always a pleasurable experience. Vowing to ensure the opposite were true, I entered her slowly.

Her eyes widened as she held onto my shoulders. The sea lapped against our bodies as I relied on years of restraint not to move too quickly. She was so tight, and the sight of her... Was this truly happening?

"Issa," I ground out, prepared to withdraw. "This would be the time to change your mind if you wish it. In a moment, you'll no longer be a virgin."

No longer able to give that gift to any other man.

Control, Marek.

"I am certain."

Without giving her time to think, to worry about the pain, I thrust deep, tearing open Issa's maidenhead and burying myself deep within her. Kissing her, a distraction I hoped would ease the sting, I did not dare to move. But when Issa pressed against me, I said, "Straddle me and hold on," lifting under both buttocks as Issa did as I'd said.

Mimicking with my tongue our movements below the water, I held onto the thinnest threads of control, the feeling of being buried deep inside her as I moved her against me... her moan of pleasure was nearly my undoing.

Faster and faster, I thrust into her, the pace well beyond normal now. Nothing about this was like any other coupling. Determined for Issa to find release, I pressed and circled against her, unable to reach between us with my hands. She was not shy about reciprocating, and soon our pace was almost as frantic as *Tidechaser* being bounced around in the Depths.

Faster and faster, we moved in the same perfect rhythm as the tides. Water splashing, our bodies grinding together, we were one. Finally. Irrevocably. Issa was mine.

"Marek," she gasped, her head falling back as she held on. I continued to circle and thrust, willing her to let go.

"Go ahead, sereia. Scream as loud as you want. Release all of yourself."

She did.

Calling my name, Issa's entire body shuddered as I buried myself deep, releasing all of me into her. Deep, unabiding, complete.

I couldn't hold onto her tight enough, her backside shaking beneath my hands as I attempted to catch my breath. It was as if we were being pulled under, unwittingly surrendering to a force greater than ourselves.

Holding each other's gaze, Issa and I remained that way for so long, I wondered how my arms weren't tired, especially after the exertion at the Depths.

"I could hold you like this forever," I said, kissing her again and again.

"I would like that, I think."

It was enough, for now. Certainly not a plan, but confirmation that, she too did not see this as a passing fancy. As a way to release all that had built up between us as we fought for our lives today.

Tomorrow was uncertain, especially given our present circumstance and the Maelstrom Depths separating us and the Gyorian coast.

But for this moment, at least, we had each other.

And it was enough.

31

ISSA

As first, when I opened my eyes, I forgot where I was at. Not Hawthorne. Not Marek's cabin on *Tidechaser*. We'd fallen asleep on the deck, the ropes our pillows. And we were moving.

I jumped up.

Sure enough, though the sun hadn't yet risen, the shore was nowhere to be seen.

"How did I sleep through our casting off?"

Marek was at the wheel, wearing the same clothing as the day before, like me.

"The water was calm, and I didn't want to wake you."

Only a Thalassari could accomplish such a feat undetected.

"I'll be back."

Scrambling below deck and making myself as presentable as possible, utilizing a bit of thornroot for my teeth and re-braiding my hair, I returned to the quarterdeck just in time to catch the sunrise.

Pulling me to his side, Marek said nothing as we watched it together.

We'd discussed our course last eve, but as we sailed away

from the safety of our temporary haven, flashes of the Depths intruded happier thoughts.

"What if it doesn't work?" I asked, unable to keep the question to myself despite having asked it more than once already last eve.

"If we continue due south, there is no chance we will come close to the Depths."

Shuddering at the thought of being sucked into them again, I hoped he was right.

"By my calculations," he said, repeating his words from last eve when Marek had shown me our route on the map, "we should reach Thalassarian shores in two days, three at most, if the weather cooperates."

Provisions consisted of dried fish and hardtack, but at least water stores were plentiful.

Marek and I had agreed that returning to the Gyorian coast was neither wise, nor necessary. Avoiding any path near the Depths seemed prudent, and once in Thalassaria, we could send word to Adren of the altered plans. From there, we would restock supplies and sail to Valewood Bay.

"Warren and Edric probably believe I've abandoned them."

"They know better than that," Marek said, as he had before.

Last eve, we'd talked extensively not just about our route, but I shared my fears about Draven's plans. We spoke of it, of our retrieval of the Crystal, of Mev and Kael and how surprised, and pleased, they would be to learn we'd retrieved it. We spoke of the next steps that would need to be taken to open the Gate, namely retrieving the Stone of Mor'Vallis, the final artifact.

We spoke of everything except us. Sitting with my back against the railing, sore all over and content to watch him sail, I pulled my knees to my chest.

"There is one thing we're yet to discuss."

By the look he gave me, I could tell Marek's response would be anything but serious.

"How enjoyable yesterday was? There's no need, sereia. I could tell from the way you called my name—"

"Marek."

"Issa."

"We already did discuss that, if you recall."

He pretended to think on it.

"Aye, I believe you are right. What else, then? My bravery as we sailed through the most dangerous pass in all of Elydor?"

I rolled my eyes. "Your modesty becomes you, captain."

"One of my many fine traits."

Sighing, I tried to think of how to begin.

"I should never have left. Not in that way. Not at all, in fact," he said. When Marek became serious, it took me aback.

"We've discussed this—" I began, wanting to move forward, but he stopped me.

"We have, but not in truth. What you did, in the Depths..." Marek now sighed, as if the weight of Elydor were on his shoulders. "You were willing to sacrifice everything for me."

I hadn't thought of it that way at the time. I only knew, if we turned back, if Marek returned on his own, he would not have made it out alive. We barely did together.

"I would never have forgiven myself." My throat tightened. Again, the thought of me standing on the docks in Grimharbor, waiting for a ship that might never return...

"That morning," he said, his voice so soft I could hardly hear him over the wind. It had picked up: a fact I tried to ignore. "I awoke before dawn and rode out to the stream. When I'm too long away from the water, an unsettledness that is difficult to ignore consumes me. I had no intentions on leaving, but as I stood there..." Marek turned to me. "I've been alive many years.

Long enough to have known our connection, my feelings for you... I was in love with you then, Issa. The knowledge terrified me. My father was never the same man after my mother died. To love a human? It was not something I had ever considered before, knowing the pain of loss after my mother died. I also knew your place was at Hawthorne, and mine was at sea. If I returned to you that day, I reasoned, our bond would only deepen. Better to keep riding and spare us both, or so I believed. I left because I was scared, and very little scares me, Issa. But falling in love with you terrified me. And if I'm being honest, it still does. We come from two very different worlds."

I wanted to go to him.

Stand up, fall into his arms, and feel the comfort of his embrace. Instead, I remained where I was, hugging my knees to my chest, considering his words.

I'd forgiven him for leaving. But forgiveness did not erase the barriers between us.

"Others have done it," I said, as much to myself as Marek.

"Mev," he said, "is demi-immortal. Nerys and Rowan." Marek turned his face to the sky, his eyes closed. When he opened them, they were as troubled as before. "I warned her, but it did little good. I think they've simply accepted the pain that is inevitable, for Nerys especially."

"Pain," I said softly. "That to her, is worth a lifetime with Rowan."

"Aye," he agreed. "One I would accept too."

It took a moment for his words to sink in. By his expression, I hadn't misinterpreted them. My heart raced, Marek's meaning becoming clear. Unfortunately, it was not the only barrier between us.

"I tended to both of my parents when they were ill," I said. "My mother passed along first, and soon after, my father. He asked that I keep Hawthorne and its people safe, Marek. His whole life, my father had fought for humans to be accepted as Elydorian. For Estmere to be recognized as a legitimate kingdom. For Hawthorne Manor to provide more than a fleeting safety from Gyoria but as a true home to all who live there. He died before that dream was realized. We are more fractured than ever."

The look on his face... it was as if seeing me for the first time.

"It seems the roles are reversed." He was hurt, and though I didn't blame him, I needed Marek to understand.

"How can I choose between you and my parents? It is an impossible choice."

He was quiet as the wind picked up. I stood, looking out to the sea, the memory fresh.

"A storm is brewing," he said behind me.

Please let it not be the Depths pulling us close. I stood at that railing as the sky darkened, the telltale signs unmistakable. Discussions of us, of our future, would have to wait. There was another storm to weather, a very real one, first.

32

MAREK

"Be careful, the rocks are slippery. Here." I held out my hand. Issa took it as we made our way to shore. Finally, after a storm that could have found its origins from the Maelstrom Depths, it was so strong, and an extra day at sea courtesy of it, we arrived precisely as predicted. I'd never been so glad to see the distant shores of my home on the horizon.

"When you said we would not be sailing into the main port, you were not jesting."

"Few know of this inlet," I said, hoping Issa would not ask more. I'd never been ashamed of my unsavory lifestyle, when not sailing with the Tidebreaker Fleet, until now. My reasons for it may have started out pure, but I'd become deeply ingrained in the underbelly of Elydorian society.

As we came upon the shore and turned from the inlet where *Tidechaser* was docked to the other side of the cliff that jutted out into the sea, I waited for Issa's reaction. Seeing Elydor and all its splendor through Issa's eyes had become a favorite pastime of mine.

"The Thalassarian palace. I've never seen it up close before. It's beautiful."

"The Palace of Tides is constructed from white limestone and coral. Once inside, you'll find open-air courtyards allowing the sea breeze to flow freely. Its inhabitants like to be reminded of the sea just outside their doors. As do all Thalassari, though most do not live in such splendor."

"I would think not."

"This way," I said, the secret entrance locked to most. As we made our way from the depths of the palace upward, eventually arriving in open corridors, I explained the origin of the many mosaics of swirling waves and celestial maps that decorated its halls. "At night, the paintings glow with phosphorescent inlays in the stone, reflecting the magic woven into Thalassaria's very foundation."

I slowed, seeing Issa's expression.

"Something is wrong?"

"I cannot present myself to the Queen of Thalassaria this way. But my belongings are—"

"Nerys will care little about that, Issa. I promise you."

But Issa did care. She was a noblewoman, trained to present herself in a particular manner. Not being nobly born myself, I often forgot the protocols that were deeply embedded into her culture.

"Captain," a servant who had aided Nerys in her transition to queen greeted me as he passed.

"Aeolis." I stopped him. "A favor, if you please."

He darted a quick glance at Issa. "How may I be of assistance?"

"Lady Isolde is a guest of the palace. We've traveled a long way, our belongings lost to us."

Highly competent, he needed no further prodding. "I will see her installed in a chamber."

"Overlooking the sea," I added, knowing she would enjoy the view even though our time here would be limited.

"Of course. And I will secure garments for you, my lady, if you will follow me."

"The queen?" I asked him.

"In the throne room, meeting with her council."

"Will you get a message to her, please, that I have returned with urgent news? I will be in my chamber. Please bring Issa when she is finished. And a meal, as well."

"Of course, captain."

"You have a chamber, in the palace?" Issa asked.

Aeolis appeared amused.

"I am an important figure here with many official duties," I said in my best highborn voice.

Issa's laugh floated down the corridor as the servant led her away, attempting to hide his smile.

I watched her go, Issa not turning back. A foreboding I couldn't shake, watching her walk away, came over me. Why did she not see that her happiness was as important as anyone's? She was made for the sea.

She was made for me.

But forcing her to make a decision she wasn't ready to make would not bode well. Instead, as I'd done these past few days, I pushed aside the future to concentrate on the present. Namely, telling Nerys and Rowan of our successful mission and gaining their support to overtake Draven.

The chamber Nerys had given me to utilize, a small but functional one above the smuggler's entrance, had one important feature. Fresh water, drawn from hidden aquifers, streamed through the ceiling, pouring into polished stone basins that drained seamlessly into the palace's waterways. Cleaning and drying myself, I changed into something more presentable: the uniform I'd worn as a corsair. Securing the leather pouch on its belt, I opened it, as I'd done so often these past days, still in awe at what stared back at me. Small enough to sit in my palm, its jagged facets shifted from deep blue to silver. Faint veins of light pulsed within, as if alive with a quiet, steady power.

I wasn't surprised when a knock at the door was followed by it whipping open. I'd left it unlocked, expecting the precise reaction from my friend as I received. Nerys ran toward me and tossed her arms around my neck.

"You're alive. Marek, I was so worried. When did you get back? Did you make it to the Depths? I can't believe you're alive."

Untangling her from my neck, I smiled at the now-queen.

"Are you simply planning to stand there, grinning at me? Marek, answer my question."

"I would but am uncertain which one you'd like for me to answer first."

"Uh." She jumped back. "You are impossible. I honestly thought I might not see you again. So you didn't make it to the Depths? Did you come here first? Mev sent word and mentioned some sort of problem."

Making my way to the door which Nerys had left wide open, I closed it and turned to her, laughing. "Queenhood has not settled you, I see."

"Marek," she warned.

I held open my hand, the Crystal inside. Nerys rushed forward, staring at it. And then me.

"Impossible."

"And yet, possible. The Wind Crystal. Retrieved from the Maelstrom Depths, as your majesty requested."

Nerys shook her head in disbelief. "How did you...? You did it. Marek, you really did it?"

"Take it," I said, offering the Crystal to her.

"It is not mine to take." She closed my fingers. "That Crystal belongs in Aetheria. Will you take it there? Deliver it safely to Mev and her father?"

I'd expected the request.

"Of course. But I have a favor to ask of you first."

In response, Nerys hugged me once again, both laughing and crying at the same time.

"So little confidence in me," I said, hugging my old friend back, glad to be home, even if it was temporary. "And much to tell you."

33

ISSA

I opened the door. Sure enough, Master Aeolis stood there, waiting for me, as he'd instructed. I hesitated. Though the garment I'd been given fit perfectly, it was unlike anything I'd ever worn before. Form-fitting breeches, soft, knee-high boots, and a teal fitted tunic with silver thread in wave patterns were capped off with a wide, leather belt, adorned with pearlescent inlays.

"I look Thalassari," I said, realizing I did so aloud when Aeolis grinned.

"You would not be the only human in the palace to do so," he said.

I pulled the door of my chamber closed. "A human king of Thalassaria. I never thought to see such in my lifetime."

As we made our way through the corridors, water flowed everywhere. Beside the walkways, cascading waterfalls like the one in my bedchamber were oddly comforting.

"Times are changing," Aeolis said. "More believe in the human cause than cling to the old ways."

"I'm glad to hear you say as much," I admitted. If only

Hawthorne bordered these lands and not those whose king continued to poison his people with hate.

"A meal will be delivered to Captain Marek's quarters," he said, stopping before one of countless chamber doors.

I glanced at the guard.

"The queen is inside," Aeolis explained. "She may enter," he said to the guard. "On orders from the captain."

With a nod, the guard opened Marek's door. I stepped through, thanking Aeolis.

At first, I didn't see them. Realizing Marek and the queen sat on the balcony, similar to the one in my chamber, I made my way to it, stopping at my first glimpse of Nerys. She sat on a wrought-iron chair in a gown of teal and silver, sheer in parts and as beautiful as the woman herself. Mesmerized as she looked up at me, I nearly forgot that she wasn't alone until Marek came into view.

He looked... magnificent. Official, much as he had in Aetheria.

Marek stood as I made my way to the door. A small shiver ran up me at his appreciative perusal, from my head down to my toes.

"Lady Isolde," Nerys said before also standing and holding her arms open to me. I was about to curtsy when the queen pulled me into an embrace.

"Thank you," she said, squeezing me. "From the very bottom of my heart and soul, thank you for what you've done for my friend and for Elydor. It was so very brave."

It was like being embraced by a long-lost friend and not royalty.

When Nerys let go, smiling at me, she indicated I should sit between them. Though Marek's chamber was smaller than the one I'd been given, his expansive balcony was positioned at the corner of the palace with views of both the sea, to our left, and the palace grounds to our right. I wanted to obey the queen, but was drawn to the balcony railing.

"It is so... beautiful."

"Marek, ever demanding, chose this view for himself. But if I accept his resignation, I am unsure I can justify reserving this chamber for him."

Resignation? I spun toward Marek, whose steady gaze confirmed the queen's words.

Sitting, I addressed the queen. "Forgive me, your—"

"Oh no, there are no formalities between us. Nerys, if you please."

"Forgive me, Nerys, but I was not aware of a... resignation."

"Marek?" Her reproachful tone made me smile.

I pushed my own chair back so that I may see both Marek to my left and Nerys to my right. Inhaling deeply, the salt air as calming as the distant sound of gulls over the water, I waited impatiently. Why had he not mentioned this to me?

"I would serve Nerys in a less official capacity," he said. "As Navarch of the Tidebreaker Fleet, I am often required on long missions and many days at sea."

"I see." Though I didn't. Beyond the hammering of my heart, I couldn't think straight.

"You two have much to discuss," Nerys said, standing once again as I made to do the same. "Sit. I will see myself out. Lady Isolde—"

"Issa," I said, offering her the same informality as she did to me.

"Issa, it has been a pleasure to make your acquaintance. I know you are anxious to return to Hawthorne Manor, but I would request you break your fast with us in the morn so that I might introduce you to Rowan, who is away from the palace right now."

"Of course. It would be my honor."

"Thank you again for keeping my friend alive. Despite myself, I am quite fond of him. As it seems you are too."

How much had he told her?

"At times," I responded, to which Nerys laughed, making her way back inside.

"Oh." She turned back toward us. "I am sending a fleet along with you to Hawthorne. Though I have confidence King Galfrid's men can secure your home against the usurper, Lord Draven, they are Aetherian, after all, and all of Elydor knows Thalassari warriors are superior."

"That is very gracious of you."

"It is the least that I can do. Issa. Marek." With that, she sauntered back inside, the very height of elegance and grace.

"There is a meal inside for you," she called back. "When you are ready."

My stomach responded to her words. We'd eaten very little of substance these past few days. But I was interested in something more than food at that moment.

"You look beautiful," Marek said, before I could ask the obvious question.

"Thank you. I would repay the compliment. You are every bit the dashing Thalassari Navarch this eve. A role you will be giving up?"

"With the role comes many responsibilities," he said. "I took it because it was my mother's dream, for me to rise through the ranks. I never desired fame or riches, though. Freedom," he said, "is worth more than coin to me. Sailing with you reminded me of earlier days when I had no crew to command. Exploring, letting the wind take me... as I told Nerys, she will always be mine to command, missions such as this one, or bringing the Crystal north..."

He let his words hang there, and I understood the deeper meaning.

"It is different for me," I said finally. "If left to its own devices, Hawthorne would fall into the hands of Gyorians who still resent that land being taken from them."

"That land was King Galfrid's to give when he first opened the Gate."

"I would agree but many Gyorians would not. Prince Terran—"

"Can rot in the Depths. He is becoming more like his father every day. It's a wonder Kael was able to get out from Balthor's grip on a bitterness that has infected his people for too long."

A conversation of Elydorian politics only masked the deeper discussion. One I was not yet prepared to have. Marek's resignation was surprising, but as I said, our circumstances were not the same.

"Shall we eat?"

I could tell the question disappointed him, but Marek did not press the issue. Instead, he rose and held his hand out to me.

I took it, falling easily into his arms for a kiss that was sweeter and softer than most others, one touched by the breeze and blessed by Thalassa, who must surely be out there, looking after us, Marek and I having survived such an ordeal.

A kiss that felt a bit too much like goodbye, the talk of his future a reminder that our paths were anything but intersecting.

34

MAREK

"She is a lovely woman," Rowan said.

He and I watched Issa and Nerys as they spoke animatedly. We had broken our fast in Nerys's private courtyard, and Nerys was now giving Issa a tour, telling her of the various enchantments like the mosaic floor that shimmered with shifting constellations tied to Thalassaria's tides.

"I assume Nerys told you everything?"

"The important parts, aye."

A part of me had hoped to remain with Issa last night, but it was clear she struggled with our path forward, if indeed there was one.

"I hurt her, badly," I said, more sorry for it than anything else in my life. "We met before," I admitted. "A long story, and one that doesn't reflect well on me."

"The past is over, Marek. The future is uncertain. Look to the present if you wish to truly live."

"Wise words," I said. "Now that you are a king, I suppose I must heed them."

Rowan laughed. "You've settled well into your new position."

"One I never expected, admittedly."

"I had a vision—"

His words were cut short by a royal attendant with a message. Rowan moved toward her as they spoke. He nodded and looked toward Issa. Sitting straighter, I watched his face carefully, convinced the message had something to do with Issa. When the attendant left and Rowan returned, he called for the ladies, who were at the far side of the courtyard now.

"Something is wrong?" Nerys asked.

Rowan didn't confirm it, not needing to. His expression did that for him.

"Is the name Ilyas Rho familiar to you?" he asked me.

"He is a Gyorian artifacts dealer," I said, remembering our last conversation. "And owes me a debt."

"Seems as if he's paid it," Rowan said. "Apparently, he's been making inquiries about you, and Issa, as well as Lord Draven's movements. I have no notion of how Ilyas and his network knew you were here, but the message found its way to the palace."

"Gyorian smugglers," I said, "and black-market traders use enchanted trade gems to signal movement of important cargo, and sometimes people."

Nerys's mouth fell open. "Trade gems? I've never heard of such a thing. Marek—"

"Perhaps not the time to be properly educated about dark magic, Nerys. You're better not knowing."

"I beg to differ," she said, looking as if she were about to strangle me.

"However he learned of it," Rowan interrupted, "Ilyas has relayed a message to you."

As expected. I had asked him to report to me, by any means necessary, about Draven's movements. Of course, we thought to return to Grimharbor, and I couldn't help but be impressed by Ilyas's tenacity.

"What is the message?" I asked, knowing already it would not be good.

"Draven has proclaimed himself Lord of Hawthorne Manor."

Issa gasped.

I would kill him.

"There is a contingency of Aetherian warriors outside the manor's outer defenses, along with those of Hawthorne's own men who managed to escape before the gates were closed." My stomach turned as I watched Rowan address Issa. "There were casualties among those who opposed him."

I ran to her, holding Issa as her knees buckled.

"Warren," she gasped. "Please, no."

"We do not have the names. But apparently, he was supported by Gyorian warriors who are now threatening King Galfrid's men to stand down."

"Draven's working with our enemy," Issa said. I held onto her even though she'd regained her footing, standing tall.

"This has the potential," Nerys said, "to spark an all-out war. Two clans and ours will make three. There's not been a battle between all the clans since the Gate was closed."

"Four," Issa whispered.

Everyone looked at her.

"Four clans. We are as Elydorian as the others."

"You are." Nerys sighed. "Four. Though I am determined to help you fight back this usurper. It is our fault, taking you from Hawthorne, that he was able to exploit his advantage."

"Nay," Issa said, gathering the strength I knew was within her. "I was blind to his ambitions. He would have taken another opportunity to seize control. Are you certain," she said to Nerys, "that you wish to involve your people in my fight?"

Nerys did not hesitate. "Your fight is Elydor's fight, even if I did not owe you a personal debt for aiding Marek. Thalassaria cannot both remain neutral and claim to care for the fate of humans. Inaction is also an action. Rowan," she said, "find Caelum and have him double the size of our contingency." Then to us: "It will take us some time to prepare, but they should be ready within the day."

"We leave at once," I said, knowing Issa would not want to wait. "Have them meet us in Valewood Bay."

"And Marek, I do not accept your resignation."

Startled, I let go of Issa, who no longer had need of my assistance. "Why do—"

"Until after this battle. You have the immunity of a Navarch," she said, and I understood her meaning. Nerys was protecting me by keeping me under her command for the time being.

I nodded and turned my attention to Issa. Her face had gone pale, worry for her commander, and the people of Hawthorne, evident.

"We will prevail," I promised her, prepared to fulfill that promise.

"At what cost?" she asked.

That was a question I simply could not answer.

"I wish you well on your journey."

I made my way back down the secret palace entrance with Nerys where I would meet up again with Marek.

"Thank you for your support, though I do worry that Gyoria will not take your involvement well."

"Then perhaps Balthor should keep his clan from supporting an unrightful claim."

"Do you think he knows of it?"

"As king, it is his duty to know. More likely, he does not care."

"Or supports any instability in Estmere."

"Aye, or that."

We emerged from the palace, Nerys's guard not far behind.

"No sign of Marek." She scanned the coast and then turned to me. "Issa," she said, her gaze open and sincere. "I have known Marek a long time. He is insufferable and unwieldy, but as you must know by now, there is nothing he would not do for those he loves. And I have no doubt, he loves you."

"I believe he does," I agreed. "It took some time for me to realize. Marek hides his true feelings well. And I love him too. But my duty is to Hawthorne. Or it was," I said. "Until I failed them."

"You did not fail them," Nerys said, steel in her voice. "I could not have taken the crown from Queen Lirael without support. Asking for, and accepting aid, is a strength and not a weakness."

She was right, of course.

"I wish you had been able to speak more with Rowan. His situation was very similar to your own," she said.

I knew some of Rowan's background from Marek, but much of it was still a mystery.

"His family lineage is long and prestigious. He too struggled with the duties to which he was born and remaining here, in Thalassaria, with me."

"Remaining," I said, watching the ebb and flow of the tide. From here, I could not see *Tidechaser*, tucked away behind the rock outcropping, but would be glad to board her once again. "Rowan is doing much more than that."

"Something he also never bargained for, and it's not always been easy. We are no Gyoria, but there are many here who cling to the old beliefs."

"Including a mistrust of humans."

"Including that," she admitted. "Some have been alive for hundreds, or even thousands, of years. Their memories are long and, sometimes, their tolerance for change short. But we have come a long way. As for Rowan and the decision he made, one you will too... the question is not whether you have failed Hawthorne, but whether you will allow that fear to dictate the rest of your life. I had to choose between my past and my future, between what was expected of me and what I truly wanted, as did Rowan. You must make that choice, too. But remember, if your heart is divided, you will never belong fully to either path. Choose, and do not look back."

If your heart is divided, you will never belong fully to either path.

She understood me in ways I barely understood myself. Experience was a master teacher, but there were other barriers between Marek and me too. Ones she and Rowan had navigated.

"His humanity? And your immortality?" I asked, unsure how to phrase the question.

"We don't have all the answers yet to that, I will admit."

I'd been hoping for more, but her candor was appreciated.

As Marek appeared, my heart raced at the sight of him, as it always did. It ached too as I remembered the message Rowan had delivered.

There were casualties among those who opposed him.

I had no doubt Warren would be among Draven's opposition.

"Take this," Nerys said. I'd seen the leather satchel she carried and wondered at its contents.

"What is it?"

"Something I believe you will need. Open it after you decide."

Could I wait that long? I was already intensely curious.

"Thank you for escorting her here," Marek said, reaching us and embracing his friend. "And for your support. I was just at the docks. You ordered the Tidebreaker Fleet to follow us."

"I did," Nerys said.

What did that mean?

"Thank you."

"Be safe," she said, letting him go and indicating to her guard she was coming. "I am confident you will prevail."

I wish I could share Nerys's confidence.

Marek took the satchel from me. "What is this?" he asked as Nerys left, and we made our way to the ship.

"I'm not certain. Nerys gave it to me and said to open it." I paused, not wanting to use her exact words. "Later."

His brows drew together, but Marek said nothing. He held out his hand as we scrambled across the rocks and didn't talk again until we'd readied the ship and cast off. Though it was cloudy, there were no signs of a storm, thankfully.

"Have you realized," I asked as we passed the palace harbor, "I knew what to do without your guidance as we set sail?"

Marek steered us expertly through the water, not using any magic. On a day such as today, none was needed.

"I have," he said, pointing toward the palace. "The balcony, where we sat last eve. Do you see it?"

It was far into the distance, but I could see the portion of the palace he referred to.

"Aye."

"A high-ranking Navarch stayed there, when I first came to the palace, who resigned not long after. He never got on with Queen Lirael. They called him the Warden. He was as respected as any sailor in Thalassaria. They say when he was put through the Stormcaller's Rite, his instructors thought he might be our next king, he was so powerful. But the Warden's magic, he told me once, wasn't stronger than the queen's; he knew better how to listen to the sea than most. He advised me to feel the rhythm of the waves, the shifts in the wind, and understand the sea's will. I thought of him when we were in the Depths, when you correctly reminded me not to fight the storm. To let it guide us."

"What happened to him?"

"The Warden lives in Ventara, a beautiful, clifftop village north of Corvi."

We were quiet for some time, sailing past first the palace and its harbor and then the capital. I could understand how the Thalassari had become independent, complacent to the struggles of humans and disconnected from Elydorian politics. These lands were a paradise, untouched by our troubles.

"I cannot stop thinking of Warren, and Edric, my maid—"

"Rowan offered wise words to me, just this morn," he said. "'The past is over. And the future is uncertain. Look to the present if you wish to truly live.' I'm sorry for it, Issa. So very sorry. But what's done is done. We will face what comes next together."

Wise words that were easier to agree with than to practice. Nothing could change the signs I had not seen, or the warnings I ignored.

"My father became infallible after his death," I said, not wanting to admit the truth, even to myself. "If I am honest, we had a difficult relationship while he was alive, though I loved him very much. I believe my memories are clouded by guilt that I could not save him, or my mother. I trusted Draven because he did, convinced my father had never made a wrong decision. He was the most honorable, and loyal, man I knew."

"We all have flaws, sereia."

"Father too."

"Aye. Even those lost to us."

Sometimes, I forgot Marek had dealt with the same pain as me. "Perhaps your mother simply made a poor decision," I said quietly. "Trusting a friend too much. Perhaps," I ventured, "those waters were not cursed but simply... dangerous. In the way the Depths were dangerous even before Galfrid hid the Crystal there."

Glad that Marek appeared open to discuss this, a topic that was difficult for him, bolstered my confidence to continue. "You said yourself the Depths do not forget. That the oldest legend tells of its long memory, as if it were a living thing."

"The sea, to us, *is* alive."

"Right. And if you remember the journal entry. 'She called upon the sea, but it answered in hunger. Not offering the tide its due. The Depths demand more than courage. They demand a heart willing to break.'"

"A sacrifice. I remembered that entry when you were willing to accompany me."

"Perhaps it was nothing more than a recounting of the legend you had heard. But maybe, it's more than that. If the Maelstrom Depths are not just a place, but sentient in some way—"

"As I'm certain they are."

"Then they absorbed centuries of magic, sacrifices, and lost souls. They remember every life taken by the sea. When an artifact as powerful as the Wind Crystal entered the water, the Depths, perhaps, absorbed its power. Taking it back was like ripping out a piece of the Depths itself. Maybe that was the sacrifice? Or maybe it simply didn't belong there, an Aetherian artifact in Gyorian waters."

Marek stared at me. "You've thought a lot on this."

"I have. Though at times, I wonder if they are meanderings of thought that bear no consequence."

His smile was slow to form, almost sad. Unlike Marek's usual easy grin.

"There is nothing I've ever wanted more than to sail the open sea, solving its mysteries with you, Issa."

My breath caught at his words. I could imagine it. The adventures we would have. Every part of me craved his touch. Craved to be with him again. But I was as certain that I could not do that, and be separated from him again, as I was that my duty called in one direction, my heart... in another.

"The Warden," he offered, so suddenly, I'd forgotten his tale for a moment.

"The Warden," I repeated, my mind meandering back to Marek's story.

"You've learned on this journey, Issa, to read the waters of your life. You no longer need me, or anyone, to steer for you. Like the Warden, you've always had the ability to navigate. Trust yourself. And whatever decision you make..."

I understood his sadness now. Marek knew well the weight that held me down.

"I will support you."

36

MAREK

"Why does everything look so much more different than I remember it?"

We stepped onto the dock in Valewood Bay, Issa looking around as if it was the first time she had seen it.

You're not the same person as when you left.

I wanted to tell her that, but Issa wasn't a woman that could be coerced or convinced into a decision. She would decide for herself what our journey meant to her, and the course of her future, without aid from me. It was one of the many things I loved about her. That fierce, independent spirit was evident on the very first day we met. She was so brave, for a human especially, and Issa had proven that in the Depths.

"I know we said we would wait for the others, but if you wish, we can make our way to Hawthorne now?" I asked, assuming Issa would be anxious to be on the road.

"With the same winds and good weather we had, they should not be far behind us, you think?"

"That's my hope."

"We will wait," she said. "Besides, we have no mounts until they arrive."

"I can get us mounts if necessary."

"Ever resourceful, as always, captain."

It was good to see Issa smile. Our journey here had been swift, thankfully, but it was difficult to see her so forlorn knowing there was little I could do to comfort her.

"Let's find out what we can."

Issa and I made our way through the port. We talked to people, gathered information. Ate a meal and eventually made our way back to the harbor to wait. Unfortunately, we learned little more than we already knew. Draven had declared himself the new lord of Hawthorne Manor, but most seemed unconcerned. It was that apathy, even for fellow humans, that had not allowed Estmere to realize its full potential.

"I know it is difficult for you," I said as we watched the sea for any signs of Thalassari ships, "with Hawthorne Manor under siege. But excuse me for saying, I've enjoyed this time here with you. We work well together, Issa."

I'd never spoken more truer words. On land, and at sea, we were of one mind which was remarkable given the difference in our upbringing, our abilities, our life spans.

"There is no need for me to excuse you," she said. "If not for the weight of my people upon me, I would enjoy making my way through port with you. It was the same in the Gyorian marketplace. Beauty, among the darkness. Happiness, despite despair. 'Tis the way of life, I suppose."

"The first more easy to appreciate given the second."

"Aye." She craned her neck, and I followed her gaze.

"It's them." Issa ran to the edge of the dock, and I followed. They were still far away, but the sight of the largest ship in the Tidebreaker Fleet was enough to cause a stir. As promised, Nerys had not just sent a contingency of Thalassari sailors. She'd sent the best. Soon, we were surrounded by onlookers.

Watching Issa's expression, I wanted to pull her to me and kiss her. Reassure her all would be well. But that wasn't what she needed. Issa had made it clear when we'd re-boarded *Tidechaser* that she wanted distance, and as difficult as it had been, I'd given it.

She's preparing to be separated for good.

I could feel her pulling away, bit by bit. Had she already made her decision and just didn't want to tell me? Could I really ride away from Hawthorne when this was over, never to see her again?

Did I have a choice?

Putting our future from my mind, and restraining myself from touching her, I watched with her as the ship pulled into dock.

"Come on," I said, nearly taking her hand, until I remembered.

"They really brought horses with them," she said as they began to unload.

"Horses, provisions. It's not the first battle of this sort they've seen. You forget, some of them are thaloran."

"I do forget," she admitted. "It's so hard to imagine living more than five hundred years. I even forget how old you are sometimes."

"I'm a child compared to this one," I said as the seven-hundred-year-old Navarch and leader of this fleet approached. "Lady Isolde, this is Navarch Kieran of Thalassaria, a sharp and steadfast sailor, despite his advanced age."

Kieran barked out a laugh. "Despite it? Because of it." He inclined his head to Issa. "My lady, it is a pleasure to make your acquaintance."

Kieran's silver-streaked hair and sea-weathered face bore witness to a life spent battling both enemies and unpredictable tides. We clashed, at times, but he was a worthy and competent ally.

"Thank you," she said, "for coming to Hawthorne's aid."

"And miss the opportunity to remind our Gyorian neighbors the strength of the sea?" He grinned, his gold tooth glinting. "It is our pleasure."

It wasn't until the ship was fully unloaded that Issa and I made our way back to *Tidechaser* to collect our own belongings. I attached them to the mounts that Kieran provided us, and with all eyes in Valewood Bay on us, more than sixty Thalassari followed as we rode from the city.

By the time we reached the outskirts of Hawthorne Manor, it was apparent things were not the same as we'd left it. Issa gasped when she first spotted the Aetherian tents, visible in the distance because of the blue light they emitted. Unlike Gyorians, who preferred to blend into their environment, Aetherian warriors believed their presence should be known, a beacon of power and protection. Their tents, woven with threads imbued with celestial energy, shimmered like the night sky.

"If it was not so terrifying, I would call it beautiful," Issa said.

"The precise feeling they hope to evoke."

We were too far from Hawthorne Manor to see it in the distance, especially in the dark. Movement from the Aetherian camp told us they were aware of our presence, so I wasn't surprised when two riders, on their gleaming white mounts, headed our way. I was surprised, however, to realize one was familiar to us.

Before I realized what she was doing, Issa had stopped and was dismounting, running to Lyra. The Aetherian warrior did the same, the two embracing as if they had been lifelong friends. In times such as these, with stakes so high, connections were forged and strengthened. I too appreciated the familiar faces, not expecting Commander Eirion to have come himself.

Grabbing the reins of Issa's mount, I rode forward.

"We've yet to advance," I heard Lyra saying.

After greetings were exchanged, I asked Eirion if their camp could accommodate sixty more.

"Indeed," he said. "Though we've a newcomer to camp, a Gyorian himself, who warns of a flank attack by a band of Gyorians. We were told those who support Draven are inside with him. Reivers, thieves... none with authority from their king. But the others are a different story."

"How far away are they?" I asked.

"Unsure. Our scout should be returning soon to confirm."

Gyorians hid their tracks over land well, but an Aetherian scout didn't rely on physical markers alone. With the air at their command, I had no doubt we would know precisely how far away this new band was.

"What's the plan?" I asked.

It was Lyra who answered. "It may change with your arrival."

I motioned ahead. "Onward then."

Issa remounted easily, reminding me how adept she was at more than just sailing.

If it was unusual for a contingency of Thalassari to join an Aetherian one to defend a human holding, it was made even more so by the presence of Gyorian scouts lurking at the tree line. I couldn't see them, of course, but knew they were there. Three separate clans had converged upon Hawthorne Manor, and the air was thick with tension.

As we dismounted, Eirion and Kieran greeted each other warmly, their individual histories intertwining more than once throughout the ages.

"This way," Lyra said to Issa and me as our mounts, and

belongings, were taken by one of my own men who had joined the mission. I raised a hand to thank him, allowing Lyra to lead us toward the Aetherian camp.

"Our newcomer," she said, weaving between tents. "I believe you know him."

Rounding the corner, we came upon what was likely Eirion's tent. It was larger than the others, five times in size. Waving her hand, Lyra opened the flap made of sapphire silk. Aetherians were nothing if not impractical, their love of beauty finding its place even in the midst of battle.

The Gyorian informant's back was to us as he spoke to an Aetherian warrior who sat at the oval table in the center of the tent.

He turned.

Issa gasped.

37

ISSA

Embracing Adren, after the shock of seeing my newfound relative here, I asked the obvious question.

"What are you doing here?"

"Pardon me." The Aetherian he was speaking to excused himself as Lyra, Marek, and I sat, Adren doing the same. On the table in front of us, a map of Hawthorne Manor.

"The day you left," Adren said, a question in his eyes since he wouldn't know it was safe to discuss the Crystal in front of Lyra, "Ilyas returned to Grimharbor, asking for you. An interesting one," he said sardonically to Marek, who shrugged. "When he realized my connection to you, he admitted that he'd been acquiring information on your behalf. It was through him I learned of Draven's declaration. I left immediately for Hawthorne."

"When he arrived," Lyra said. "Before Adren knew I was at camp and could vouch for him, he was nearly killed."

"A risky move," I agreed. "Coming into an Aetherian camp alone. Or did you bring others?"

"I am alone. There are men of Kael's I trust but also knew

from Ilyas about the Aetherian encampment and thought it best I come myself."

"Wise," Lyra agreed. "And likely what saved you."

"You risked yourself to be here?" I asked.

"Hawthorne Manor is yours, my lady, not Draven's. If circumstances were different, if Kael still led his men, I'd have taken them, and Hawthorne, back already."

"But Kael is in Aetheria, as unlikely as that seems, and us here." Lyra turned to me. "Did you not sense the Crystal there?"

Raising his hand, Marek gathered moisture from the air, creating a silencing mist. Then standing, he reached into the pouch on his belt. Taking the Crystal carefully from it, he opened his hand, revealing its contents to Lyra and Adren.

Their reaction would have been amusing if our situation were not so dire. He put it back, the mist intact, and recounted as quickly as possible our experience in the Maelstrom Depths. He overstated my role, clearly proud. "I would not have retrieved it without her," he finished.

"You'd be at the bottom of the sea without her," Adren said.

With a swipe of his hand, Marek evaporated the mist.

The four of us stared at each other, the full importance of what we'd accomplished finally settling.

"And now we turn our sights to Hawthorne," Lyra said. "From what we've gathered..." she began, and then hesitated.

That's when I knew.

I *knew* with the certainty of my ancestor's senses, even though I wasn't using them.

"No," I said, willing it not to be.

"I'm told from the few who got out before Draven fortified the outer defenses, Sir Warren Calder was not only your commander but a friend."

Was.

"I am so very sorry, Issa. Draven had him killed, using your commander's death as leverage to bring the others in line. There was an uprising—"

"No." I could not breathe. Could not listen to this. I pushed back the tent flap, inhaling the night air. Except it didn't help.

Marek's arms were around me from the back before I was even aware he'd joined me. Spinning me around, he held me as I allowed myself to fall apart in his arms.

"He loved me," I managed. "He loved my father. My mother. Hawthorne. His family."

Marek said nothing for there was nothing to say. So much death, and by the hand of a man I'd defended. "I should have—"

"Stop." Marek took me by the shoulders. "This was not your doing. It was Draven's. And there are more inside those walls who need you now. This isn't over yet."

He was saying, without uttering the words, that I could not fall apart. Not yet. My people needed me.

Wiping my eyes, I took two more deep breaths.

"I'm ready," I said, lying but wishing it were true.

He leaned forward, kissed me, and led me back into the tent.

"You were saying?" I sat back down, not wanting Lyra's and Adren's pity. My face flushed with a sudden vision of driving a knife into Draven's treacherous heart.

"There were others," Lyra said softly, "though I do not know their names. By one account, three are dead. By another, up to seven. Some managed to escape. The others are now taking orders from Draven, who is secured inside with the Gyorian mercenaries. They've not yet struck our camp, perhaps realizing the war they will incite. We've been debating our next move—"

"If we take it back with force," I interrupted, "Hawthorne will be decimated."

None disagreed with me. It was well-known, when a battle

broke out in Elydor, little of consequence remained in the aftermath. With all three clans, not counting the humans, involved? Elydor had almost not survived the War of the Abyss, so named afterward for what had nearly become of it.

I began to pace back and forth in the small space afforded to me in the tent. "My father often said the tree cover to the west which runs from the outer defenses all the way to the keep should be removed, though he never did it."

"We could attack from above," Lyra correctly guessed.

"As could we," Marek argued, to which Lyra burst into laughter.

"Can a Thalassari climb a tree?"

"I've never seen it," Adren agreed.

"I can climb a tree," Marek grumbled, making even me smile.

"As I was saying," I continued. "It is well known the Aetherians are accustomed to striking from high above and could seek such an advantage. The silencing mist you used," I asked Marek. "Do all of your men have such a skill?"

"More than half do, aye."

"They can silence your movements," I said to Lyra. "And when Draven appears, you can strike. Without him, my men will revolt."

"No."

That, from Marek.

"They are my people. This is my home."

"I've missed an important piece of information, it seems." Adren adjusted himself in his chair.

"I will draw him out. Insist he speak with me. When I do, you can strike," I finished, although now even Lyra was shaking her head.

"It could work..." Adren said.

Marek glared at me. "You forget about the Gyorian mercenaries."

I ignored him. "Adren, will they listen to you, if Draven is incapacitated?"

"Dead," Marek clarified.

"Dead," I agreed. There was little chance of him walking away from this alive after what he had done.

"They may," he said, thoughtful. "I can claim to have the king's authority. But if they don't, I am happy to engage with them."

"We will support you from above," Lyra said.

"As will the remainder of you and your men," I said to Marek. "It should be easy enough for you to gain entry with the others occupied."

"No," he repeated. "You will not put yourself in such danger. Too much can go wrong."

I stopped pacing. Crossed my arms.

"This. Is. My. Home."

"I understand, but—"

"Marek. I took an oath. And will not be denied a confrontation with the man who betrayed me, betrayed my father's memory, and killed someone I considered like family."

He looked to Lyra and Adren, but neither said another word against the plan.

"I will not be waylaid. Resistance is futile."

Lyra chuckled.

As Marek and I stared at one another, an understanding seemed to pass between us. A mutual respect. It was what began as an interest that grew into an attraction. One which had built to a crescendo on that beach and settled into what it was. Still uncertain. With more questions than answers.

Love. It was love that passed between us, an unspoken one but love, nonetheless.

"I am coming with you," Marek said finally.

"Very well."

"We would do well to move before they've realized you've joined us," Lyra said. "We can get into position before dawn."

"Which means there's much to discuss before then." Adren pulled the map toward him. "First, we should—"

The tent flap opened.

Adren fell silent as Commander Eirion stepped inside.

"We have visitors."

38

MAREK

"He's alone," the commander said as we walked through camp. Adren and I followed as the others remained with Kieran to continue formulating the plan of attack. One I disliked heartily. "He refused to come any further, insisting we meet him here."

"Could it be a trap?" I asked.

"No," Adren said. "Terran is many things, but he is not dishonorable. When he fights, he will do it with fair warning."

Very little comfort since, according to Kael, his brother was the "only one, besides my father, who could best me, on a good day."

I saw him clearly, lights from the Aetherian tents behind us offering enough illumination to make the night appear almost day. They didn't know the meaning of subtlety, I would give them that, at least.

"So it's true," Terran said, his voice similar to Kael's in inflection. Though they were twins, Terran was slightly larger, his hair, shorter. Other than that, it was like looking into the face of my friend. Except, Terran was not a friend. Not to me, and not to our cause. "Defected, again."

He spoke to Adren.

"Never," he responded to his prince. "My loyalty has always been to Kael."

Terran's harsh laugh sent chills through me. "Loyalty to one who doesn't know the meaning of the word. Kael is a traitor to our clan." He shot me a look. "Who are you?"

Disliking his tone, I considered not responding. Better to defuse than instigate. So instead, I smiled.

"Marek of Thalassaria." I bowed with a flourish. "At your service."

"I've no need of a water-wielder in my service."

Prince Terran's demeanor tracked with his reputation. I shrugged off the insult, waiting instead to hear his purpose for being here.

"My grandmother was a Hawthorne." Adren's bark matched Terran's, reminding me why I spent so little time in Gyoria. "I will not see its lady's inheritance stolen from her. I mean to help her defend it."

Terran clearly wasn't prepared for that explanation. His dark eyes narrowed.

"You are—"

"Half-human."

Awareness dawned, Adren's ever so slight aging, an anomaly among full-bred immortals, likely now clear to the prince. His jaw flexed as Terran ground his teeth together.

To his credit, he remained silent, taking in the new information before speaking.

"I would ask why you are here," he said finally to Eirion. "But Aetheria has always been the bitch to humans."

Eirion stepped forward.

Adren stopped him. "Do not let Prince Terran's hate affect the outcome here. He merely does the bidding of his father."

That didn't please Terran, though I supposed it wasn't meant to. If anyone was the bitch here, it was the prince to his king.

"But you?" He turned his attention to me. "What business does Thalassaria have in human affairs?"

The truth would not do. In fact, no answer would be acceptable to one with such hatred in his heart, so I appealed to the one thing Terran apparently loved.

"As a favor to your brother."

It was well-known Kael and Issa were friends and that was a partial truth. Terran didn't question my explanation, but his nose flared in anger at the mention of Kael.

"Lord Draven executed Lady Isolde's commander and several of her men," Adren said, "with the aid of Gyorian mercenaries. We are not butchers, Terran."

If my words angered the prince, Adren's incensed him.

"Who?" he demanded.

Adren offered names, not improving Terran's demeanor. I watched as the two spoke, wondering how Mev was able to turn Kael so firmly to the side of justice if he was even half as brainwashed by King Balthor as his brother.

"Help us," Adren finished. "How many do you have with you?"

"We do not... aid humans."

"You would allow them to be butchered? Hawthorne decimated? For no cause but one man's ambition?"

Eirion and I watched the exchange, silent. I knew what the King of Gyoria's response would be. He had made his stance clear by cutting off humans from their loved ones without remorse. But his son? Was Terran redeemable?

"They will be dead soon with or without our aid. And you would all do well to remember it. You are no longer welcome in

Gyoria, Adren. Tell my brother the next spy he sends will not be met with mercy."

With that, he turned and walked away.

We watched him leave. I, for one, considered it a victory. If Terran wished to interfere, he could have easily sparked a war here. One that would likely occur eventually. If not today, then the day King Balthor realized his stolen Crystal had been taken. Or when Kael attempted to retrieve the Stone of Mor'Vallis. A reckoning was coming, either way.

Adren sighed. "That was his father speaking through him."

Eirion snorted, a very un-Aetherian sound, to be sure. "Maybe it was once, but those words came from Prince Terran. He is not who Kael believes his brother to be. Not any longer."

"Perhaps." Adren sighed. "He will not interfere, either way. Terran is a man of his word."

You are no longer welcome in Gyoria. That's what he had said. If Terran was a man of his word, Adren was as without a home as Kael.

And that's when it hit me...

39

ISSA

And so, it began. The battle for my home, one I never expected or asked for. But sometimes, challenges meet us despite our wishes, and this was one of those times. I refused to be humbled, being forced to ask for permission to enter from a guard who had accompanied me hunting too many times to count. Draven was at fault, and he would pay for his treachery.

"If he or any of the Gyorian mercenaries—"

"I know, Marek. I will stand behind you and Adren. We've discussed this many times."

Adren looked to the trees. We could not see them. Though their tents might shine like stars in the sky, the deep-blue color of the Aetherian warriors' clothing blended seamlessly with the trees.

Thank you, father, for the idea. I will secure Hawthorne once again in your and mother's memory. That is a promise.

The portcullis lifted. Though I hadn't expected the two Gyorian warriors standing on the other side. They were also clearly just as surprised to see Adren.

"You, remain," the taller one said. His nose looked as if it had been broken many times. The other was small, for a Gyorian warrior, though still larger than most human men.

In response, Adren strode forward, blatantly disregarding the order. Marek and I followed his lead. At first, I assumed they would stop us. The two flanked us instead, grumbling but otherwise saying nothing as we walked through the empty outer courtyard. As planned, we stopped before heading through the second gatehouse.

"This is far enough," I said. "Fetch Draven."

The broken-nose one laughed. "We do not take orders from you. Draven is Lord of Hawthorne Manor. You are to be brought to the keep."

"Either fetch Draven," Marek said, "or our combined forces outside the gate will make their way inside and kill every one of you bastards who colluded with him, leaving Draven to rule over a pile of ruins."

The shorter one took a step toward Marek. In response, in a movement I barely caught, he somehow created a chord of water that he wrapped around the mercenary's feet. While his companion stumbled to the ground, broken nose raised his arms as Adren barked, "Don't do it."

"Remove the binding, now," was his response, on behalf of his friend.

Adren sighed as if the entire incident bored him. I turned to see my guards, positioned as usual at the gatehouse, staring down but otherwise not moving. They were clearly terrified, and I didn't blame them. Getting between Elydorians in battle was not wise for humans, no matter the circumstance.

"We will not be going to the keep," I said in my most commanding voice, hoping it didn't sound as shaky as it felt. "I would prefer not to meet the same fate as my commander. Fetch Draven," I repeated.

"There is no need."

My entire body tensed.

He emerged from the early-morning shadows; Draven's ability to manipulate auras meant he could conceal his energy. Slinking in the shadows was something he did well, no doubt having served him throughout the years in ways I never realized.

"Release him."

Marek did, the Gyorian not at all pleased at being so easily incapacitated. Though Marek must have gathered moisture from the air, how had he managed it without anyone noticing?

"Is it true?" I asked, looking my father's old friend straight in his eyes. "Did you kill Warren?"

Draven sighed, as if I bored him. "He didn't have to die. Warren chose his fate."

So it *was* true. The ache in my chest intensified. Ignoring it, I pressed him.

"Who else?" I demanded.

"Issa, my dear—"

I lunged toward him at the condescending tone. Would have reached him, too, if Marek and Adren hadn't pulled me back. At Draven's laugh, I lost all sense of where I was and what was happening. I would kill him before this was through.

"She always did have difficulty controlling her emotions. Women can be so... ah, ah, my Thalassari friend, I would not do that."

Whatever Marek had been about to do, he stopped as the outer courtyard was suddenly filled with five, ten, more than twenty Gyorian mercenaries. I'd tangled with them enough times over the years to know, and appreciate, their sheer strength.

At the first gust of wind, Marek yelled, "Behind me, Issa."

I did as he said, my fingers still itching to slice Draven's throat.

It took the Gyorians a moment to realize what was happening, that they were being swept off their feet from above.

As expected, chaos reigned. Adren stomped his feet, splitting the ground beside Draven open. But instead of falling into it, he jumped to the side, saving himself at the last moment. Marek was engaged with two Gyorians as others shouted orders to dismantle the stone wall and use it to attack the trees.

Hawthorne would be decimated, just as Adren predicted.

Marek, forgive me.

Pulling my knife out from my belt, I bolted toward Draven, ignoring Marek's shout for me to stop. Draven, anticipating me, grabbed my wrist so completely that I thought it might have snapped. The knife dropped harmlessly to the ground, which rumbled beneath my feet. A quake, meant to disrupt. Disarm. I held my ground, pretending I was on the deck of *Tidechaser* during a storm.

Not just any storm. We were in the Depths. Violent winds from above, calls of "Thalassari" from behind. And the man who'd started it all, dragging me by the wrist, away from the fray.

Promise me, Issa, you will look after our people.

My father's words echoed in my ears. I would not allow Hawthorne to be reduced to embers, a once-flaming beacon of hope for all humans that we could survive even with Elydorian opposition at our doorsteps.

If we fight, we lose.

I stopped struggling. Allowed Draven to believe he'd subdued me. With my free hand, I reached down to my boot, dragging behind me in the dirt. Taking a deep breath, summoning every bit of strength left in me, I began to wriggle and kick so Draven was forced to stop.

When you strike, make it count. A wounded stag is dangerous.

I would make it count.

Circling my arm and aiming for his chest, I didn't hesitate. The knife embedded itself with a sickening thud that I would never forget. One moment, my wrist felt as if it were being crushed in a vice. The next, it was free and my head bounced off of the ground.

The next, Draven was above me, screaming in pain and rage. But then, he was lifted from the ground and tossed as if he were a sack of wheat. Adren stood above me, watching him. But he didn't move. Even when Draven attempted to stand, something I couldn't do. Instead, I watched from my dirt bed, the courtyard grass tickling my cheek.

Marek.

His hand was lifted, though I couldn't see what was happening. Adren scooped me up into his arms, and for better or worse, I had a clear view now of the same water ties he'd used on the Gyorian being tightened around Draven's throat.

"He's gone, Marek," Adren called to him.

He either didn't hear him, or didn't care. His fingers twisted and I looked away.

"Draven is dead," Adren yelled, so loud, it was like a clap of thunder.

A twist of water, like a beacon, rose from in front of Marek up into the sky. With it, the winds stopped. Everything stopped. My head throbbed. My wrist, I was all but certain, was broken. I'd close my eyes, just for a moment.

And then, blessedly, it all went black.

40

MAREK

"Don't get up too quickly."

Issa's hand flew to her head.

"Ouch." She looked past me. "I'm in my bedchamber."

"Astute," I teased. "What's my name?"

"Marek, be serious."

"Close enough."

Jesting aside, it was a relief that she was alert. I'd seen head injuries fell the best of warriors, and from how long she had been out, she must have hit the ground hard.

"My wrist." She lifted it into the air. It was wrapped with silk-spore, Hawthorne's healer as adept as they came.

"Adren noticed the bruises. We don't believe the bone is broken but—"

"What happened?" she interrupted me, attempting to sit up in her bed. I pushed her shoulder back gently.

"Not yet," I reminded her.

"Marek—"

"Hawthorne is safe. The mercenaries were run out, none

willing to sacrifice themselves with Draven dead. No one else was injured. At least, not seriously injured."

"Except Draven."

Bastard. When I saw Issa's wrist, I'd wanted to kill him again. "You follow orders well, my human warrior," I said not holding back a large measure of sarcasm.

"I'm more accustomed to giving than receiving them." Her small smile fled as quickly as it formed. "He killed Warren."

I tucked an errant strand of hair behind her ear. "I know he did and am sorry for it. I should let you rest. You're under strict orders not to move for the remainder of the day, but there are people who will want to know you're awake. Edric, your maid..."

"They are well?"

"Aye, they are well."

"I really do feel fine."

This time, I kept her in bed by leaning down and kissing her. It was a kiss to remind her that I would be patient. But it was also one to soothe my own soul that had nearly been torn to shreds when I saw her being dragged by Draven.

Patience, unfortunately, had never been a strength of mine. Despite her injury, I wanted to continue to probe. To ask Issa what she thought of us, of a future together. Of days that included helming *Tidechaser*, or walking through ports and marketplaces together. There were ways such a thing could be possible, but it was not the time, nor place, to discuss them.

I love you, Issa.

A knock at her door stopped me from saying it aloud. Reminded me we were no longer alone on *Tidechaser*. Issa was home, surrounded by people she loved and who loved her. Though they were terrified of Draven and his hired Gyorian thugs, it was clear they adored their lady.

"Please rest. I promise all is well." I stood. "The castle is surrounded, though I doubt very much the mercenaries will return. My lady has amassed quite an array of allies across Elydor."

I bowed, for emphasis, eliciting a giggle from Issa. A glorious sound.

Issa stopped me halfway to the door. I turned to see her very clearly disregarding my request to remain lying down. Sitting, though she remained abed, Issa was also unrepentant.

"Thank you," she said simply.

I stood there, looking at her, wondering how in the tides I could have ever left this woman.

"With pleasure, sereia."

* * *

"They aren't coming back."

Lyra stepped onto the battlements with me, looking out onto an empty field.

"That they felt emboldened to overrun a human holding, in Estmere... the tides are turning against the humans."

"They have been for some time," Lyra said quietly. "Thalassaria just has not noticed."

I wanted to refute her, but couldn't.

"We've been... apathetic to their cause."

Lyra didn't disagree.

"I would say, having risked your life to retrieve the Wind Crystal, you've made up for it. Given them a chance."

"I could not have done it without Issa."

"So, what's next for you, Marek of Thalassaria? Commander Eirion tells me you've given Queen Nerys your resignation from the Tidebreaker Fleet."

"What is next for me," I repeated. I didn't know Lyra well, but she was a friend to Mev and Kael, and therefore, a friend to me. "That will depend on Issa."

"Mmm, I am not surprised. It's evident you care for each other."

"Her place is here, or so Issa believes."

"You don't agree?"

I wanted to say, no. Issa was an explorer. An adventurer, like me. She was made for the sea, had taken to it remarkably well. But being here, hearing how her people spoke of her, how they revered her... it was a fool's dream to think, even for a moment, she might leave Hawthorne.

"It is not my place to agree, or disagree," I said instead.

"You have experience she does not. The benefits of multiple human lifetimes."

It was true. But that did not make me superior. "Issa has done well with the human life she's been given."

"Indeed, she has. And will always have an ally in King Galfrid. We will defend Hawthorne Manor as if it is Aethralis."

I'd known as much already, but it was good to hear Lyra say as much.

"And for you? Lyra of Aetheria?"

"I serve my king. And Princess Mevlida, now."

"Your loyalty is admirable."

"His cause is just. My parents both serve him also, in their own capacities, and believe in his vision of Aetheria. One in which humans play a vital role."

Sighing, I considered what needed to be done next. "How will Kael possibly retrieve the stone if it sits upon his father's head?"

Lyra shook her head. "I do not know. But I will help him and Mev however I'm able."

"What in Elydor's name," I asked, more to myself, having

turned toward the courtyard just in time to see her, "is Issa doing out of bed?"

41

ISSA

Thus far, I'd visited the kitchens, the servants' quarters and the armory. It had been surprisingly difficult to track down Edric, who was typically in the keep. I'd been told he visited my chamber earlier, when Marek was with me, but no one had seen him since.

"There you are," I said.

Edric turned from the entranceway of the stables and ran to me. I embraced him, holding back tears. Grateful he was alive, I thanked the steward for all he had done.

"I'm told you were a voice of calm amid the turmoil."

Edric pulled me out of view, between the stables and hay supply.

"I'd not recount the events in front of the stableboys. They were particularly shaken."

Of course they were. They were children, and would carry the scars of seeing the fallen bodies of my people paraded through the courtyard, a particular fact that I could not shake from my mind since hearing it.

"I'm sorry, Edric. For leaving—"

"My lady, had you been here, you'd likely not be alive."

My eyes widened. "What do you mean?"

"I overheard Draven speaking with one of the Gyorian merce-naries, their leader, on the day after Warren was killed. I'd spare my lady the details of the conversation but... I am glad you were not here."

I wanted to ask him to recount the conversation, but there was a part of me that did not want to hear it. To hear of Warren's fate now...

"We knew the Aetherians had arrived. He was nervous, and rightly so. I thought Hawthorne Manor would be no longer after the fighting began. Many of us did."

"Elydorian battles are notoriously brutal," I conceded. "But we knew, without Draven, and in the presence of both Aetherian and Thalassari forces, they would likely retreat."

We spoke more of the days leading up to Draven's coup. I assured him my next visit was to the families of those who had been killed, and our conversation turned to Hawthorne's future.

"Edric, have you heard of a Lady Evelyne?"

I could tell, from the look in his eyes, he had.

"A cautionary tale, an old myth, of a Hawthorne who fell in love with, and was murdered by, a Gyorian. It's a name I've not heard for many, many years."

"Not a myth at all," I said. "She was real. And was not murdered but fled Hawthorne, in fear, living out her days in Gyoria."

He was confused, as I'd expected. So I told him Adren's story, one he clearly did not believe.

"Come with me," I said, grabbing the old man's hand. He followed me as we searched for Adren, finally finding him in the healer's cottage.

"You've been hurt?" I went to him. Adren frowned and

pointed to Hawthorne's healer. "She is relentless," he accused. "It is a scratch, nothing more than—"

"Not a scratch," Mistress Delia shot back, looking at Adren in a way I'd never seen her look at any man. "I found him limping along, refusing treatment, despite a broken ankle."

"I've suffered many broken bones," he said. "It will heal."

Elydorians healed more quickly than humans, it was true, but in the meantime, a broken ankle would be as painful for Adren as it would for anyone. Not surprisingly, it was now wrapped. No one, simply no one, refused Delia. My mother had always said the healer was the only person at Hawthorne who terrified her. A comely widow who had served Hawthorne well, Delia was as revered as my father had been. Perhaps more so.

"Is he finished?" I asked the healer.

Delia's grimace confirmed he was, though not of her liking. "His shoulder—"

"Is fine." Adren stood. "Thank you, mistress." His fist to chest in parting was not overlooked by the healer, who understood its significance.

"We would speak to you," I said, Adren standing and attempting to mask the fact that he was indeed injured.

We left Delia's cottage, Adren glancing back to the healer one last time before she closed the door, and we walked a short distance when I stopped them both.

"Thank you," I began. "Call it duty, or say what you will, but I owe you my life."

"Marek was there," Adren said, predictably. "He'd never have let Draven pull you away. More importantly, it was you who delivered the first blow."

We would likely debate the details of Draven's death for many years to come, but that was not what I wished to discuss.

"Adren," I said. "Will you show Edric the pendant?"

He hesitated.

"He has been Hawthorne's steward for many years. And has heard of Lady Evelyne, but believed her story to be a myth."

"She was no myth," Adren said, producing the evidence. "Lady Evelyne was my grandmother. She gave this to my mother."

Edric took the pendant, inspecting it. After a long while, he looked up.

"This is why you offered Hawthorne aid against your own?" he asked, handing it back.

"I offered aid because Kael is my friend. Issa is my friend. And aye, for this too." He put the pendant away. "They are not mine," Adren finished. "Those mercenaries are like Draven. Ambitious, dishonorable—"

"It is well known," Edric interrupted, "Gyorians do not like humans."

"Our king does not like humans. And aye, there are some who agree with him. But not all. Just as not all humans would betray their lord, or lady, to seize power for themselves."

"Adren," I said, not knowing how else to broach the topic. "You have been excommunicated from your clan by Prince Terran for remaining loyal to Kael, and offering us aid."

He grunted his agreement.

And now came the more difficult question.

For a brief moment, when Draven was injured but not down, I had only one thought.

It was not of the vow I'd made to my father but one of never having Marek embrace me from behind as *Tidechaser* cut through the water, open seas and blue skies before us...

"You have a strong claim to Hawthorne Manor," I rushed to finish, seeing Adren's hesitation. "This is my home. These are my people. But it was never my dream to remain here, something

Edric, and my parents, knew well. But they became sick and..." I swallowed, thinking of them. Of Warren and the others. "You've served Hawthorne well this day. And can bridge the divide between our clans, I believe, and re-shape its future. Along with that of Estmere and Elydor too."

He understood, even if Edric did not. Yet.

"Do not give me an answer until you think it through. But if you'll have it, Hawthorne Manor is yours."

Edric gasped.

Adren simply stared at me as if I'd gone mad.

"I love this land, and my people," I rushed to add. "But I also love Marek of Thalassaria. Remaining here was my parents' dream," I repeated, "but never my own."

Edric looked from me to Adren. "I will say, this is most unexpected."

A heavy ache pressed against my ribs. Would he, and the others, not be able to look past the fact that Adren was Gyorian? Would they feel abandoned by me?

"Although Warren would not have thought so," Edric continued. "He knew, we all knew, you were in love with the Navarch. He worried for you, while you were away, but I think he knew this might happen. You stepped into your parents' role here, and did Hawthorne Manor well, my lady. We will miss you."

"He didn't yet accept," I reminded Edric as we turned our attention to Adren. "Perhaps being lord of a border holding is not your dream."

Adren appeared thoughtful. "I do not need to think it through, Isolde. I serve Kael of Gyoria, but there is no longer such a person now that he's pledged himself to Aetheria. I've no notion of what comes next— for Mev and Kael, the Gate, for Elydor— but if your people would have me, I would honor my grandmother's memory by protecting Hawthorne Manor and the humans."

"You would?" I asked, incredulous.

"I would be honored."

"Does Marek know?" Adren asked.

"Not yet. If you'd said no... there are few that Hawthorne would accept in my stead. But a rightful heir... They are a proud people, their customs old."

"I am Gyorian."

"And Draven was human."

Neither had an argument to that. With luck, the people of Hawthorne would see it that way too.

"There you are."

"Oh dear," I said at the sound of Marek's voice.

Edric and Adren exchanged a glance.

I explained to them. "Marek asked that I remain abed, despite that I am not injured."

"Your head—" Marek said.

"Hardly hurts. I fell, not for the first or last time."

"Your wrist—"

"Is no reason to stay abed."

"Issa—"

"Adren has agreed to inherit Hawthorne Manor, accepting his rightful claim through his grandmother."

With that, we were no longer speaking of my bodily injuries.

"You would... when did you..."

I had never seen Marek struggle to find words before.

"I thought it would be difficult to fulfill my duties as Lady of Hawthorne Manor from *Tidechaser*."

He looked at Edric. And then Adren. And then back to me.

"Come," Edric said. "You'll be wanting a tour of the manor, my lord."

Adren was about to argue the use of his title, so I offered him some advice. "You will become accustomed to it. Accept the title. It is a small boon for the troubles you will face."

"Do not scare our new lord from his duties already, my lady," Edric argued. "If you will." He gestured for Adren to walk ahead of him. It would take some time for him to become accustomed to the new role. We watched them disappear into the courtyard.

Marek pulled me toward him, covering my mouth with his. It was a hungry, all-encompassing kiss that left me barely able to stand when he finally pulled away. His lips, still wet. His eyes, desire-filled. But there was something else there too.

Disbelief.

"I thought of it not long after he told us his story," I said. "Immediately dismissing the idea, not prepared to leave Hawthorne. But when Draven had me... Marek, I love you. As painful as it will be to walk away from this place, I've no doubt watching you leave would be tenfold more painful than that."

"I'll admit, I thought of Adren as well, but I wanted you to decide for yourself."

"And I have. I choose you. I choose adventure and freedom and the sea."

Marek crossed his arms, his eyes narrowed. "Do you only choose me for *Tidechaser*? Will I return to the ship one day to see you sailing off with it?"

"Perhaps," I teased. "If you do not construct a bigger bed in the captain's cabin, I will be forced to take it over. Oh, and the emergency provisions... there is much we need to discuss."

In response, Marek scooped me up into his arms and began to carry me through the courtyard.

"People are looking," I whispered, wiggling to get down. "What are you doing?"

"You know precisely what I'm doing, as do they."

"Marek!"

"Unless, of course, you truly are more injured than you claim."

Mortified, I buried my head into his shoulder, giggles following us, my people likely as mortified as me.

"My head is fine," I mumbled. "My wrist is sore."

"You won't need your wrist."

Carrying me into the keep, Marek did not pause as he took the stone steps to my chamber by two. I wanted to continue to berate him for the display... but I wanted him more.

The way he snatched me from the courtyard, I expected a frenzied tangle of kisses and limbs, but it was just the opposite. He put me down, but didn't let go. Instead, Marek held my face between his hands in a way he never had before.

"I'm sorry that I left you, Issa. I'm sorry I didn't have the courage to love you when we first met or later in The Moonlit Current. I will remain thankful each and every day that you've given me a second chance. You've sacrificed what you love most, for me, and I will never forget that."

I looked into his eyes. "I didn't, Marek. I love you most. I promised to take care of the people of Hawthorne, and they're now in the hands of someone strong and honorable. I've fulfilled the promise to my father. And now I live for me. For us."

This kiss was soft, like a gentle wave's caress. I wanted to be closer to him, but when I tried to wrap my arms around Marek, he guided them down by my sides instead. He knelt down before me then, and looking up, removed first one boot, and then the other. Every movement was slow and deliberate. With each article of clothing he removed, the anticipation grew. When I tried to hurry him, Marek would not have it. Instead, he stood back and began to undress.

"You are so beautiful, sereia."

It should be strange, standing in front of him wearing nothing but a silkspore wrap on my wrist. But it did not. Watching him undress, staring at me as if I were as awe-inspiring as the open sea, his words washing over me like a caress...

"Are you Thalassa?" he asked, tossing aside the last of his clothing. "Surely the sea goddess is not so perfectly formed," he said, reaching for me.

"Is that not heresy?" I asked, thinking the same of him. He was perfect.

And mine.

"I only speak the truth." His lips touched mine, Marek's tongue insisting I open for him. Welcoming the caress, I made a sound of contentment as his hands explored, dipping down to my waist and then back up to cup both breasts. Running his thumbs over each nipple, Marek worshipped every bit of me.

There was no other word to describe it, as if he was thanking me for a sacrifice that felt like anything but. By the time I became aware that we were moving, we were at my bed. Once again, he lifted me up, as if Marek didn't trust I could crawl into it myself without hurting my wrist, and placed me onto it.

"I will not break," I told him. "I've had worse injuries than this." I lifted my hand.

"If it were up to me," he said, kneeling between my legs, pulling them apart. "I would have you remain in this chamber, away from harm, locked inside with me from now until the end of our days."

"No *Tidechaser*? No water? I think not."

His only response was to smile just before his head went

between my legs. After that, I forgot to think. Or tease him. Or do anything other than enjoy the sensation until I wondered...

"Marek, could I do that to you?"

In response, his head lifted.

"By the tides, Issa. I am trying to take this slowly, but you're making it difficult."

I pulled on his arms. "I want you inside me, Marek."

With a curse, he moved forward, enough that I was able to reach between us to feel him. "I'd wondered what it was like," I said as his hands closed around mine, guiding me. With a groan, he pulled my hands away, positioned himself and then, little by little, filled me until Marek was buried deep. There was no pain this time. Only the tenderness that was his care of me and the tug inside my chest.

"I love you, Marek."

His head dipped back, at my words, he pulled out slightly and then filled me once again.

"I love everything about you, Issa."

Out and then in, Marek moved more quickly now. He reached his hand between us, circling his thumb just right. His mouth partly open, watching me, filling me...

"Marek." I said his name over and over again. "Please," I begged him, this time, knowing what I begged for. I wanted that same tidal wave, its all-consuming power taking over my entire body. This time, I could anticipate it. And I wanted him to feel that too.

Thrusting my hips up toward him, I matched his increasing speed and pressure, my fingers digging into the skin of his arms. Each tensing of his muscle, each time he said my name, I inched closer and closer until... we both came crashing down.

I called his name, and he called mine. I held onto him, not daring to let go.

I would never let him go, ever again.

43

MAREK

It seemed like all of Hawthorne Manor was at the small chapel. Its priest stood at the door, prepared to escort us inside. There were about to be more than a few disappointed villagers since most would be left on the doorstep for the ceremony.

"Can we exchange vows here?" I asked him.

The dour man was exactly as Issa had described. He peered up at me as if I were less than deserving of the woman we waited for. In fact, he'd told me as much when we met three days past.

"Lady Isolde... and a Thalassari sailor."

I had hushed the man before Issa could hear him, and thankfully, he held his tongue.

"That would be highly unusual," he said now, clearly annoyed.

My charm didn't seem to work on him, so I appealed to Adren, who stood beside me.

"Do you not think the people of Hawthorne would like to bear witness to their lady's marriage?" I asked, using the human term. "My lord," I added.

Adren's scowl every time I said it made me wish to repeat the moniker more often.

"I believe," he said, despite my needling, "Lady Isolde would like that very much."

Father Dour Face frowned but didn't strike down the idea.

In the days since we arrived, he was one of a very few that I hadn't taken to at Hawthorne. As Issa met with everyone from the manor staff to Hawthorne's villagers, introducing them to Adren, I had also been busy. After sending a messenger to Aetheria that we no longer needed them to research as the recovery had been successful, I traveled to Valewood Bay's port after learning that Cassandra had been instrumental in alerting the people of Hawthorne Manor of Draven's intentions. Sir Warren had relocated nearly all of the women and children within the castle grounds to the village, although a few, including the healer, had refused to leave. Unfortunately, my sister was no longer there, having left for Thalassaria a sennight earlier.

Now, the day before we would leave Issa's home for our new one, *Tidechaser* waiting for us at port, we would make it official. Last eve, we talked well into the night about Issa's mortality, one problem we could not easily solve, as well as others that were more easily addressed with time and trust.

"She's coming."

Whispers reached us, even though I could not see her from where I stood. Climbing up a step, just below the priest, I craned my neck to peer above the crowd. Eventually, the chatter became gasps and for a moment, I thought something was wrong.

And then I saw her.

Issa wore a Thalassari gown that shimmered like the ocean at dawn. Iridescent silk shifted between shades of deep sapphire and seafoam green with every movement. Delicate strands of gold thread, resembling waves, were embroidered across the bodice and cascaded down the flowing skirt. Pearls and tiny opalescent beads adorned Issa's neckline and cuffs, reflecting light like droplets of seawater. A circlet of pearl and coral wrapped around her head, Issa's hair flowing freely beneath it.

At the center of the headpiece, my mother's pearl.

Adren must have returned the pearl to her, but the gown? It was not possible Issa could have had it made. That gown was designed and created by a master Thalassari seamstress, some of its materials not readily available in Estmere.

After what seemed like forever, Issa finally reached me. I held out my hand, hardly able to speak.

"I've never seen a sight more magnificent in all my days, sereia."

"And you look equally as handsome, captain."

"Where—"

"Ahem."

Resisting an eye roll, I capitulated to the priest, who explained that we would hold the ceremony on the chapel's steps for all to see even though the idea obviously displeased him. Adren really would have to find Hawthorne a new priest.

He made it short, at least, Issa and I exchanging vows and making the children at our feet giggle when I kissed Issa at the end—without permission from the priest. It was only as we made our way back to the keep for the banquet when we slipped away momentarily from the crowd that Issa finally solved the mystery.

"It was in the satchel Nerys gave me, along with some other clothing more appropriate for a Thalassari than a human."

"Nerys," I repeated. "She knew."

"Knew. Suspected. Hoped. I am not certain. But I am grateful. It is a beautiful gown."

"Not as beautiful as the woman wearing it." My eyes traveled to her headdress. "Adren?"

"Aye. He gave it to me, with your message. You did not expect to survive the Depths."

I thought back to that day and was unsure how to answer.

"Expecting failure is never advisable but I knew the odds were against me."

"I will take it off after today so you can have it."

"No," I said immediately. "It is yours. A token of my love and thanks for the sacrifice you were willing to make that day and the one you make in leaving your home. Searching for answers about my mother's death led me to you, so I will never regret it, but I too must stop living in the past. You are my present and my future." I smiled. "And my wife, as you humans call it."

"Husband, partner... the name is less important than the commitment and love I have for you. Wherever the sea takes us, I will be by your side for the adventure."

"Our fate was sealed the first day I rode through these gates. If only I had known it then."

"We know it now, and that is all that matters."

Our fate, our future, was just beginning.

EPILOGUE

ISSA

The Ascension, Aethralis, the palace… despite having been here before, it was as awe-inspiring as the first time. As we walked into the Celestial Hall, I reminded myself it was still day. Here, the high ceiling illuminated to replicate the Elydorian night sky. We'd come during The Trial of the Tempest, an annual Aetherian festival that tests the abilities of its participants on everything from storm summoning to wind whispering. According to the guards, it was the last day of the trials, and those who had shown exceptional skill that day were being celebrated this eve.

We had been taken to our shared chamber, Marek and I enjoying the waterfall room together before dressing for the evening. Mev and Kael were apparently soon returning from the Sky Pinnacle, a sacred mountain where winds were at their strongest and today's test had been held. Now, having been escorted here, I remained in awe of Aetherian architecture.

"How do they manage it?" I asked. It appeared the roof was open to the night sky, but I knew such a thing was not possible since it was still daytime.

"Much of Aetherian magic is still a mystery to me, even after all these years. Ask Lyra; perhaps she'll know."

The Aetherian in question walked toward us.

"Marek. Issa." She hugged us both. "Apologies you were not personally greeted into the palace. Mev, Kael, and the king should be returning any moment."

The hall was already filled with participants and their parents, with Aetherian council members and honored guests, also according to the guard.

"Everyone is dressed so... beautifully," I said, their shades of silver and white hair matching gowns of the same colors mixed with deep blues and celestial inlays.

"This is one of the most revered nights of the year in Aetheria. Your Festival of Tides is similar," she said to Marek.

"I don't believe there will ever be another one quite like the last," he said as Lyra gestured for us to walk with her. We made our way to a door that I hadn't even seen, it was so seamlessly cloaked into the wall around it.

Stepping through it, we entered an antechamber that was similarly decorated as the hall. It was, however, quite empty.

"Is it true?" she asked. "We received your message."

"That we are married?" Marek teased. "Aye, it is indeed."

Lyra's smile was as serene as her movement, as if she was an angel come down from the sky. I really did need to ask her how they managed it. "Was that really not the actual sky above us?"

"It is true," I said, not willing to leave Lyra in anticipation. "We have it."

"There you are."

Mev burst through the same door we'd come through, running toward us. She looked every bit an Aetherian princess, her all-white gown shimmering with silver threads. Grasping us both at the same time, she held onto Marek and I as if she would never let go.

"You will suffocate them," a gruff voice said from behind her. Kael.

"I don't care."

"Is that a way to repay your friends?" another male voice boomed.

The king.

Mev let us go, turning toward the others.

Marek didn't make them wait. He opened the leather pouch on his belt, the one that once held his mother's pink pearl that now rested on my chest on a necklace fashioned by Hawthorne's silversmith.

Taking out the Wind Crystal, he handed it to the king.

Each of them stared at the artifact in King Galfrid's hand.

The king looked up to Marek and me. "Thank you. I am forever indebted to you."

"I cannot believe you did it. We want to hear everything," Mev said, moving toward the Crystal. "I didn't expect it to be so small."

"Small things can be great too," her father said, wrapping his fingers around the Crystal and looking upward. With a wave of his empty hand, we watched as the stars in the "sky" disappeared. Dark turned to light and clouds rolled in as if a storm were approaching. With a clap of thunder, they turned grey as distant lightning flashed through the sky before the "storm" suddenly disappeared, replaced by sunlight. Though we could hear birds chirping, I didn't see them. And just as suddenly as it all began, the "sky" once again darkened, stars appearing, twinkling as they had in the beginning.

Everyone, including Mev, stared at the king but he was looking at me.

"You did wonder about the ceiling, did you not?"

"But... I asked... you weren't there."

The king smiled.

"Aetherian whispers," Marek said beside me. "Are there not those just as skilled who might hear us?" he asked.

"No," the king replied. "You have your silencing mist, and we have our ways as well."

There was an Aetherian equivalent to the silencing mist? I'd never heard of that before.

"I was told the Celestial Hall's magic was ancient and irreplicable," Mev said to her father.

"Both are true," he said. "Without this"—the king held up his closed fist, indicating the Crystal—"it would not be possible."

"Bummer. That means you can't teach me to do that?"

"I cannot. This only works for the most powerful in Aetheria. Though your skills have come a long way, daughter."

"Thanks," she said, clearly proud.

"But we've much to discuss now." He turned his attention to Kael. The final artifact. The Stone of Mor'Vallis which currently sat in Kael's father's crown.

But before either could continue, something occurred to me.

"Your research," I blurted. "We reached the Depths before receiving any word from you," I explained to Mev and Kael. "Quite by accident." I began to tell them what had happened as Marek chimed in. When we were done with the story, I circled back to my initial question. "What did you find? About the Depths?"

Mev and Kael exchanged a look of apprehension that made the hairs on my neck stand straight.

"We found references in an ancient text," Kael said, "which seemed to coincide with the journal and our earlier discovery. One that spoke of dark magic and a sacrifice needing to be made with the use of any of the clan's most powerful artifacts. Listening to you now, I believe the Crystal's presence intensified the unnatural magic that already existed there, though we're unsure who or how it originated. As you suggested, it did not belong in those waters and made it especially dangerous, even more so than it once was."

"We did send a message," Mev whispered.

I swallowed, seeing her expression. Mev looked to her father, who sighed so heavily, it could only mean one thing.

They had been resigned to our failure.

"What was the message?" Marek asked.

Part of me didn't want to know.

"Not to risk it. That it was our belief," Mev said solemnly, "that while the Crystal could be taken, the true cost of reopening the Gate had yet to be paid."

* * *

MORE FROM C. L. MECCA

The next book in C. L. Mecca's Heirs of Elydor Series, *Realm of Stone and Starlight*, is available to order now here:
https://mybook.to/RealmBackAd

ABOUT THE AUTHOR

C.L. Mecca is the author of historical romance and also writes contemporary small town romance as Cissy Mecca.

Sign up to C.L. Mecca's mailing list for news, competitions and updates on future books.

Follow C.L. Mecca on social media here:

facebook.com/MeccaRomance

instagram.com/meccaromance

tiktok.com/@clmeccaauthor

ALSO BY C. L. MECCA

Heirs of Elydor Series

Whisper of War and Storms

Tide of Waves and Secrets

Fate of Echoes and Embers

C. L. Mecca writing as Cissy Mecca

Cedar Falls Series

Fallen Hearts

Desired Hearts

Boldwood
EVER AFTER

x♡x♡

JOIN BOLDWOOD'S
ROMANCE
COMMUNITY
FOR SWEET AND
SPICY BOOK RECS
WITH ALL YOUR
FAVOURITE
TROPES!

SIGN UP TO OUR
NEWSLETTER

HTTPS://BIT.LY/BOLDWOODEVERAFTER

Boldwood

Boldwood Books is an award-winning fiction publishing company seeking out the best stories from around the world.

Find out more at www.boldwoodbooks.com

Join our reader community for brilliant books, competitions and offers!

Follow us
@BoldwoodBooks
@TheBoldBookClub

Sign up to our weekly deals newsletter

https://bit.ly/BoldwoodBNewsletter